LET'S GET IT ON

LET'S GET IT ON

Jill Nelson

Amistad

An Imprint of HarperCollins*Publishers*

This book is a work of fiction. References to real people, events, establishments, organizations, or locales are intended only to provide a sense of authenticity and are used fictitiously. All other characters, and all incidents and dialogue, are drawn from the author's imagination and are not to be construed as real.

HarperCollins books may be purchased for educational, business, or sales promotional use. For information please write: Special Markets Department, HarperCollins Publishers, 10 East 53rd Street, New York, NY 10022.

FIRST EDITION

Designed by Lisa Stokes

Library of Congress Cataloging-in-Publication Data has been applied for.

ISBN 978-0-06-076330-5

09 10 11 12 13 ov/rrd 10 9 8 7 6 5 4 3 2 1

For Nicki Rickman, Helen Hyde, and the September sisters,
who taught me that Friendship, laughter, and libido
have no expiration date.

ACKNOWLEDGMENTS

Thanks to my editor, Dawn Davis, for her patience. To my agent, Jennifer Rudolph Walsh, for the story about the hummingbird. To Valerie Wilson Wesley for her talent, time, and generosity. Once again, thanks to Faith for her expansive, essential friendship. And to all the sexual healers out there who wanted more.

And to Flores, who exceeds both my expectations and imagination.

LET'S GET IT ON

Wanda

Y OU KNOW THAT SAYING "PAYBACK IS a bitch"? Well, you can believe it. And in the case of *Marshall v. McGruder-Forbes et al.,* the bitch in question is me, LaShaWanda P. Marshall, and I'm proud of it.

Not that I wasn't nervous as hell an hour ago when those twelve jurors filed in. When the bailiff instructed the courtroom to rise, my knees felt wobbly and I could feel puddles of sweat form between my breasts and behind my knees, and begin to flow downward, and I'm not a sister who ruffles easily or takes kindly to perspiration. Then C. Virgil Susquehanna, the presiding judge, swept into the court and I couldn't keep a slight smile from my face. Six foot four, black as a cast-iron skillet, with chiseled cheekbones, a broad forehead, liquid brown eyes, and full lips, C. Virgil strode into the courtroom exuding confidence and power. Did I mention he is gorgeous? In his early sixties, he not only bears out the old adage "Black don't crack," he is living proof that it gets better with age. During the three weeks he'd been hearing my suit to recover $2 million in commissions plus interest stolen from me by my former employer, the Wall Street investment bank McGruder-Forbes, I'd tried to read him, with no success. He was at all times courtly and attentive, and kept a serious poker face. Even when he was overruling an objection from the battery of evil attorneys McGruder-Forbes had arrayed against me or sustaining one from my lone attorney, Debi Mountain, it was impossible to get a sense of which way he was leaning. I guess he took seriously those scales of justice and the need for fairness, but damn, sometimes a sister can use a break.

By the time the court officer handed him that paper from the jury, I'd surrendered to the sweat in every crevice of my body, and being a plus-size sister, there were more than a few of them. Big-ass pigeons, not delicate, ladylike butterflies, were wreaking havoc in my stomach, and if my fingers, each nail adorned for luck with red, black, green, and gold four-leaf clovers painted by my wild cousin Sukey, nail artist extraordinaire, hadn't been firmly planted on the table in front of me, my legs alone wouldn't have been enough to get me up. As different as our respective lines of work are, both me and the judge are in businesses where failure to rise is a serious offense. I didn't want to be cited for contempt of court.

My ears were ringing so hard and my stomach churning so loud the only way I knew that Judge Susquehanna asked if the jury had reached a verdict and that the forewoman said yes is because I've watched enough episodes of *Law & Order* to know the drill. I couldn't hear a thing. You know how when you fly, your ears clog up and don't pop until you touch down? Well, that's what happened to me. Touchdown came when the judge read the words, "In the case of *LaShaWanda P. Marshall v. McGruder-Forbes*, we find the defendants guilty." Suddenly the pigeons in my stomach went home to roost with those chickens Malcolm X talked about in 1963, that sweat dried up in its own tracks, and I could hear again. Not only that, but I was $2-million-plus-interest richer, more than enough money to replace the suit on my back.

I glanced over at the jurors, eight women and four men, and they were all smiling. A couple of the women even gave me a thumbs-up. Beside me, my lawyer squeezed my hand and murmured, "See, Wanda, I told you the American system of jurisprudence works." I wasn't about to go tell that to the innocent people in prison or those who are poor, colored, or both and serving disproportionately long sentences. It also wasn't the moment to remind Debi, a pal of that enemy of the people, Supreme Court Justice Clarence Thomas, who I'd hired not because I agreed with her politics but because she'd never lost a case, that she was being paid many pretty pennies for representing me. If you want justice your way, it don't come cheap. Anyway, it was true that in this instance, for this woman, this time, the system had worked. That was definitely something to celebrate. I could hear Lydia Beaucoup, my friend and, technically speaking, employer, who'd moved with me from Reno to San Francisco so she could come to court to support me every day, yelling, "All right, Wanda! You go, girl! Go!" That's exactly what I wanted to do, go. Out of that damn courthouse, straight to the bank with my check, and on with my life. If living well is the best revenge, I now had the funds to do just that. I've never been a woman who wastes time.

"The court will come to order." Judge Susquehanna's creamy baritone silenced the room. "Many of you know something of my journey to the bench. I was born and raised by a hardworking single mother in Mississippi during the meanest years of segregation and Jim Crow.

I worked after school, weekends, and long summers as a golf caddy at a segregated country club from the time I was twelve. I was able to fulfill my mother's dream of education and betterment when several members, impressed, I believe, with my hard work and nonthreatening demeanor, chose to contribute funds to, as one of them put it, 'Send the little coon to college.'

"I doubt they thought this 'little coon' would finish college. I am positive they did not think I would continue, on full scholarship, to law school. Surely they did not suspect I would become an attorney for the Baptist Brotherhood and Boule and Racial Solidarity Now! during their heyday in the 1960s. Or that I would go from there to the NAACP and eventually head the Inner City Conclave, struggling for political and economic equality and justice for not only my people but all Americans. Over the years I learned that the battle was not only in the streets but in the suites. After all, what good does it do to integrate an establishment if my people cannot afford . . ."

C. Virgil kept on talking, but my mind started wandering, trying to remember what the Libor index had been the day before in order to compute exactly how much the interest on my recently recovered $2 million would be. I've always got some sort of music playing in my head, kind of a self-induced Muzak, selected by my subconscious to fit my mood and circumstances. It was no surprise that the current sound track in my head was the exuberant voices of the chorus in the musical *42nd Street* warbling, *"We're in the money, we're in the money, / We've got a lot of what it takes to get along!"*—their voices rising to such a crescendo that they drowned out the judge. That was okay with me; since I'd already heard the words I most needed to hear, "guilty, guilty, guilty, guilty, guil-tee!" everything else was extra. I just sat there, listening to the chorus jamming in my brain, trying not to nod my head to the beat, and watching C. Virgil's lips move as he talked.

What pretty lips they were, full, dark, perfectly shaped. Since even in a court of law, honesty is the best policy, and though I'm no longer on the witness stand, I remain sworn to tell the truth, I confess that even if he's old enough to be my father and, at least up until now, I've been partial to younger men, I couldn't keep from fantasizing about those lips of C. Virgil's. Kissing that warm place behind my ear, slowly traveling down my neck, gently licking, then drifting lazily south to fasten onto that small place between my neck and collarbone where, when kissed, sucked, and nibbled just right, it felt so good it made me simultaneously giggle and cringe in ecstasy. Power is an aphrodisiac, and C. Virgil had my whole world in his hands: it's no wonder I was turned on.

Hey, standing in court daydreaming about being made transcendent love to by a handsome judge—or, truth be told, anyone else—may sound strange, but sex is my business. I'm the chief financial officer of A Sister's Spa, located just outside Reno, Nevada. In business just over two years, we're wildly successful, and not just because we offer massage, aerobics, herbal wraps, and a relaxing place for stressed-out women to spend a few days. In addition to great food, wonderful atmosphere, and every spa treatment imaginable, A Sister's Spa also sells fabulous, safe sex delivered by gorgeous young men trained in the art of pleasuring women. Come for either the In and Out, our shortest package—a massage and sex expertly delivered in four hours—or the Total Healing Deluxe, two nights, three days, unlimited spa services, and sex with as many sex workers as you can handle in the combination of your choice. And we guarantee you'll leave relaxed, loose, and planning your next visit. Not to mention with a Cheshire cat smirk on your face.

But before I go any further, let me be perfectly clear: my career plan after I graduated from Yale wasn't to work in a spa-brothel. Like thousands of smart, aggressive, and debt-ridden college graduates in the 1990s, my American dream was simple: to work on Wall Street and get rich. I was well on my way there until I was framed by at least one of the directors of McGruder-Forbes, the New York investment bank where I worked, to cover their own unscrupulous dealings. That's when I'd packed up my shit, fled west on my own buppie trail of tears, and settled for a job as executive assistant to the vice president of Old Western Bank while I schemed on how to get my money back.

Sounds grim, but as my granny used to say, "If life deals you lemons, make lemonade," to which I'd add, then bottle it, slap on a fancy label, and get paid. Granny's point, and mine, is that bad things can sometimes lead to good things. If I hadn't been set up and driven out of town, I never would have moved to San Francisco, taken a crappy job at the bank, and met Lydia Beaucoup and Acey Allen when they came in to apply for a business loan, for which they were turned down. I wouldn't have been at Sapphire's, my favorite restaurant in San Francisco, during happy hour having a much-needed after-work drink and waiting on my always late girlfriend Muffin Dixmoor, and I wouldn't have run into Acey and Lydia a few days after their unsuccessful visit to the bank. Not that I was looking for them. When they'd come for the meeting about the loan, Lydia stepped to me like I was something unattractive standing between her and jackpot door number three, and even though her best friend, Acey, had tried to clean it up, I was not impressed. I read them as two bourgie black women wearing expensive clothes and nonthreatening hair coming to beg the man for money, with no clue how the system worked, and about to get their asses kicked. I didn't like Lydia's assumption, even though the only thing standing between her and the banker who could make her a loan was me, that I was powerless, someone to be stepped over, and if necessary, on, before the main event.

But hey, I've been black, female, and several sizes above a fourteen most of my life. I've learned to ignore negative assumptions or make them work for me. If someone thought my race, gender, weight, weave, or red, black, and green fingernails made me stupid, that was their mistake. I sent those bitches in to see my boss, Gardiner Roberts III, flipped my waist-length extensions, and promptly forgot about them. It wasn't until several days later when I ran into them at Sapphire's that we got to talking seriously about their unique business idea. The truth is, I'm not a spa person. With apologies to Jane Fonda, Billy Blanks, and Joe Pilates, sweat is not my friend. I spend way too much money on hair and nails to willingly engage in any activity that might chip my polish, sweat out my roots, or cause these shoulder-length kinky twists I'm wearing now to unravel. With the exception of great sex, that is. Let me get with a man who's got the equipment and knows how to work it, and I don't give a damn if my nails break off down to the pads of my fingers while I'm clinging to the headboard or his back. As for the hair, I've had sex so good that not only did my roots nap up, beads and shells flew off my braids so fast and hit the walls so hard you'd think you were under sniper attack. And more than one man has found himself with a handful of some poor Asian woman's hair in his fist when he held on a little too tight. The next morning I had to crawl out of bed, put a baseball cap on my head, and hobble to the beauty shop for an emergency touch-up, but I'm not complaining. Now, let the church say amen.

Short story long, I'd hooked them up with Muffin, she'd delivered the capital they needed to open the spa via her elderly, right-wing, rich-as–King Midas hubby, Dick Dixmoor, although I'm sure he didn't intend for his grants to be used to open a brothel for black women. Anyway, realizing my financial savvy, they'd offered me a gig as CFO. We've been successful from day one, having tapped into what I intended to gamble was a national, even global, women's fantasy: fab safe sex on demand, no strings attached.

It hadn't been easy. Along with Lydia, Acey, and me, our gang of four included Odell Overton, a fine-as-hell chocolate-brown brother who Lydia met when he was the UPS delivery man at the ad agency she'd worked for. Both Lydia and Acey swore Odell was a fantastic lover, but not having had a taste, I had to take their word for it. What I did know was that he was smart, cool as a cucumber, and not looking to put in another twenty years and then retire from UPS. It was also clear to me that it'd help to have a man in his thirties working with us in a business in which most of our employees were young and male. Sexual glutton that she is, even Lydia had to admit that it was physically impossible for her to identify and screen the forty sex workers we needed to open the spa. That's how Odell became the director of human resources, responsible for finding, hiring, and managing the rainbow coalition of sex workers responsible for pleasuring our clients.

Did I say that A Sister's Spa was a success from day one? We were offering women multiorgasmic sex without the complications of mating, dating, or a relationship, and they were hungry for it. Unfortunately, no good deed goes unpunished, especially when it benefits women. We had to beat back attacks from the Reverend T. Terry Tiger, a minister and former leader of the Negro people who'd been rendered virtually obsolete, fallen on hard financial times, and tried to use attacks on A Sister's Spa to rejuvenate his shrinking ministry and fatten his coffers. Muffin's husband, Dick Dixmoor, a right-wing manufacturer of munitions and pharmaceuticals, had funded the spa, ostensibly as a way to employ said predators, but it turned out that his involvement with the spa was really his own secret Tuskegee Experiment. That's the study where, from 1932 to 1972, the United States government withheld penicillin and let four hundred poor black men suffer, and some die, of syphilis so that doctors could study the disease. In the end we won and prospered. The business of boning is booming, and in addition to delivering that bitch of a payback, my plan is to use the money I just recovered to open up the first franchise of A Sister's Spa.

Yep, the four of us had accomplished a lot in the last two years, and had much fun and even more sex doing so, but I'm ready for something, though I'm not exactly sure what. It's not that I'm unhappy or anything, I just miss something or something's missing. Maybe it's the same feeling people who complain about winter and cold weather have when they finally move to an island where it's in the eighties and sunny 360 days a year, and then move back to the cold within a few years. "I missed the change of seasons," they often say when you ask them why they came back. Sounds simple, but the truth is I always thought *change of seasons* was a euphemism for missing things far more complex, although right through here I can't be any more specific.

I'm staring dreamily as C. Virgil's lips open wide, wider, widest, half listening to what he's saying as I mentally retrace the route that got me here and ponder where I'm going next, when his lips part and he snarls, "Abomination!" That's when my interior sound track screeches to an unceremonious halt, and I'm back in that courthouse listening to the final comments of Judge C. Virgil Susquehanna in the matter of *Marshall v. McGruder-Forbes et al.*

"To her great credit, LaShaWanda P. Marshall did not become bitter, she did not get mad. She believed in the system and came to this court to get justice. This jury's decision should stand as a warning to all those who would seek to deny the dream of America to anyone, whatever their race, religion, gender, sexual orientation, or class. Beware attempting to rob the people of their dreams!" C. Virgil Susquehanna roars. The courtroom is absolutely still except for the muted sound of whimpering. Is there an infant in the courtroom or could it be one of McGruder-Forbes's lawyers?

"For the first time in my ten years on the bench, I am going to use my judicial prerogative and assign McGruder-Forbes, in addition to the two-million-plus-interest the jury has awarded, punitive damages of one million dollars for Ms. Marshall's pain and suffering. Beware tampering with the American dream. You do so at your own peril, whether you are a street punk stealing a worker's wallet and week's pay, or a Wall Street mogul exploiting a junior executive. I thank the members of the jury for their service. Good afternoon." With that, C. Virgil Susquehanna, for the first time in the six weeks of my trial, grins. Those pretty lips pull so far back I can see every one of the thirty-two enormous, sparkling white teeth in his mouth. He looks toward the jury and gives a slight, courtly bow, tosses the defendant's attorneys a final glare, and turns toward his chambers, robes swinging. That's when he looks at me, winks, pivots, and sweeps out of the courtroom. The absolute silence he's commanded erupts into a cacophony of voices and applause punctuated by the groans and agitated mutterings of the McGruder-Forbes lawyers as they shove papers into their briefcases and likely desperately calculate by how many tens of thousands their annual bonuses will be diminished by the loss of this case.

Beside me, my lawyer, Debi Mountain, slides papers into her briefcase, a smug, vaguely canine grin on her face. Debi is superbly trained, cutthroat, and profoundly amoral, one of those people who doesn't concern herself with right or wrong but is simply determined to win. Maybe that makes her the perfect lawyer, but you sure wouldn't want to have her over for dinner and a heart-to-heart. "Thank you so much, Debi." I step forward to give her a hug. I'm not surprised or disappointed when she backs away and extends her hand.

"A pleasure, LaShaWanda, a pleasure. Justice has been done," she purrs, pumping my arm and squeezing my hand so hard the bones shift and a sharp pain shoots up to my elbow. "I'm sure we both hope there won't be the need, but please feel free to call me for future legal assistance," she adds, turning back to her briefcase. Before I can take offense, a hand grabs me and spins me around, and my girl Lydia's arms are on both my shoulders and we're doing a strange little jig in the federal courthouse to the tune of Lydia's could-never-be-in-the-church-choir singing, with apologies to the godfather of soul, James Brown, *"That's where I laughed, for the big payback, the big payback!"*

"Oh my God, Wanda, you kicked some serious ass here today. You know those lawyers will never get over it," Lydia crows, laughing. As she has been every day of the trial, she's dressed in red, this time a brilliant Versace suit with a short jacket and skirt the color of an over-ripe pomegranate. Shortly before the trial began, she'd announced that during a vision—an extremely rare occurrence for the devout, but al-most unheard of for a cynical agnostic like Lydia—it had been revealed to her that red was the color women warriors wore during the hunt. She'd explained to me that since my case was in pursuit of my stolen cash—i.e., a twenty-first-century hunt—she planned to attend the trial daily in red to ensure success. Hey, at the time I'd just given her one of those "whatever" nods and laughed. But given the outcome of events, maybe Lydia had a point. I'm glad I let her convince me the night be-fore to wear my red suit for luck.

"Nor should they get over this day, ever," Lydia says loudly enough for the last humiliated lawyer scurrying out of the courtroom to hear and slapping me a high five. "Shit, court's barely adjourned and those sniveling creep lawyers are probably already in a dank, dark bar some-where looking at the want ads in the *National Law Journal*. In this lousy economy, good luck. And how about C. Virgil? Who knew? I always thought he was one of those uptight, born-again Republican, it's-all-a-meritocracy Negroes, but there's a brother buried up in there someplace, and he sure came out of the closet today. I could not believe it when he started telling that 'little coon' story. Damn. And an extra million in punitive damages? Where are you taking me to lunch? I've always wanted to try some Cristal."

"Where else but Sapphire's?" I ask, slipping my arm through Lydia's. "As it was in the beginning, so shall it be in the end."

"Great. We need to celebrate. And, Wanda, you've been refusing for weeks to talk about what you'd do with the money if you won, claiming it'd be bad luck. But now that a check for three-million-plus-interest's in the mail, it's time to give up the goods." I laugh, but Lydia's serious. "Listen, Wanda, whatever you decide to do is your business, and I'll support you unconditionally, blah, blah, blah, but I hope you're not going to leave A Sister's Spa. Not only do me, Acey, and Odell love you, we need you. Where else are we going to find a CFO who's as smart and cool as you?"

"Nowhere." I laugh. "And since I know you well enough to know you're incapable of waiting until we get to lunch to talk and you'll be bugging me like a no-see-'em on a beach in the Caribbean unless I toss you a bone, I'll say this and no more. I have no intention of leaving A Sister's Spa. I love the work, the money, and not to get sentimental, the three of y'all. Yes, there're some things I've been thinking about doing, but I think we can work all that out to our mutual benefit." Lydia starts to say something, and I put up my hand. "Not now. I want to leave this courthouse, get a good drink, and take off these damn shoes." Lydia's mouth is flapping like a guppy at feeding time, ready to spit out a zillion questions as soon as I pause for breath. "That's all she wrote. For now. At the moment there's nothing I'd like better than to go spend some of my millions at Sapphire's. The four of us can talk about the future after we're home and rested."

Lydia's already pulling me toward the exit. Then she grabs my arm and stops in the aisle of the nearly empty courtroom. "I know you're not big on sentiment, Wanda, and neither am I, we can leave all that to Acey. But I've got to say that I am really proud of you and happy for you. You hung in there, fought for what was yours, and won in the end." I can hear a slight catch in her voice, and when I look into Lydia's eyes, damned if they don't look a little teary. I'm scrambling to think of what to say that'll let Lydia know how much her support means to me and also squelch her impending tears so we don't both end up sobbing like banshees in federal court when I hear the door open and a familiar voice holler, "Wanda-babe, oh no you didn't, no you did not!" And it could be none other than my cousin Sukey, who's always late and definitely the only person who calls me Wanda-babe as if it's both one word and the name my parents gave me.

I turn and there she is, running toward me as fast as she possibly can wearing four-inch Jimmy Choo sandals, which isn't very fast at all. She's wearing a navy-blue, severely cut business suit, but the hem of the skirt falls closer to her pubic region than her knees and she's softened the look with a purple lace bustier. Her hair, cut in short layers and streaked with gold highlights, stops just above the nape of her neck, and as she moves she brushes away bangs that fall into her eyes. Even from twenty feet away I can see her two-inch French nails, each finger painted with a red, white, and blue American flag that seems to undulate, as if blowing in the wind, as she advances.

"Suks, as Oscar Wilde famously said, 'Better never than late,'" I greet her, smiling and stepping into her open arms. Five foot three and petite, the only big things about her are her breasts, the genetic legacy of the women on my mother's side of the family, and her hazel eyes flecked with gold. Even though at twenty-nine she's just five years younger than I am, the dynamic between us has always been more that of a mother and child than cousins separated by just a few years. The way she now throws herself into my arms and burrows into the space between my breasts, the same way she's done since these double D's miraculously appeared when I was twelve, makes me—single, childless-by-choice, under-thirty-five-year-old sister that I am—damn near maternal.

"Wanda-babe, I don't know Oscar whoever, but I just met some guy with a uniform in the hall, Bailiff, who told me what happened. So is it true? Did you win the million bucks, not once but three times? Remember how we used to love watching reruns of that show *The Millionaire* on TV when we were growing up in the Bronx, always hoping that uptight butler in the buttoned-up suit would knock on our door in the projects and give us a million-dollar check? Now you gotta be on *Survivor, Fear Factor,* or some other crazy shit, work your ass off, and risk your life to get paid. Back then, all you had to do was be a good person. Whatever, it all worked out in the end, huh? Because, Wanda-babe, you're rich, I'm hungry, and you know I can always use a drink. Where we going to celebrate, cuz?"

"We're on our way to Sapphire's, and as always, your timing's perfect," I tease as I reach out and grab Sukey's hand. Enclosed in my fingers, it vibrates gently. The intensity of the trembling in Sukey's hands has become a litmus test for reading her state of mind since she arrived in San Francisco in October 2005 with nothing to her name but a valise stuffed with scissors, clippers, files, and nail polish, the few tools of her trade she'd been able to salvage before the waters came. Driven from her home in New Orleans at the end of that August by the winds and rain of Hurricane Katrina, broken levees, and government indifference, she'd been abandoned and ignored, then shipped to shelters in

Vermont, Iowa, and finally Dallas, Texas. It was there, in Dallas, and not for the first time, that hope died. Sukey finally understood that there was nothing left of the Big Easy she'd known and loved, that everything—not just her house and tiny nail salon, but most important, the people—was gone. They couldn't return even if they wanted to; there was nothing there for them and hardly anyone interested in putting it back. She'd hitched a ride to San Francisco with a trucker working for a subsidiary of Halliburton hauling dry ice from Seattle to Dallas. She'd arrived unannounced and I'd thanked him for delivering my cousin—clutching that battered suitcase, still full of life and talking trash—to me safe and, for the most part, sound.

"You've missed all the preparations and arrived just in time for the party," I say as the three of us walk from the courthouse into the dazzling sun of San Francisco in early spring. I absentmindedly slip my other arm through Lydia's, my thoughts on Sukey. We grew up in the same housing complex in the Bronx, but Sukey left home at fourteen, living in a series of homes for incorrigible girls and working part-time at salons around the neighborhood, where she picked up the fine art of decorating nails. By the time she was eighteen and legally independent, she'd made a name for herself and was making a living working on women's hands. By then I was twenty-three, a Yale graduate, had moved to Manhattan to work on Wall Street, and rarely visited the Bronx. I spent my time working, working, or hanging out with my more affluent clients and colleagues, the better to observe how the other half—the one I intended to become a part of—lived. Sukey'd drifted in and out of my life as she saw fit, simultaneously effusive and elusive. One of those people who could step to you so warm and strong you thought you'd found your best friend for life and then disappear the next day without a word, not to be seen for months or years. As she was always high-strung and mercurial, surviving the hurricane and its aftermath, being labeled a refugee in her native land and treated accordingly, had exaggerated these characteristics. The trauma had done things to Sukey that I only knew were there and whose intensity I could only guess at by the tremor in her fingers.

We were family, grew up close, and when she suddenly showed up it was as if a prayer I didn't even know I had was answered. It was good to have blood nearby, and Sukey was happy to have a home again, some stability, and she'd easily found a job in one of San Francisco's many nail salons. Sukey was good at what she did, the clients loved her, and she was usually booked. When I told her I expected the decision today, she'd asked me to wake her up early that morning and sworn she'd meet me at court. I'd known Sukey long enough not to bet on her showing. I read the fact that she'd arrived at all as a sign of her deep affection.

"Hey, I would have been here earlier but I was finishing up the client from hell. Some tired babe from Texas with one of those champagne-colored hair helmets in town for a Republican fund-raiser. Woman had to have the face of the last ten Republican presidents, up to and including the current jerk, painted on each nail. Girl, I barely know who the last three presidents were, don't care, and really didn't want the gig, but an old client referred her and when I said a thousand dollars for the job she didn't blink, so—"

"Wait. She paid you a grand for you to do her nails?" Lydia interrupts. Sukey responds with a sniff that is both offended and haughty.

"Lydia, let me explain this to you one more time. These women who work in storefronts and charge nineteen ninety-five for a manicure and pedicure, scrape your feet with a funky razor, have your cuticles hanging by the next day, and send you out in half an hour, they 'do nails.' I am a nail artist. I paint stories on nails, tiny visions made real, and like any other creative artist, I deserve to be paid well for my work."

"I apologize, Sukey. I mean, I know you're good, I've seen the nails you've done—I mean, created—for Wanda. It just seems like a lot of money."

Sukey laughs. "It is, but I'm worth it. Besides, if Wanda'd lost her case, I'd have plenty money to take you both out to a commiseration lunch. Anyway, I hope we're not walking. These shoes are cute as hell, but comfort is not their strong suit."

"Taxi stand." I point as we descend the steps, gesturing to the left where a line of cabs, engines running, belch exhaust into the brilliant blue sky. The three of us jump into the first taxi in line. "Sapphire's," I say to the neck and close-cropped back of the head of the driver as he pulls into San Francisco's noontime traffic.

"I'm exhausted." I lean my head against the back of the seat, rolling my neck from side to side in an effort to work out the stress kinks, as John Legend's "So High" drifts from speakers behind my head. "Happy as a pig in slop, but tired as hell. I'm looking forward to an evening of relaxation and heading back to Reno tomorrow for some sexual healing." I exhale and smile, thinking about which of our many multitalented sex workers I'll give the pleasure of working away my body's knots. I close my eyes, visualize a man's head between my legs, but when he looks up it's not the face of one of the spa's youthful sex workers I see but C. Virgil's. The thought puts a grin on my face. And they say sisters are hard to please.

Next thing I know, Sukey's shaking my shoulder. "Wake up, cuz, we're here." And we've pulled up outside Sapphire's. I reach to open my purse, but Lydia stops me.

"I've got it, Wanda. You can spend that big money for lunch and libation. How much is that?" she asks, leaning toward the driver.

"Twelve dollars and eighty cents," says a voice deep with the tones of the continent. Lydia, the generous but disorganized, begins digging in her purse for her wallet.

"So, where're you from?" she asks, making conversation as she tries to excavate some cash.

"Africa."

"That's obvious. I mean what country?"

"Kenya."

"I've been there, what a beautiful place," Lydia says. Wallet located, she's now searching through credit cards and miscellaneous receipts for money. "My best friend and I spent two weeks at the beach in Mombasa a few years ago. Gorgeous. Warm. Beautiful people. Have you been there?" The driver shifts around in his seat to face us. Damn, *fine* would be an understatement. Full lips so dark they are almost purple, high cheekbones, white, white teeth, sculpted neck, and eyelashes so long I see their shadow on his cheeks. Since Lydia's still fumbling with those bills, his eyes gaze into mine. I swear I can feel his glance clear through my panties.

"Yes. Mombasa is my home," he says proudly. Lydia looks up, triumphantly clutching a twenty-dollar bill. Her mouth falls open and she gapes. Okay, the brother's a hottie, but fabulous men are our business. Get a grip, girl.

"Afrodonis!" she yells. The driver looks confused.

"I beg your pardon?"

"You. Afrodonis. Don't you remember me?" The driver's expression is simultaneously puzzled and wary.

"Have we met?"

"Of course we've met. Mombasa, two years ago on the beach by the Serenity Beach Hotel. I was on vacation with my girlfriend Acey. We'd just arrived for some much-needed rest, relaxation, and strictly girlfriend time. You asked us if we were interested in any nightlife and—"

"And you laughed until tears came," the driver says slowly, a smile teasing at the corners of his mouth. "Not the response I usually receive. I remember you. Where is your friend?"

"Acey. In Nevada, running our business. Remember I gave you an employment application on the beach?" Afrodonis smiles full-out. I swear the day gets appreciably brighter.

"Ah, yes. At that time I had no plans to come to the United States."

"What're you doing here now?" I ask.

"Homey's driving a cab, that's obvious," Sukey, already outside the taxi and leaning against the roof, snaps. "Can we go inside? I need a drink." She impatiently drums her nails on the taxi's roof.

"Relax, Sukey. Go on inside, find us a table, and order one. Lydia and I will be right in." Swinging my legs out of the cab, I make a mental note of her use of the word *need,* as I struggle to my feet. Beside the door, Afrodonis extends a helping hand, and of course, I take it. "I'm LaShaWanda P. Marshall. And you are?"

"I am Jamal M'Benge-Min, at your service." He bows slightly, and it's all I can do not to leap up, wrap my legs around his waist, and holler, *Serve me, brother! Serve me!* "What brought you to America, Jamal?"

"I came to find my future," he says softly, seriously.

"Have you found it?"

"Not yet, but I will. Perhaps today, perhaps tomorrow." He gives a deep, short chuckle, looks into my eyes. Then he stretches in the midday warmth like a big cat on the African plain, and I can't resist grinning as I watch the muscles in his arms and legs ripple. I'm afraid to look at his package or I just might make a fool of myself.

"Well, maybe we can help you out." I glance at Lydia and she takes time from her entranced gaze to nod enthusiastically. "Do you have a way I can contact you?"

"Of course. Here is my cell-phone number." Jamal M'Benge-Min hands me a card with his name and number on it.

"Perhaps we can get together later tonight," I say. Suddenly, catching the last flight back to Reno tonight doesn't seem important. Getting together with Mr. M'Benge-Min might be a way to take care of both some professional and personal business at the same time. Jamal frowns slightly.

"I have a meeting I cannot miss, but it should be over by eight o'clock."

"Maybe we can meet you for a drink or something afterward?" Lydia suggests. Jamal nods agreeably. Holding up one hand, he curls the three middle fingers inward toward his palm, extends thumb and little finger outward, and holds his hand up to his ear, the international "call me" symbol. Then he slides behind the wheel of his taxi and pulls off.

"Right, thanks, we'll be in touch," I call after him, shake myself out of my stud-struck reverie, slip my arm through Lydia's, and pull her toward the entrance to Sapphire's. She laughs.

"Can I get a witness, my sister? I told you he was beyond good-looking, Wanda, and I know you thought I was tripping. Here the man came to America to find his future, and we run into him on the very day you get paid enough that all things are possible. How fortuitous is that? Maybe there is a God after all." She snickers.

"Must be. God, higher power, karma, whatever you want to call it, can't all be coincidence."

"Whatever." Lydia waves a hand as if erasing any further discussion from the menu. "Back to Jamal. I'm sure we can find something more rewarding for him to do than driving a cab."

"I know I can. But let's not fight about who gets him, though I guess we could share custody."

"Share custody? Wanda, what's up?" Lydia demands. And since I know the sister will wear me down sooner or later, I decide to spare myself the torture and her groveling and tell her my plan. Then maybe I can relax over lunch and a strong drink.

"Well, you know we've always agreed that women all over the world deserve magnificent, affordable, safe sex. How if we had the money, it'd be wonderful to have A Sister's Spa become a franchise—"

"Cut to the chase, Wanda, it's me, the former copywriter, I wrote the spiel, remember? You interested in opening a franchise in a different county in Nevada?"

"Actually, I've been thinking about opening one back east."

"But the only state where prostitution's legal is Nevada."

"I know that. I've been doing some research. I'm thinking we could pull it off as long as we didn't put it exactly in a state . . ."

"Outside a state? Like on the space shuttle? That'd give a whole new meaning to the word *liftoff*." Lydia snickers.

"No, like on the ocean," I say. "As in a big, luxurious yacht moored three miles offshore, which puts the spa in international waters and outside of state jurisdiction everywhere but Florida and Texas. We could drop anchor, do some business, and if necessary simply pull up anchor and, like that old song by the Floaters goes, 'Float, float on.' Poof, now you see us, now you don't."

"Isn't that illegal? Last thing we need is the feds after us."

"The feds are responsible for everything two hundred miles out, but I don't think that'll be a problem. Let's be real: they're so busy talking tough on terrorism, wiretapping American citizens, and looting the planet, I'm gambling we could slip in under the radar. We'd simply be one of hundreds of wealthy yacht people enjoying the fruits of our labors. People like that validate the American dream C. Virgil was talking about, so why mess with us?"

"Wanda, you have been doing your research. I guess you've also decided exactly where this boat of ill repute will be moored?"

That's when I let a smug smile slide onto my face, because I certainly have.

"Yep. I've found the perfect location to try out my floating-spa idea. A place where for three months a year there are lots of women without men, scads of yachts, tons of disposable income, and a constantly changing population intent on having fun. From my research into lifestyles of the rich, famous, and infamous, this place also has a substantial population of women who are well-heeled, discreet, and alone. The men are either in the city working and unavailable, not interested, or so old that even Viagra or Levitra won't help. Did I mention our pool of clients live on an island? Honey, we'll have a captive audience ready, willing, and able to appreciate all of the services A Sister's Spa offers."

"Where is this paradise? It sounds perfect. I might have to go with you and help put it together." Lydia laughs.

"In Massachusetts, just over three miles as the eagle—and I do mean the ones on U.S. Treasury notes—flies. A short and scenic watershuttle ride from the island of Martha's Vineyard."

CHAPTER 2

Lydia

SOME SAY THAT PATIENCE IS A VIRTUE, but clearly no one ever told that to Sukey, or if they did, experience had taught her that the people pushing that line were usually the same ones pushing past her. My behind has barely depressed the leather of the corner banquette inside Sapphire's, Wanda's still got one arm in her jacket, and Sukey's saying, "Lydia, could you catch the attention of the waiter next time he passes by? I need another drink." It's after lunch but before the four o'clock happy hour, so the place, usually packed with the important, self-important, and wannabe either one, is nearly deserted. In the booth in the corner opposite us is a woman about my age, and while I like to leave that in the forties for official purposes, the truth is forty-five arrived some months ago and fifty's breathing down my neck. The woman is whispering intently to a man who could be her son, although that's definitely not the case. One of her perfectly manicured hands clutches his forearm, the other appears to be embedded in his crotch, and tears roll down her cheeks, digging furrows in her perfectly applied makeup. Him? He sits looking at her impassively, that tired, bored look of a man who's gotten what he wanted and is ready to move on without drama. It's a familiar scene, one which I'm sorry to admit I've starred in a few times myself, and a key reason why Acey and I started A Sister's Spa. After years of trying to find it without success, we created a place where women can come and indulge in fabulous sexual satisfaction absent the complications and head games of feeling compelled to convince ourselves—or be convinced—that the only way to feel comfortable getting our freak on is to pretend we're in either love or a meaningful relationship. Hey, if this wasn't Wanda's party, I'd probably go over to that woman's table and give her a card for the spa. Better to look away and let the sister humiliate herself in private. My eyes pass over three drunks scattered along the length of the bar. Whatever's bothering them, they're keeping it between themselves and Jack or Johnnie, or whoever's in the sweating glasses they clutch like lifelines. Speaking of lifelines, I catch the waiter's eye, motion with my hand for him to bring a round for all of us, and turn toward Wanda.

"Are you serious about opening a spa on the Vineyard?"

Wanda waits until the waiter returns with three icy martinis and takes a big sip before responding. "*Off* Martha's Vineyard, and absolutely, girl."

"Of all the places in the world, why the Vineyard?"

"The Vineyard? So, that's what you island girls call it?" Wanda teases. "Only the nouveau boogie say Martha's Vineyard, huh?"

"Actually, yes, but that's beside the point, Wanda. Answer the question: why the Vineyard?"

"Funny you should ask. I got the idea to locate it on Martha's—sorry, I don't want to play myself as a wannabe—the Vineyard from you."

"And you got the idea to locate it on the Vineyard from me exactly how? You've never even been there, Wanda."

"You're right. Growing up in the Bronx, I was lucky to get a few days at the funky beach at City Island." She laughs. "But I've been hearing about Martha's Vineyard for years from prep school and Yale friends who've been summering there for generations." When she says *summering,* her voice goes low, nasal, and if I weren't looking right at her, I'd swear I was talking to the ghost of William F. Buckley. Wanda snickers. "Honestly, it wasn't until I started hanging around you and Acey that I realized that it wasn't just a handful of black folks with money there but a substantial colony of colored elite. Then, when you and Acey went to visit your godmother, Mrs. Nicola, at her home in Oaks Bluffs this past Labor Day—"

"Ma Nicola, not Mrs.," I interrupt. "And it's Oak, not Oaks, Bluffs, no *s.* Adding that *s* is a sure sign of a newcomer, Wanda."

"Yeah, whatever," Wanda snaps. "Anyway, I heard a lot about the black folks on the Vineyard as you were preparing to go and even more about the goings-on there once you got back. The clay cliffs of Aquinnah, lobster rolls, the beautiful beaches, the month of August, when the daily round of parties starts at brunch and doesn't end till after midnight. All the drinking, card playing, networking, and so-cializing that goes on, the famous and infamous who summer there, sounded like big fun. Yet the constant refrain I heard from you two was 'No men! No men! No men!' Seems that with all the Vineyard has to offer, dating and dick is not on the menu—unless you bring your meat with you."

"You got that right. If you see an attractive, unattended man on the island, I guarantee he's taken, underage, gay, or a mirage."

"So I gathered, and a little bit of research backed you up, in spades. Lydia, what better place to franchise and open the ultimate exclusive sex spa for women than in international waters three miles off the coast of a wealthy resort island overflowing with babes with plenty of disposable income, active libidos, and a shortage of men?" She reaches for the fresh martini glass the waiter's slid in front of her, sips daintily, and looks me in the eye. Beside her, Sukey butters a sourdough roll and peers at the menu as if she's trying to decipher hieroglyphics, seemingly oblivious to our conversation.

"Kind of like *How Stella Got Her Groove Back* goes stateside, huh?"

"Yeah, except this time Stella's straight-up paying for the pleasure, and her man ain't gay." We laugh and high-five.

"I've got to give it to you, Wanda, you've done your due diligence. And you're right, sex and the lack thereof is a constant subject of conversation on the island."

"Yep, I've got the perfect remedy and the perfect entrée: you and your godmother. Judging by the way you've described her, she's unconventional, rich, connected, and about as high up the social ladder as it's possible to climb without getting vertigo. I'm hoping that she'll help introduce us to our prospective clientele, with all due discretion, and we can take it from there. Once they visit the spa and partake of the services we offer, our product sells itself."

"Us? We?"

"You know a girl from the Harriet Tubman Houses in the South Bronx can't roll up to Martha's Vineyard and expect the doors to swing open, even with a bagful of cash. I'm gonna need some black bourgeois leverage. That's where you and that fabulous godmother of yours come in. Don't front and play hard to get, you know it'll be a ball."

"That's true. The Vineyard's always had lots of sun and socializing, just not enough sex."

"Listen, Lyds, I've been collecting data on the women who've come to the spa since we opened, and it's clear that women in search of multiorgasmic, no-strings-attached sex cross all demographics. Our clients range in age from twenty-one to ninety. Thanks to the diversity of services, the different packages we provide, and our liberal payment plans, we're able to attract women from all economic brackets. Our clients are a United Nations of sexually active women. They come in all colors, shapes, and sizes." Wanda tosses her head and the sensuous twists of her hair undulate gently.

"According to my research, the only area in which we fail to have real diversity is geographically. Seventy-two percent of our clients come from the Midwest or West because it's more convenient and less expensive to fly to Reno from those locations. And they spend between twenty-two and fifty percent more money at A Sister's Spa than clients who come from further away. Now picture the Floating Spa, staffed by our ready, willing, and able male sex workers on a luxurious yacht three miles off Martha's Vineyard, an island where the average income of summer residents is in the high six figures and women outnumber men fourteen to one. Wonderful sex and pampering await you, just a twenty-minute water-taxi ride away. It's a no-brainer. The way I see it, there's money lying—no, floating—around waiting for us to scoop up. We'd be fools *not* to franchise," Wanda says triumphantly.

"Damn, Wanda, I'm impressed."

"Thanks, but Mavis did most of the research, after I made her swear not to mention it to you or Acey and agreed to pay her fee and a substantial bribe for her silence." My mother, Mavis Ransom Beaucoup, soon to turn eighty, is a retired research librarian who hasn't lost her thirst for information or much else. Armed with a laptop I gave her a few years ago, she can find out anything. When we first came up with the idea of A Sister's Spa, it was my mother who researched the history and legality of brothels in Nevada. She's one of those people with so much energy that if she were younger, you'd have her tested for crack, crank, or a thyroid condition. She wakes early, goes to bed late, and when she doesn't have enough to do calls me too often. I hadn't wanted to look a gift horse in the mouth, but Wanda's research project explains why I'd had substantially fewer dawn phone calls in the last six months.

I look at Wanda wide-eyed and slowly shake my head in wonder. The woman is truly amazing. She's simultaneously been able to prepare for her trial, function as CFO of the spa in Reno, supervise my mother's research, create what appears to be a tight business plan in order to franchise to the East Coast, and maintain always impeccable hair and nails. Me, I'm no slouch and take care of my share of business, but I'm constantly being reminded by Acey and Odell to show some restraint in partaking of the merchandise. As for hair, the best I can maintain is a short natural. Nails? Well, I *can* say mine are always clean and never bitten.

"If you're gonna sell nails with the nooky, ya got to have Miss Sukey," a singsong voice interrupts. I've been so deep in conversation with Wanda I'd just about forgotten Sukey, who now snorts, puts down her glass, and reaches for the last roll in the basket. Damn, I hate these young girls who eat whatever they want and don't gain a pound. I take comfort in the knowledge that soon after she passes thirty her metabolism will turn on her like it has the rest of us. "I am the greatest," she adds through a mouthful of roll and, judging from her slurred words, an alcohol buzz.

"Yeah, you may be the greatest nail artist in the world, Sukey, but that don't mean shit if you're late, lazy, and just plain trifling." Wanda laughs. "We're trying to make money, cuz, not run a private welfare agency for relatives." For the first time since we've been at Sapphire's, Sukey puts down both her drink and the piece of roll she has in her hand and stops chewing. She turns her body 180 degrees in the booth so she's looking straight at Wanda.

"Dag, Wanda-babe, when does it end?" she asks softly. "I mean, yeah, I know I fucked up in the past, but I've changed, I've changed. I know how to handle my business now. I mean, I *handle* my business," she says emphatically. "Come on, Wanda-babe, lighten up. We're family," she emphasizes, as if that's the magic word, her hands reaching toward Wanda like a kid looking for a candy handout, not an adult looking for a job.

"Cut the drama, Sukey," Wanda snaps, unsuccessfully attempting to stab flaccid pieces of Boston Bibb lettuce with her fork. Sukey drops her hands and sits back against the banquette, the look on her face suddenly soft and blank, a little girl waiting to be reprimanded and hoping she won't get beat. "One reason I want to move back east and open a spa is to be closer to family, so I don't need any lecture from you about family spirit. I'm all for it, but this is business. If you come and work for me, you'd better handle your business and mine, too, you understand me, Sukey?" A look of relief passes over Sukey's face.

"I hear you, Cousin Wanda, and I know this can work. I mean, I know your spa's all about the sex, and I respect that. But sometimes Miss Kitty's gotta rest, you know what I'm saying? The pussy gotta take a breather and the body's got to get pampered, and that's where Sukey comes in. Sexed-out sister comes to the salon, picks her colors and design, climbs up in my vibrating massage chair, closes her eyes, and less than an hour later she's on her way. Body rested, nails fly as shit, ready to enjoy some more of what the spa has to offer. Instead of just rolling over in bed and snoring, she's coming to Sukey's, adding value to her stay and more revenue to the spa. You could add another three or four hundred dollars to the cash box every day."

Wanda's head jerks up. When it comes to money, she doesn't miss a trick or lose a dime. That, along with a product that—once you get over women's hump about paying for sex—sells itself, is how A Sister's Spa moved from the red to the black in less than two years. I don't doubt that Wanda can make a success of the Floating Spa back east, and I could use a change of scenery for a few months. Even though me and my lifelong best friend, Acey, started A Sister's Spa and I love her dearly, she's still conflicted about enjoying sex outside of marriage, not to mention selling it. At heart, Acey's a preacher's daughter looking for love, marriage, maybe even babies, although her biological clock is steadily winding down. Me, I've got no such reservations or aspirations. I've been married once, and *unsuccessful* doesn't begin to describe what a failure that was. Dating was a lot of work with low returns. And to be honest, and excuse me if I sound un-American, but I don't like kids. Since we opened the spa, I'm the most content I've ever been. I've got a fabulous career, a phat salary, and the pick of a couple dozen fantastic sex workers at my fingertips. Ya can't beat the benefits. My gig has some of the best perks in corporate America.

"Are you sure about this, Wanda? We have a good thing out here," I say.

"Yeah, we do, and yeah, I'm sure. It's time for me to do something different, and branching out is the obvious next step. Like I said, I'm going to need some serious help to get the spa up and running by Memorial Day, when the season starts on the East Coast, so I'm hoping Acey and Odell can take care of A Sister's Spa in Reno for a few months, and you and Chef Marvini can help me get the new business up and running. After that, we'll see . . ." Her eyes look into the distance and I can tell there's no use trying to talk her out of it, she's already on the East Coast putting together her franchise. Hey, if you can't beat 'em, join 'em.

"Sounds great, count me in," I say. "It'll be fun to spend the summer on the Vineyard, I haven't done that since I was a teenager. It won't be easy convincing Acey to let Chef Marvini go, but it'd be great to have him watching our backs, not to mention feeding our faces." Officially, Chef Marvini is in charge of all food services at the spa, from preparing delicious meals and snacks for several hundred famished clients a week to making sure that our thirty-six sex workers eat regularly and receive the nutrition they need to keep up their looks and sexual stamina. Unofficially, Marvini is a protective big brother, kindly uncle, resident pot head, and soothsayer. Me and Acey met him when we were in college. An American-history major, he started out as a great weed connection and began baking after a trip to Amsterdam over spring break junior year, during which he attempted to sample every pastry incorporating hash or marijuana he could find. Once he'd perfected baking, he moved on to other areas of cooking, sans cannabis, and his little house was where we ate many of our undergraduate meals. When we opened the spa, we offered him the job as chef. Even if he couldn't cook, we'd have hired him to just be there, observe the goings-on, watch our backs, and occasionally offer advice in that low-key "excuse me while I light my spliff" way of his. He'd saved us from ruination at least once. To my mind, Chef Marvini was good juju enveloped in a pungent cloud of reefer smoke.

Wanda laughs. "Somehow, I think they'll manage without us."

"Which means?"

Wanda shrugs, drains her martini glass. "She's your girl, you tell me. Whatever." She waves her hand dismissively. "What will be will be. Let's stay on point talking about the franchise."

"Does this mean I'm hired?" Sukey asks. Wanda ignores her.

"How many workers will we need to start up?"

"I figure eight or nine. That's about all the boat can accommodate."

"Let's make a list of five or six sex workers we can bring out from Reno for the start-up," I say, reaching into my purse for a pad and pen. "That way we won't have to train everyone from scratch. Not that I mind, but I don't think there's time if we want to open Memorial Day weekend."

"Coffee? Or would you ladies like to see the dessert menu?" I hadn't noticed that we'd finished our meal or the waiter hovering beside the table.

"Forget the coffee and cake, bring me another—" Sukey begins. Before she can finish, Wanda cuts her off with a hard look, reaches across the table, and gently wraps her plump fingers around Sukey's long, slightly trembling ones.

"That's enough, Suks." Wanda squeezes her fingers gently and the trembling diminishes. "Bring us a large bottle of Pellegrino and three double espressos." Wanda dismisses the waiter, pulls a legal pad out of the briefcase on the seat beside her, and slaps it on the table. "Enough eating, drinking, and being merry, it's time to get down to business," she declares, turning to Sukey. "You want to work for me, then sober up and tell me how much it'll cost me to set you up in a salon on my love boat. And were you talking shit or can you really generate another couple thousand dollars a week doing, uh, nail art?"

CHAPTER 3

Odell

"So I put on one of my favorite CDs for bangin', R. Kelly or maybe 50 Cent, and lie down on the bed next to her, rub up against her so she can feel I'm hard, then put her hand on it and let her rub it, you know, get an idea what she's in for. Once I'm good and hard, I roll her onto her back and fuck her until she comes and begs me to stop. But you see, here's the twist: when she does, I just keep fucking her until she passes out or runs out the room, that's when I know I got her good," Tony finishes, laughs triumphantly. He grins and his white teeth sparkle, set off by his olive complexion and dark, curly hair, a good-looking man with a big dick but not a bit of finesse. I lower my head, place my hand across my forehead, and massage my temples with thumb and forefinger, simultaneously trying not to laugh or go off.

"Do you ask the clients what they enjoy?" I ask.

"For what, Mr. Overton?" Tony shrugs. "You're a man, we both know what they enjoy, getting fucked. Why else would they be way out here in the desert paying me the fat cash to give it to them? Bada-bing," he adds, making a fist and pumping his arm from the elbow. A good-looking Italian kid, he's clearly been watching too many reruns of *The Sopranos* and doesn't understand there's a difference between making love to a woman and a Mob hit. Sitting beside me, Acey Allen, cofounder of A Sister's Spa, looks taken aback.

"What about your bunkmates, er, Tree Man and Rashid?" I ask, glancing down at the room chart in my hand. When they do sleep, which isn't that much, sex workers sleep three to a room, an arrange-ment born of necessity, since all of our clients require private accom-modations. But I believe that in the best of circumstances roommates can develop into friends and support systems. Help one another navi-gate both the physical rigors of the job and the emotional adjustments that might be necessary for some of our workers when they realize that they are, probably for the first time in their lives, purely sex objects and that the women are totally in control. I try to match newer employees with those who've been with us for a while in the hope that being in close proximity they'd help one another out and keep complaints to management, me, to a minimum.

"What about them?"

"Have you talked with either of them about some of the challenges of doing this kind of work?"

"Naw, not really. I hardly see Rashid, he's always working. Didn't he win employee of the month three times in a row? And Tree Man? He don't have shit to say. When he's not working he's reading or exercising." It's clear from his tone of voice that he considers his roommates' behaviors a waste of time.

"The reason I put you in with Rashid and Tree Man is because they know the ropes. Tree's been with us from the beginning, and Rashid for over a year, during which time he's excelled. I thought the three of you would work well together."

"Yeah, well, we might look like the United Nations, a black guy from Africa, a giant black man from down south, and me, an Italian, but it don't work like that, we ain't holding hands and singing 'We Are the World.' They go about their business and I do the same."

Acey crosses her legs, folds her arms across her chest, and clears her throat. "Mr.—er, Sanucci, is it? I hope you don't mind if I ask a few questions. Am I right in assuming that if you don't talk to your clients, you watch how they respond to your, er, well, let's call them techniques for want of a better word." He doesn't respond immediately, and I don't believe it's because he's thinking: the look he gives Acey is blank. I figure he's not listening to her, either. Beats me why a man who doesn't talk to or listen to women or read their body language would come to work at a place where providing sexual pleasure to women is the only required skill, but then what would life be without surprises? Although I prefer the more pleasant kind.

"Tony, you understand this is a serious problem, don't you?" I ask. "This is the third time we've received complaints about your work."

Acey glances down at the stack of customer comment forms in her hand. I can tell from the almost imperceptible thinning of her lips and the slight edge in her voice that she's getting fed up.

"I got no idea what you mean by complaints," Tony mumbles. Acey lets out a soft sigh of exasperation, leans forward, rhythmically taps the forms against the side of her thigh.

"Okay. What about this: 'Sex with him was too long and painful,' one woman says. 'If I wanted boring sex I could stay home,' that's another comment. 'He's like being fucked by a jackhammer with a broken off switch. The only way I could get him to stop was to lock myself in the bathroom.' These are some of the comments from the women you've serviced over the past week, Tony. Is there a problem?"

"Maybe some of these babes have a problem, I don't. As a matter of fact, I never had any fucking complaints about my boning until I started working here. Maybe the women who wrote that shit are frigid lesbian dykes or some shit." He absently pushes back a lock of hair that's fallen onto his forehead. Just under six feet, with a buffed body, good teeth, and a complexion that testifies to the Moors' time in Italy among his ancestors, Tony certainly looks the part of a strong earner for A Sister's Spa. But looks can be deceiving, and no matter how much women may like a man's looks when he's vertical, it's what goes on when he's prone that pays the bills.

"It's not your business or mine what the sexual orientation of our clients is, Tony," Acey growls. "Your job, and the job of all the men who work at A Sister's Spa, is to please and satisfy our clients, who, by the way, are always right. So if they say the sex isn't to their liking, that's your problem, and if you have a problem that affects the cash flow, then A Sister's Spa has a problem, too."

"Damn, Odell, help a brother out." Tony comes out of his slouch, turns toward me, and spreads his knees. Suddenly we're not only brothers but on a first-name basis. He's using that familiar man-to-man body language that draws an invisible circle around the males in the room, exiling Acey to a frozen zone outside.

"How so?" I ask Tony coolly. He shrugs, grins.

"Shit, you a man, you know the deal, some women just can't be satisfied, they're not built right, or they just want to complain after they get their freak on, whatever." He shrugs dismissively. "I know my shit is tight."

I'm trying to maintain my professional demeanor and listen to Tony with all due respect, but between his blinding ego and Acey rolling her eyes and making faces behind his back, it's hard not to laugh. I manage, because while Tony's youthful arrogance and ignorance are funny in a pathetic way, I know that what's about to go down needs to be carefully handled. Even though the women who are our potential clients and the men who we hire as sex workers at A Sister's Spa often laugh when they first hear about our brothel exclusively for women, from the perspective of me, Odell Overton, director of human resources and recruiting, it's strictly business and no laughing matter. Besides Chef Marvini, who keeps those healthy gourmet meals cooking, and the small maintenance staff, I'm the only man who works at the spa who doesn't provide sexual services to our clientele. Don't trip, I'm into women and like sex as much, maybe more, than the next man, but I don't have any interest in making my living pleasuring women. I made it clear when they offered me this gig that I was interested in a management position, period. My job is to find, recruit, supervise, and to the extent possible, train the men who will provide sexual services to our clients. Any sexual auditioning is taken care of by Lydia or LaShaWanda. Acey tends to stay comfortably on the administrative side of the business, although every now and then I suspect she partakes of the spa's wares, discreetly, unlike Wanda and Lydia, who behave like kids let loose in a candy store.

With a busy week coming up, the last thing I need is to be short-staffed. I'm hoping Tony's just had a brief bad run and that he can get over it and come back strong. A miracle would work, too. Just something to not leave me with one fewer worker and make my job more difficult than it already is.

"I'm trying to help you," I say, smiling. "Tell me this, before you started work, did you do a dry run, to use an inappropriate term, with Wanda or Lydia?"

"Naw, man, they didn't have time, remember? Y'all hired me right before all those union women arrived for the Labor Day weekend retreat. There wasn't time for any tryout, although Wanda did look at my shit and tell me she liked what she saw." Tony's grin is so wide it takes up most of his face, but my heart's sinking. It's clear the guy was a bad hire and has got to go. I've learned working at the spa that when it comes to a man's ability to suppress his own physical needs and ego and focus solely on pleasuring women, beauty is often only skin deep.

"Get with it, Odell," Lydia told me once when I mentioned my surprise that Christian, a short, balding brother from Guadeloupe with a slight paunch, was one of the sex workers who returning clients most often requested. "Chances are a tall, handsome, buffed brother like you is going to pull the women without really trying, because before you open your mouth or get near a bed, you've stepped into a sister's fantasy. Now, brothers like Christian are like Avis, popular opinion says they're second best, so they've got to try harder. Now, the perfect man looks great *and* is a champ in bed, but perfect ain't easy to find."

"Tony, we're going to have to let you go," Acey says as I'm still trying to find the right words. This is the difficult part of the job, not least because in a way you're firing two distinct entities, the man and his penis. It's a double whammy men take very personally; I know I would. Tony's grin freezes on his face. He looks like an animal caught in the glare of headlights.

"What? Let me go where?" He's not only a lousy sex worker but far from the brightest bulb in the box.

"I'm sorry, but it's just not working out," Acey continues, her voice modulated and firm. "This is, what?" She glances down at his file in her hand. "The third notice we've given you concerning negative feedback from the women you've serviced?" She looks Tony in the eye, one perfectly shaped eyebrow slightly arched. I watch her admiringly.

I mean, damn, this sister is cool and beautiful. If I didn't know her better, I'd think this was a casual, friendly conversation, not the end of the road.

"Hey, wait, maybe I just got a bad crop of clients, need a little more time to get into my rhythm—"

Acey interrupts, an undertone of impatience in her voice. "You've made my point, Tony, that you're just not suited for the mission of the spa. First, there are no bad clients. Second, you've been with us, what, two months? And if that's not enough time to, as you say, 'find your rhythm,' I'm sorry for you.

"We'll give you two weeks severance pay and a ticket back to—did you say you're from Providence?" Acey plows on calmly. I remember where the wannabe Italian stallion came from: Acey and Lydia had flown into Providence airport the previous summer on their way to visit Lydia's godmother on Martha's Vineyard, and Tony drove the shuttle bus to the ferry. No doubt they'd chatted, Lydia had flirted, and they'd left him with a nice tip, an application for employment at A Sister's Spa, and nine months later here we were, about to send Tony back to where he'd started.

"Thanks so much for your service and I'm sorry it didn't work out," Acey says, standing and extending her hand. Tony rises and takes it. He looks shocked, as if he's not quite sure what's happening. She squeezes his hand, smiles warmly. "I wish you the very best in life; now, go on to the men's dorm and start packing your things. The car to the airport will be out front in an hour."

Tony stands silently, his bottom lip hanging, still holding Acey's hand and looking startled, as if he's hypnotized by her voice or so surprised at being fired he's mute. I stand, reach for his hand, and he snaps out of it.

"We at A Sister's Spa sincerely wish you the best in your future endeavors," I begin. Still clasping his hand, I place an arm around his shoulder, I reach for the doorknob, open the door. Standing outside are two of my biggest workers, Tree Man and Enrique, who double as security on the rare occasions when someone has to be escorted off the premises. When security is called it's more often because a client's enjoyed herself so much she refuses to leave. Our rule is that once you book a service, that's it, when it's over it's over. Clients are always welcome back, but they have to go home first and regain perspective. A Sister's Spa isn't the real world and our clients shouldn't confuse lust with love.

"Hey, Odell, man, you're making a mistake," Tony says, grabbing the edge of the door and stopping. "You don't want to send me back home, that's going to cause serious problems, man, my mom'll kill me. Lemme have another chance." The arrogance is gone, and he's close to pleading.

"I wish I could, but it's too late." I place a hand on his shoulder, simultaneously patting and pushing him into the able clutches of Tree Man and Enrique. For a few moments the four of us are frozen in a doorway tableau, then Tony releases the frame.

"You're making a mistake, man, a serious mistake." He turns to me, shaking my hand off his shoulder and walking out the door. Neither Tree nor Enrique touches him, following discreetly as he walks toward his room.

I close the door and turn to congratulate Acey on a job well done. She's fallen back into her chair, her rich brown skin looks suddenly ashen, her breath comes quick and hard, and there's a troubled look in her eyes. "Are you okay, Acey?" She slowly nods her head yes. "You sure? You don't look so great. Let me get you some water." As I walk around her to the small refrigerator behind my desk, a whiff of her perfume wafts into my nostrils. I twist the top off a bottle of Fiji water, pour some into a chunky crystal goblet, and hand it to her. She wraps her slender, manicured fingers around it, takes a long sip.

"Thanks, Odell. I needed that."

"Everything okay?"

"I guess so."

"You guess?"

"I just hope we did the right thing."

"We gave him every chance to save himself, Acey. He didn't."

"I know. I know Tony had to go. I guess I just have a bad feeling about it."

"That's normal. It's never easy to fire someone."

"No, it's not. But I've fired people before and didn't feel like this."

"Like what?"

"I just have a bad feeling."

"Bad how? He'll be off-site in an hour. I've got a list of approved applicants to choose from to fill his spot. I've sent all the clients who complained a note of apology and invited them to come back and enjoy a night of free services." Acey smiles, reaches up, and soothingly pats my cheek as she moves toward the door.

"I'm not sure, Odell, but I'm going to think and pray on it," she says. "I'll let you know if I come up with anything. Until then, don't stress. It's just a feeling and my feelings are—"

Before she can finish, the phone on my desk rings. Reflexively, I pick it up on the first ring and a familiar voice crows, "Odell, I might just have to clone your ass! I won my case big-time and I'm about to become the first to franchise A Sister's Spa!"

Wanda's talking so fast I can't catch everything she's saying, in addition to which, Acey's pushed up against me, standing on tiptoe with one ear against the other side of the telephone receiver, and most of what's being said is lost in the middle. The truth is, I'm distracted by

Acey's left breast pressing against my right elbow and the warm, faded scent of her perfume. I don't think I've been this close to her since that day two years ago when we made mad love in the bell tower of her father's former church after Sunday service. Right after that, Lydia and Acey offered me this job. This job provided the opportunity to leave my job driving for UPS, make way more money, and build a business from the ground up. Like Lydia, Acey, and Wanda, I'd moved to Reno from the San Francisco Bay Area, which had made it easy for me to keep an eye on my triplet brothers, DeJuan, DeQuan, and DeMon, then undergraduates at the University of Nevada, Las Vegas. They'd even worked at the spa on weekends when they were finishing school, and since graduation they'd worked here full time while they waited to hear from grad school or a positive response to their job search. Our clients spoke rapturously of their sexcapades with "The Triplets."

When I hooked up with Lydia and Acey, I was about to turn thirty, been with UPS for five years—not exactly intellectually stimulating work—and was past ready to do something besides delivering packages and having sex with the female recipients. Behind more doors than you'd imagine was the same jackpot: a woman yearning for sex and attention and more interested in the package between my legs than the one in my hands. At first this seemed like a man's cornucopia, but once I got my ego in check, I figured out that not only didn't these women care about their packages, they didn't care about me. I was a safe, hard dick, period. No one was interested in my feelings, how my day was going, or my dreams or aspirations. Not that I was interested in those aspects of them, either, I just didn't realize what a user I was until the script was flipped. When I took the job with A Sister's Spa, I'd recently ended what passed as a relationship but was really anonymous, meaningless sex, no intimacy, only with the same woman. I was ready to open a new door, wasn't sure what it was, and then these two smart, sexy business sisters invited me to join them in creating the first-ever bona fide brothel for women. I wasn't sure that women would be willing to pay for what they were used to getting for free, but Lydia convinced me that catching was too iffy and the emotional and psychological price exacted from women was already exorbitant. Add to that the implicit risks in deciding to have intimate relations with a virtual stranger who could turn out to be an abusive maniac, bad in bed, diseased, condom-phobic, or all of the above, and the costs increased. Then there were all the rituals of courtship, difficult to dispense with even in the most straightforward and cynical of sexual transactions. Dating, making small talk, sharing brief, highly edited biographies, and feigning interest to get to the sex. Listen, after Lydia described the torturous routes women had to travel in search of satisfaction, I was convinced.

A Sister's Spa opened almost two years ago, and business has been, if you'll excuse the word, banging. Judging from the rate of recidivism, bowlegs, and smug looks of contentment on their faces when they check out, for the most part our clients are pleased with our services. We ask all our guests to fill out detailed exit questionnaires and we take their comments seriously. A Sister's Spa's motto is "Women's pleasure on women's terms." If an employee can't or won't embrace that concept, it's time for him to move on.

The past few months I've been wondering if it's time for me to do the same. For the last two years, the major relationship in my life has been with A Sister's Spa and that's been pretty much all work and no play. Besides our clients, the only women regularly on the premises are Acey, Lydia, and Wanda, my business partners. Call me old-fashioned, but I'm not the type to avail myself of the services of the dozens of brothels for men that dot the Nevada landscape, so for the most part I live a fairly celibate life. When that gets to be too much, I take a quick trip back to the Bay Area. I've kept in touch with a few of the women I met on my UPS route, and we've maintained open, honest relationships of casual friendship and mutual sexual opportunism. Still, in the last few months I've found myself thinking about what's next.

"Ask her when they're coming home!" Acey instructs, tugging on my sleeve and pulling me out of my head and back to the present. "Tell her to hurry up. I want to hear every detail of the trial, the decision, and C. Virgil Susquehanna."

"Did you hear that, Wanda? Acey says to tell you two to hurry up and come home so she can get the 411." I try to decipher the torrent of words that rush from Wanda's mouth, since it's no use asking her to slow it down.

"You're going where? To do what? Ran into who? Yeah, I'll tell her, but first tell me—" But before I can ask when she and Lydia expect to be back in Reno, Wanda crows, "Ciao, Odell, baby. Gotta go get me a piece to celebrate my victory!" and the line goes dead.

CHAPTER 4

Wanda

"Y OU KNOW I LOVE ODELL TO DEATH, BUT the brother needs to learn to loosen up," I say to Lydia, flipping my cell phone closed with a sharp *thwack*! I toss my hair away from my face and over my shoulders in a gesture now available to women of all colors and hair textures thanks to the magic of twists, locks, weaves, and extensions. I'm convinced that one of the reasons black women love extensions and weaves is that they finally give us something on our heads to toss. And leave it to us to create a whole vocabulary of hair throwing. There's the angry toss, the seductive, "I know you want to run your hands through this shit" toss, and the passive-aggressive toss, which involves making sure the hair makes impact with a body part, preferably the hand or face, of the offending individual. But for true, my favorite move is the one I just made, which I like to call the "just because I can" toss. That's when a sister tosses naturally, organically, reflexively, as if she's had tossable hair all her life, a toss of pure pleasure.

Which is exactly what I'm feeling at the moment, and I don't want anything to interfere with that emotion. That includes any further conversation with my cousin Sukey and getting into a ménage à trois on the telephone with Odell and Acey, trying to fill them in on the court decision and my plans. There'll be time enough for that between now and Memorial Day weekend. At the moment my stomach's full, I'm buzzed on martinis, and I'm rich. Right through here all I'm interested in is getting out of these court clothes, into a long shower, and hopefully, some great sex.

"Cuz, you really going to hire me?" Behind me, Sukey tugs on my sleeve as we move through the dim late-afternoon light of the restaurant toward the doorway.

"You're hired on a three-month trial basis, Memorial Day to Labor Day. Start closing out your affairs here, be ready to move when I call you, and you've got to stop drinking, Sukey. It'd also help if you started working on some new nail motifs especially for the Floating Spa, maybe with a nautical theme." Sukey can be a pain in the ass and needy as hell, but when it comes to painting designs on nails, she's the absolute best. I don't doubt that she can bring a needed service and a nice piece of cash to the weekly revenues of the East Coast spa if she's committed and focused.

"Suks, I love you, but let's get this straight. I am hiring you because you are very good at what you do, not because you're blood. That said, I believe you can offer a needed service and increase revenues. I'm also hiring you because the spa is on a boat and I know you can't swim and are too afraid of the water to try and row yourself to shore. You'll be living and working on the boat. You won't be able to do your disappearing act or sneak drinks, and when you work for me there's no such thing as being late. I love you dearly, Sukey. But this is my business, and if you mess up, I will not only fire your ass but set you adrift on the ocean."

Walking beside me, Lydia snickers. I cut her a look and she nips that chuckle in the bud. As was my intention, Sukey looks chastened.

"Okay, Wanda-babe. I hear you. I'm not going to let you down," she says.

"You best not," I say, squinting as we exit the dim cocoon of Sapphire's, almost blinded by the hard white sun of late afternoon. I turn, open my arms, and Sukey scoots into them.

"I won't. You'll see, and thanks for giving me a chance. You won't regret it." Her body feels frail and skinny in my arms, but when I hug her tight I feel the hardness of muscle and bone underneath and her seeming frailty disappears. I release her, hold her at arm's length, look into her face.

"You're welcome. Now, if you'll excuse me, I'm going to go make some mischief with my girl Lydia, then we're headed back to Reno in the morning. Wrap things up here, and when I call be ready to empty the fridge, lock the apartment door, and head east. The next time I see you it'll be on the Floating Spa. Can we drop you somewhere?" I'm relieved when Sukey shakes her head.

"I'm gonna walk some, clear my head, and start thinking about those nautical motifs you mentioned. See you in a month, Wanda-babe; you, too, Lydia," Sukey says, waving and heading toward Market Street. I watch her initially wobbly walk straighten up as she goes, and say a silent prayer that she'll actually handle her business and help expand mine. But enough. By the time she turns the corner a block away, she's out of sight and out of mind.

"Okay, let the games begin!"

"Exactly which games are we talking about?" Lydia asks, laughing.

"Definitely ones that involve me getting out of these heels and panty hose." I laugh. "Is it only because I'm a big girl that after a full day in stockings I feel as if I'm wearing a girdle from the waist down and being slowly suffocated?"

Lydia, who at the moment wears a ten but fluctuates between eight and fourteen, laughs. "Wanda, size has nothing to do with it, at least when it comes to panty hose. After more than a few hours, it's just wrong."

"Speaking of size, what's with that African brother Jamal, the taxi driver?"

"I don't know. When me and Acey met him on the beach in Mombasa, we were both too exhausted to check him out. As you may recall, that trip was about R and R, sisterhood and bonding, not chasing the dick."

"Bitch, please." I can't help laughing. "You know if you'd been alone or with me, you woulda jumped the brother's bones. I mean, what do you think these folks mean when they talk about 'going back to your roots,' a trip to the hair salon? Tell a sister this: how you going to go all the way to Africa and not check out the brothers? That's plain crazy."

"Maybe, but it's the truth. Look at it this way, the good news is that the brother's here and just a phone call away." Lydia reaches into her purse and extracts the business card Afrodonis gave us earlier, fans her brow with it. "What can I say? I'm getting hot already."

I'm way ahead of her. I've already got my phone out, my X-ray vision on, and am dialing his number. I hand the phone to Lydia. "Tell him to meet us at the hotel after his meeting. Meanwhile, let's hop in the first thing smokin', go back to the room, and chill until he gets there."

"No answer, but I left a message," Lydia says, sticking her hand up. A taxi screeches to the curb and I slide in first, pushing aside a newspaper left by the previous passenger and cursorily reading the headline, PREZ TO ANNOUNCE NEW DOMESTIC PLAN SOON. I suck my teeth reflexively, the only possible response barring homicide when I'm reminded of George W. Bush, and stuff the paper underneath the driver's seat. Lydia scooches in beside me and leans forward to give the cabbie the address as I let my head fall back against the seat.

Before Lydia's closed and locked the door to the two-bedroom suite we're sharing at the Ritz-Carlton on Nob Hill, I've unbuttoned my suit jacket, hiked my skirt up around my waist, and am halfway out of my stockings as I hop toward the bathroom and a nice long shower. I'm in that weird zone where I'm exhausted and wired simultaneously; my mind and body are so overstimulated that I'm like a car whose gas pedal is floored but the brake's on and I can't go anywhere, my wheels are just spinning. I'm hoping that a long shower, a nap, and some spectacular African sex will either help me come back to earth or transport me to a place where being in overdrive feels normal. Either way, I'll be good. Shit, the truth is that whatever happens, I'm great. I'm a millionaire with no dependents, the chief financial officer of a business that's lucrative, and about to open my very own franchise back east.

I pull my twists off my face and back in a ponytail, secure then with a purple scrunchie, step into a glass-walled shower as big as the room I shared with my sister in the Bronx, and turn on the water. Water sprays from six jets on each of three walls, massaging my body from ankles to neck. Above me, a flat showerhead the diameter of a large pizza sprays water onto my upturned face. I adjust the temperature to hot and turn around slowly, letting the water gently caress my body. I reach forward, bending slightly to make the water a little hotter. A jet of water pushes suggestively against my pelvis. I turn toward the source, bend my knees slightly, position the triangle of my vagina and the thick, tight curls of hair that cover it directly in front of the squirting stream. The water pulses steadily against that part of my vagina that conceals my hooded clit, gently coaxing it to emerge. The sudden, shooting pleasure of desire rushes through my body, radiates from between my legs upward to my stomach, breasts, mouth, and into my brain. Leaning back with one hand, I brace myself against the shower's marble wall, simultaneously lifting and shifting my hips to meet the warm stream of water. With the other hand I reach forward, fumble against the wall in front of me trying to find the waterproof CD player I know is there. I open my eyes but can see little through the steam, feel a button, and push it. *"Everybody get together gonna love one another right now."* Lizz Wright's sultry voice fills the small space and wraps itself around me as she sings. I let her voice and the water caress me, push up on abbreviated tiptoes, and open my legs a few inches wider to allow easy access to my love nugget. My breath quickens and I open my mouth as I breathe, warm water falling against my lips and tumbling into my mouth. I reach out and place the palm of my left hand flat against the tiled shower wall to steady myself. My right hand reaches for the bottle of Warm Spirit mango shower gel I travel with and I squeeze a dab onto my pubic hair, letting the bottle fall and disappear into the swirling steam. I reach down with my hand, parting the hairs and the lips of my labia as my soapy fingers begin to massage that most sensitive of all places. I caress my clit with gentle circular motions as the water kneads my body on three sides. I can feel the lips of my labia begin to swell and get wet as I increase the pressure of my hand, thrusting my hips forward to meet my hand, pushing against my fingers. The movement places my nipples directly in the path of water and I close my eyes, imagining that each pulsation is a warm tongue gently sucking, sucking, sucking . . .

Pressing the middle and index fingers of my right hand together, I gently push apart the bit of skin still covering my swollen clitoris. I feel it roll like a ball bearing just beneath my skin as I massage with two fingers. The waves of orgasm begin to build inside my body, the heat around my earlobes that always comes when I am sexually aroused shoots up. I increase the pressure and motion of my fingers, moving them rapidly in small, tight circles. The steam of the hot shower envelops me and all I can hear is the water hitting my body and the floor and the sound of my own short, rapid exhalations as my climax builds. I am almost there, almost, almost, almost. Between the heat of the shower, the steam, my body's response to my touch, and Lizz Wright singing about "Chasing Strange," my breath comes short and fast, on the verge of orgasm I am near breathlessness. Reflexively, I open my mouth wide to gasp for air, but instead take in a mouthful of water and begin to first choke, then cough. So there I am, all one-hundred-eighty-plus pounds of me, buck naked in a shower with a clit that feels as big as a plum, swollen nipples, and water coming out of my nose as I cough so hard I wouldn't be surprised if one of my lungs flew out of my chest. My orgasm? It's retreating as fast as a man who ain't ready when you mention marriage. The good news is that unlike a marriage-phobic man, I'm sure my orgasm will be back.

And you know, once I finish coughing, I have to laugh at myself and count my blessings that I didn't slip and bust my head wide open on this fabulous day in the life of LaShaWanda P. Marshall. I can see the headlines now, WOMAN MASTURBATES HERSELF TO DEATH AFTER LEGAL VICTORY. I turn off the water and step out of the shower, wrap myself in one of the thick, fluffy bathrobes the hotel provides, and gently pat my hair dry with a towel. Lizz Wright's finished, and through the bathroom door I can faintly hear the funky rhythm and deep beat of James Brown's "Lickin' Stick." Involuntarily, my body starts moving to the music as I dry off. Maceo Parker's sax comes in during the break and my hips sway from side to side. Before I know it I'm singing along as loud as I can, *"Mama come here quick / And bring me that lickin' stick / Lickin' stiiiiick! Lickin' stiiiiick."* As with most of his songs, I have no idea what James is talking about but know exactly what he means.

"Lydia! What's the plan? Did you reach Afrodonis?" I holler, stumbling out of the steamy bathroom and down the hall toward the living room.

"Yeah. I gave him my number and he'll come by after his meeting. I figure we can have some drinks, feel him out, and if we so desire, take it from there—wherever that may lead us," she adds, grinning.

"Sounds good to me, and that gives us a couple hours to relax." I grab a champagne from the bar and plop down in an overstuffed arm-chair. Lydia sits curled up on the couch across the room. One hand is on her feet as she massages her cramped toes, recently released from their expensive and stylish Christian Louboutin prison, a more upscale relative of the panty hose lockdown from which I've recently sprung myself, back to life.

CHAPTER 5

Lydia

HARD AS I TRY TO IGNORE THE INSIS-
tent bleating of my cell phone or incor-
porate it into my dream, it won't cooperate. By
the time I fumble around the dark hotel room, lit
now only by the ambient streetlight that sneaks
through the curtains, find my pocketbook, and
dig around in search of that annoying little
sucker, I'm wide awake.

"Hello?" My voice is raspy from sleep and a
dry mouth.

"Lydia? Jamal M'Benge-Min at your service."

"Ah, Jamal. Right. What time is it?" Now I'm
feeling around for the lamp switch, my glasses,
and something to wet my throat.

"Just after eight. Shall we meet now?" Still

fiddling with the lamp, trying to find the damn switch, with my other hand I feel around on the end table, grab a glass, gulp. Ahhh, water.

"Sure, sure, come on." Finally, the light comes on. "See you in . . . ?" I pause, listening. "Okay, a half hour."

Still sleepy and discombobulated, I plop down on the couch and take a long drink. As I try to remember how I got to this time and space, my eyes drift around the room, noticing Wanda's shoes kicked off by the door, her briefcase on the floor beside the couch, my high-heeled slippers on the end of the couch, where I'd worked them off while sleeping, several empty champagne glasses on the coffee table. Right, right, me and Wanda'd been lying around celebrating, reliving the high points of the trial and making plans for the new spa. Then Wanda'd gone into the bedroom to take a nap and I'd decided to continue celebrating by myself. I reach over and pick up the bottle of Veuve Clicquot from the table. Empty. About all I remember is that it was still light outside when I poured that last glass.

I pick up the remote, click on the television. The flat screen nestled in an armoire above the minibar blinks on to CNN. "And for more on the president's remarks at today's Republicans for Right, we go to our correspondent Barbaralee Edison," the anchorman is saying. The camera jumps to a statuesque sister wearing a zebra-print cat suit, a tiny black leather jacket that ends just below her ample breasts, and enough fake hair to make Beyoncé feel insecure.

"Thanks, Rob. This is Barbaralee Edison outside the hotel where earlier President Bush spoke to the Republican faithful, unveiling his new domestic agenda. As you know, the president has been criticized for not paying enough attention to domestic issues. Some say his speech today was an effort to signal that he's got more on his mind than the war on terror. Let's listen to a bit of what he said . . ."

The picture switches and there he is, the president, looking as if he were separated at birth from *MAD* magazine's mascot, Alfred E. Neuman, although Alfred obviously kept all the brains. I feel my stomach clench looking at his flat, smug, empty visage. Since he stole the presidency in 2000, being an American has become a profoundly depressing experience.

"Democracy is not easy to defend. Terror is not easy to defeat. Sometimes it takes terrifying measures to combat terrorism. Unconstitutional measures to protect the Constitution. There are those who say we go too far. That surveillance of our citizens, torturing suspected terrorists, jailing American citizens and foreigners without charges, is wrong and illegal. It is my belief and the belief of my advisers that no action taken by the president to protect America from those who hate us because we have thongs, MTV, and freedom is wrong or illegal. The enemy is out there, waiting to strike. We will employ any means necessary to protect America from those at home and abroad who wish to destroy our democratic freedoms.

"It is time for all Americans to get involved in this fight. Before you left-wingers start cheering, let me say unequivocally that I do not plan to reinstate a military draft or raise taxes. No way. Today I unveil the most important domestic program of my presidency, No Child, No Behind: The Crusade for Families and Abstinence. Why? Because the purpose of intercourse is not recreation but reproduction. Do you think those infidels who hate us have sex because they enjoy it? No, they fornicate with a purpose, and that purpose is to produce more soldiers and suicide bombers to join the jihad against our great democracy. No Child, No Behind is designed to promote sex for procreation. To build America. In a few weeks I will submit a bill to Congress with details. We will offer a tax credit to couples who agree to stop using birth control and reproduce. We will offer a reward to patriotic Americans who identify those who indulge in sex for purposes other than procreation. Our mandate is to strengthen the role of God and morality in our country and produce children who will grow up to continue the glorious crusade against the infidels that we have begun. We must fight fire with fire. We must procreate. We must make love to make war!"

Thankfully, the camera cuts away from boy George just before I throw my high-heeled slipper at the president's head and find a charge for a destroyed flat-screen television on the bill when we check out. "So, if I heard him right, Rob, the president plans to outlaw recreational sex," Barbaralee, a good journalist and an opportunist of the first order, murmurs into the camera. "It'll be fascinating to see how he plans to pull that off. He can't be in all of America's bedrooms simultaneously. Or can he? One thing about this president, you can't count him out. Who would have thought when he took office that Americans would go along with preemptive war, loss of habeas corpus, extraordinary rendition, the largest budget deficit in history, or four dollars a gallon for gasoline? Actually, next to that list, banning sex for fun might be easy. If there's one thing George W. Bush has proven, it's never underestimate the power of fear. We'll keep you posted on No Child, No Behind. Back to you, Rob."

I can feel my blood pressure begin to rise and a snarl start to form on my lips, a sure way to ruin what could be a perfectly lovely evening. In the interests of self-preservation, I bang the off button with my thumb and throw the remote on the couch before Rob can open his mouth in an effort to sum up, explain, or justify the president's latest insane scheme. Or even worse, before he can toss that dubious honor to the usual motley panel of pundits on retainer as they scamper onto the set in their familiar effort to spin this latest presidential idiocy into gold for themselves. I walk around the suite's living room, plumping pillows with my fist, tossing half-empty bottles of water into the trash, throw-

ing shoes, briefcases, and everything else into the closet in the foyer.
I pause in front of the mirror, check my face, pick a few pieces of lint
out of my short natural, go into the bathroom to rinse my face, brush
my teeth, reapply a bit of makeup. I stop outside the door to the dark-
ened bedroom, listening, carefully turn the knob, ease the door open,
blink into the darkness. When my eyes adjust I can make out Wanda
sprawled on the king-size bed, her ample breasts rising and falling as
she breathes. "Wanda. Wanda. Hey, Wanda!" I hiss into the darkness, my voice increasingly insistent. Wanda moans, murmurs, turns
away from me in a sleepy gesture of dismissal, but I'm having none of
it. "Wanda. Get up. Jamal will be here in a few minutes," I whisper.
She grunts, snuggles down into the plush robe, trying to burrow away
from me. I raise my voice slightly, give her one last chance. "Wanda,
Jamal is on his way over to give us some of that fabulous African love.
Get up or you'll miss it." Wanda just pulls her legs toward her chest
into the fetal position. The light from the hallway falls on her face,
and for the first time in weeks, she looks absolutely relaxed, incredibly
content, the lines of tension and worry invisible as she sleeps. I creep
into the room and pull the lightweight down comforter at the foot of
the bed over her, watch as her body relaxes into the cocoon of warmth
it provides, and softly back out of the room, pulling the door shut behind me.

I've just finished pulling on an African-print caftan I'd bought in
Kenya and freshened my lipstick when there's a gentle tap on the door.
Opening it, I'm startled once again by how attractive Jamal is. He's
wearing a short-sleeved gray linen shirt and loose slacks just a shade
darker. His skin is that dark, rich brown, near black, that seems to absorb and refract light simultaneously. Against his tight biceps the gray
of his shirt is bright and iridescent.

"Hey, Jamal. Come on in. You got here fast."

"Yes, I hurried. I was eager to see you." He walks into the room, glances around. "Where is your friend Wanda?"

"Whipped. She fell out a few hours ago and I don't have the heart to wake her up. I'm sure she'll be sorry she missed you." He shrugs easily, confidently.

"There will be other opportunities."

"For?" I turn to look at him.

"For whatever it is she needs. Tonight we will focus on your needs."

I laugh. "Yeah, well, right now I could use a drink and a foot massage," I say, taking a bottle of bubbly and glasses from the bar and removing the foil from around the cork.

"Relax. Sit down, let me take care of that." Jamal comes up behind me, encircles my arms with his as he reaches around and takes the bottle from my hands, easily pops the cork with a flick of his thumb. I can feel heat emanate from his body, smell the faint scent of musk mixed with man, the ultimate aphrodisiac. I close my eyes and inhale deeply, vaguely startled when Jamal leads me to a chair and sits down on the ottoman in front of it. He reaches down and lifts my feet, cupping the heels in the palms of his hands and settling them gently against his crotch. He begins to squeeze both feet, working his way slowly from heel to arch to ball of my foot and finally to my toes. He kneads them firmly, first all five toes, then one at a time, increasing the pressure until the feeling is so good it is almost excruciating. Involuntarily my feet try to squirm away as Jamal lifts my foot, bending my leg at the knee, his long, lithe body leaning toward me. I hear Jamal chuckle at the same moment I feel his warm breath on my foot, then feel the wetness of his tongue as he inserts it in the space between my big toe and the one next to it. He firmly caresses the toes of my left foot, still resting against his crotch, in one hand while he makes love to the toes of my right foot with his mouth. His tongue licks up one side, then the other, outlining each toe before his lips close over it. He moves slowly from toe to toe, licking, sucking, caressing. I relax, give myself over to this oral foot massage, feel the muscles of my vagina tighten as I begin to get wet, and smile to myself at the lovely easiness of sex without pretense or embellishment or aspiration, the pure physical joy of it. Jamal moves on to the other foot and I reach down and lazily caress the hair that lies tight against his scalp, run my forefingers along the rim behind his ears, gently roll his earlobes between thumb and forefinger. Against the heel of my foot I feel his penis throb and swell, shift my foot so that I caress his dick with satiated toes. He finishes with my foot, lifts both my legs, and drapes them over the arms of the overstuffed chair. He slides his hand underneath my ass, tucks the flowing fabric of the caftan underneath me so my legs are bent and spread wide, my pussy exposed. With his long arms he reaches to either side and grabs a foot, squeezing and caressing as he lowers his mouth to the space between my legs. There is only a moment between feeling his hot breath on my inner thighs and the first touch of his tongue as he licks from the bottom of my vagina up to the clit in long, slow, even strokes. With spread fingers I hold the sides of his head and try to push his head down as I rise to meet him. He licks me slowly, evenly, thoroughly, refusing to be rushed or rush me, letting the long swipes of his tongue linger against my labia, finding sensation in places I did not know there was any. The sultry dragging of his tongue against my clit, now swollen and protruding from the protective folds of skin, makes me want to cry out. I do not know how long this goes on, only that after a while it is as if my whole body is weeping with orgasm and I am glad I sit on yards of voluminous fabric, not wanting to ruin this lovely chair.

"Slide down," Jamal whispers through a mouthful of pussy. I scooch down until he stops me, my legs spread wide along either arm of the chair, my ass nearly hanging off the seat. "Hold on to the back of the chair," he softly instructs. I raise my hands over my head, sink my fingers into the thick upholstery. I hear the sound of fabric rustling, the metallic click of metal against metal as a zipper opens, the soft rip of plastic as a condom wrapper is torn, then feel the heat and pressure as Jamal presses the fat head of his penis against my dripping pussy, eases himself inside me piece by piece by piece by piece, pushing until he is all the way in, settled. Then he begins to stroke slowly and methodically, resisting the efforts of my hips to pick up the pace, smothering the demanding words I try to speak with his full lips, long tongue, deep kisses.

"Relax, Lydia, relax. I will make you come like the rains on the roof of my father's thatched hut in Kenya," he murmurs. He says other things, but I damn sure can't hear him, his words are drowned out by the rushing of my blood and the tingling of all my senses, by the pure feeling of orgasm that eats up all words, thoughts, everything that isn't in this moment. And even though when Acey and I were in Kenya we stayed in a modern hotel with a tile roof, the only thatched hut in sight a plastic facsimile over the pool bar, and it didn't rain once during the two weeks we were there, when I come it is in torrents that go on and on and on, not just a passing rain in Kenya but the torrential downpour of rainy season.

"So, have you found your future?" I tease Jamal M'Benge-Min a few hours later. We're lying entwined together on the couch, a tangle of legs, arms, and satiated libidos, each sipping from a large glass of water. The bottle of champagne we'd open earlier sits ignored on the coffee table, warm and going flat, but as much as I enjoy the bubbly, I've got no regrets. Given the fabulous experience of the last few hours, liquor seems decidedly superfluous. We've been hydrating ourselves and talking in that easy, desultory way that comes after great sex. Even though I'm ready to hire him to work on the Floating Spa right then and there, I'm trying to find out a bit more about him, if only so I'll have something to say and won't have to look sheepish and embarrassed when Acey and Wanda give me the third degree. He's got a degree in international relations from the University of Nairobi, and is the oldest son of a mother who's a Kenyan diplomat and a father who's a high school principal. So much for the stereotypical, tired backstory I'd dreamed up for him: son of a poor goatherd who'd run away to the big city, in this case Mombasa, to escape an oppressive life of poverty, fighting to protect his herd from lions on the Serengeti, and several wives and a dozen children.

"Not yet," Jamal responds to my question, flashes a brief smile. His eyes twinkle and I catch a glimpse of white teeth, deep pink tongue.

"Which means?"

"Which means I am open to new opportunities," Jamal says enigmatically.

"How about a new job?"

"That would depend on what kind of work is required." He smiles that sparkling smile again, and I feel my heart seize in my chest and the muscles in my pussy clench impatiently. It's time to cut to the chase. After the sex we've been having for the last hours, beating around the bush is a total waste of time.

"Sex work, Jamal. We're opening a spa for women on a yacht off Martha's Vineyard, an island off the coast of Massachusetts, in a few months. And if you're, excuse the expression, up for it, there's no doubt that you can do the work."

Jamal laughs. "Tell me more about this place and this business." I give the abbreviated version, and when I finish he is quiet, his face relaxed and thoughtful. I take a long drink of water, prepared to answer more questions.

"When do we leave?" Jamal finally asks. I'm startled, then I start laughing.

"So, I guess you've found your future, huh? At least for now."

"It would appear so," Jamal says in his deep, sexy voice.

"Wonderful. Any more like you looking for their future, too?" I tease.

"I have several friends who would probably be interested. They are hard workers as well." He grins.

"Wonderful. Here's to the future." I raise my glass.

He does the same, extends it toward me. "To our future," he says. I lean forward awkwardly, intending to gently tap my glass against his. But I've not yet fully recovered control of my sex-fatigued muscles; my arm slips, and the impact of the glasses sloshes water down the front of my caftan.

"No worry. Let me help clean that up." Jamal bends down and licks water from the fabric across my breast as his tongue follows its trail toward my navel. Why fight the feeling? I let my head fall back against the pillows and watch through heavy-lidded eyes as his purple lips kiss their way down south. I can't speak for Jamal, but my future looks delectable.

CHAPTER 6

Odell

AMONG THE MANY, MANY THINGS I'VE learned about relations between the sexes since I came to work at the spa is that most of the time it's best for me keep my mouth closed and listen. Working with Lydia, Acey, and Wanda—not to mention the thousands of female clients—has been an ad hoc, accelerated course in understanding the minds and desires of women and trying to figure out where and how I fit in. I haven't answered the sprawling, cosmic question of what do women want—besides great sex on demand, that is—I'm still working on that. But what's evident to me is that what they don't want is the response that comes most naturally to me—in fact, I think it's hardwired into men's

DNA—to be the fixer. I finally understand that for women, talking is a kind of action and that words create motion and serve to move them forward. Talk isn't cheap but an essential part of how they understand and order the world.

Which is why I'm silent, focused on my Pilates routine and sweating slightly as I listen to the animated conversation taking place around me.

"Acey, you know it's a sign, was meant to be. I mean, come on, what are the chances of catching a cab driven by the brother we met in Mombasa on the very day Wanda wins her case and announces she intends to franchise, which means we'll be needing an infusion of sex workers. This could not be chance. It's got to be fate. Tell her, Odell," Lydia says, looking down at me, an imploring expression on her face. This isn't my argument and I know better than to get involved at this point in the discussion. For right now my best bet is to play the same position Clarence Thomas does on the Supreme Court and say nothing. I tuck my head between my knees and roll like a ball, making sure to keep my head down and massage each vertebra as I inhale.

The four of us—me, Lydia, Acey, and Wanda—are sitting on the patio outside the spa. It's just past sunrise, and the desert air is still cool enough to be outdoors, although in a few hours the rising heat will make it unbearable. The water of the tiled pool in front of us shimmers slightly as the day heats up, and a few birds sip water from the gutters on the far side. We are surrounded by the landscaping so familiar in this desert part of the country: colorful rocks and stones of different sizes and shapes laid in patterns replace grass. Drought-resistant plants in shapes that look as if they were created by Dr. Seuss for the entertainment of children grow amid sand and rock in small, sculptured clumps. We often meet here to talk early in the morning when the spa is still quiet, our clients and sex workers exhausted and sound asleep, recovering from the previous day and night of passion. In a few hours the spa will be bustling with clients checking out and checking in, sex workers changing shifts and eating the big, healthy meals cooked by Chef Marvini.

"Besides, I thought you didn't believe in fate, Lydia, just hard work," Acey teases.

"I guess I stand corrected," Lydia concedes. "Maybe there is some sort of divine order at work, Acey. It's as if all the dominoes have been put in place and are falling our way. Wanda wants to franchise and she wins her case. We need sex workers and Jamal M'Benge-Min appears out of Africa, seriously ready to get down to business, and he says there's more like him looking for work. The Floating Spa can't miss."

"He was that good, huh?" Acey asks, raising a skeptical eyebrow. When I first met them I thought their friendship was incongruous, Lydia being so impulsive and Acey much more reserved. But first impressions are deceiving, and over the last few years I've seen not only the ways that they complement each other, but also that there's a softer side to Lydia's voracious bravado and a core of steel in the center of Acey's genteel facade.

"I wouldn't know," Wanda says with a sniff. She pushes herself upright on the chaise where she's been laid out under an umbrella, reaches for the tall glass of Red Bull on ice, her preferred morning beverage, on the glass-topped table next to her. As always, Wanda's perfectly turned out, this morning in a leopard-print swimsuit, a matching sheer sarong tied around her waist, and a strip of the same fabric holds her hair way from her face. She ostentatiously fans herself with one hand. It's impressive how women have an outfit for everything, even if, like Wanda, they have absolutely no intention of going in the water or doing any other kind of outdoor exercise. "I was exhausted from beating back the man and slept through Jamal's performance."

"Wanda, you know I tried to wake you up."

"Apparently not hard enough, greedy."

I stretch out on my back and start doing crunches, watch as Lydia and Wanda exchange a high five.

"Can we get back to the subject at hand?" Acey asks.

"You know, at first I was skeptical, figured he was talking smack, especially when he promised he could make me come 'like rain on the thatched roof of my father's hut.' But he could, I did, and now I'm a believer. Yep, he's definitely got a way with him." Lydia smirks.

"And what way is that?" Acey asks grumpily.

"Hopefully, it's the way to the bank on Martha's Vineyard," Wanda chimes in.

"Without no doubt," Lydia adds.

"Knowing you two, it was the way of the sacred poontang," Acey sarcastically suggests.

"It was definitely the way of the flesh." Lydia laughs. "And that's what we sell: flesh. What better way could there be?"

"Listen, the bottom line is we're going to franchise, we need workers, and Lydia says Jamal will do nicely. What's the problem, Acey?"

"Yeah, Ace, what's up?" Lydia adds. Acey whips off her sunglasses, pushes away the coffee mug on the table in front of her, looks hard at Wanda and Lydia. Down on the mat, my abs burning and on crunch number fifty, I don't even warrant a glance. That's cool, I remind myself. I'm not the fixer, just a member of the team.

"What's up, as you'd know if you hadn't been busy boning Mandingo, is that you-know-what is hitting the fan. While you were partying we had to fire Tony, the air-conditioning system had to be replaced, one of our clients tied up her sex worker in what he thought was role playing, then barricaded herself in her room and held him hostage for four hours until Odell talked her out, and now this!" She unfolds a newspaper and throws it on the stone floor of the patio, open to the front page. Between crunches I scan the headlines: GAS REACHES

$4 A GALLON; "TORTURE AND TRILLIONS NECESSARY TO PRESERVE DEMOCRACY," CHENEY SAYS; *AMERICAN IDOL* AUDIENCE REACHES I BILLION; PREZ: JUST SAY NO TO BUSH; P. DIDDY AND BRITNEY TO WED; UNEMPLOYMENT SURGES TO 15 PERCENT; HUGO CHAVEZ CALLS BUSH "A LOON." Wanda laughs.

"Ya gotta love that Hugo Chavez. I guess when you got all that oil and it's twelve cents a gallon, you can say whatever you want."

"Damn, we have been out of it, Wanda. I didn't even know P. Diddy and Britney were dating, did you?"

Acey stretches out one leg; the high dancer's arch of her foot, toenails painted a bright red, passes so close to my face I have to resist the urge to kiss it. Her big toe lands on the newsprint with a crackle.

"Forget Hugo, Diddy, and Britney!" she snaps. "Check this out." She pats her big toe on the words PREZ: JUST SAY NO TO BUSH.

"Does this mean he's finally going to work out his issues and stand up to his daddy?" Wanda snickers.

"No, Wanda, it doesn't mean that. It means it's his last year in office and the little rat's gone berserk. It wasn't enough for him to start two wars, ruin the economy, rape the Constitution, and ensure most-loathed-nation status for the United States. Nope, now he wants to outlaw recreational sex in the name of the war on terror. In other words, no babies, no fucking. Apparently the only acceptable reason for Americans to have sex is to birth Christian crusaders to fight against the Islamic jihad. And in case you've forgotten, we sell sex. We're doomed." Acey sits back in her chair, winces slightly as her back touches the hot wrought iron. Seventy-four, seventy-five . . . I silently count crunches as Lydia and Wanda lean over, reading the article.

"That's impossible. What an idiot."

"He can't outlaw fucking."

"Red-blooded Americans won't stand for it."

"Really? That's what we thought about invading Iraq in search of nonexistent weapons of mass destruction, ignoring the Geneva Convention, doing nothing for the half a million Americans displaced by Hurricane Katrina. I could go on, but have I made my point? Like your mother always says, Lydia, never underestimate the stupidity of the American people."

"Okay, okay, I get your drift. But on the real side, how is the government going to regulate sex?"

"No chicken in every pot, but a camera in every bedroom? Come on."

"Joke if you want, but this is serious. Read on. Even if he's an idiot, the ideologues around him aren't. They're planning to appropriate money from Social Security and offer ten thousand dollars a pop to anyone who turns in what they're calling 'recreational fornicators.' And if you know of some fornicators, don't turn them in, and the government finds out, they plan to fine you ten thousand. I mean, between the financial incentives in a collapsing economy—did you notice unemployment's at fifteen percent?—and the financial consequences if people don't go along with the program, it's the perfect American motivational storm: fear and money."

I finish my crunches as Lydia and Wanda huddle together around the newspaper. I feel the exhaustion and tension emanating from Acey as clearly as I see her hunched shoulders. I stand up, strip off my soaked T-shirt, use it to wipe the sweat off my chest and hands. I walk behind Acey's chair and knead my fingers into the ridge along her shoulders, feel the muscles begin to relax, knots untangle. Finished reading, Wanda and Lydia are silent, staring out past the manicured patio into the earth-colored expanse of desert. In the loud silence of our thoughts, the only sound is the distant howling of a coyote. Acey opens her eyes and tilts her head back, looking into my face.

"So. What do you think, Odell?"

"I think that, as Wanda's favorite judge, C. Virgil Susquehanna, once said, it's not either/or, but and/both."

"Which means?"

"Which means that I think we should proceed with caution."

"Franchise, but keep it on the down low?" Wanda asks eagerly.

I grin. "Those aren't the words I would have chosen, but yes."

"I'm with Odell," Lydia says. "This No Child, No Behind bullshit could do for the spas what Prohibition did for the Mob, make us bigger and richer."

"Maybe the sign is that we should call it a day and move on. We've all made some money. Maybe we should pool our resources and think about getting into another business."

"Like a day-care center for all those babies we be birthin'?" Lydia asks in a not bad imitation of Butterfly McQueen's famous line in *Gone With the Wind*. Acey doesn't laugh.

"Even good things must come to an end."

"That's true, Acey, but I don't think the spa's time is now. I'll be damned if I let the government take away my livelihood," Wanda declares.

"Not to mention sex," adds Lydia.

"Which is our livelihood." They both chuckle.

"You two want to make everything into a joke, but this isn't one," Acey hisses. "Bush and his boys are serious."

"Damn, Acey, we know that. No one needs a lec—" Lydia starts to say.

I interrupt before this becomes an argument instead of a strategy session, turn to Wanda. "You've done the research and are confident the spa will be under the radar in international waters?"

"As confident as possible. I mean, as far as most people know, we'll just be another group of rich folks enjoying a summer on our yacht, and because we're on the water, it's not as if anyone can walk in and surprise us. We'll make sure that the only people allowed to board are clients who've come through us; Ma Nicola, Lydia's godmother; or referrals from repeat visitors."

"And if there's any trouble, we can always hoist anchor and sail into the sunset."

"What about security?" Acey asks.

"The ocean provides a natural barrier, like a moat."

"Let's give it a try, Ace. The Floating Spa is Wanda's dream, just like A Sister's Spa was ours." Acey listens intently and looks thoughtful. I can almost hear the gears of her supple mind moving as she tries to shift her way of thinking and seeing. Her dad was one of those hell-and-damnation, fire-and-brimstone preachers who believed that the man was meant to lead, the woman to follow, and that sex outside the confines of marriage and procreation—at least for women—would lead to nothing but misery. Over the years we've worked together, we've had more than a few deep discussions about religion, sexuality, the way we were raised, and how easy it can be to understand intellectually that our sexuality is healthy and to be celebrated, yet how much longer it takes to accept it emotionally and integrate it into our own lives. On the flip side, it often seems as if Lydia and Wanda are freer. They trust their feelings, often lead with them, and have faith that the rest will follow. Odd, since you'd think Acey would be the one with the surplus of faith, passed down through the genes of her father. Finally, she nods her agreement, slowly.

"I see the Floating Spa as a smaller operation, but I'm going to need eight sex workers to open the end of May," Wanda says.

"That's just eight weeks away."

"I know that, Odell, which brings me to my point about Afrodonis, also known as Jamal M'Benge-Min, aka the African love warrior.

He's the missing, and most important, link. Even though I've been working on the idea of the Floating Spa for months, up until two days ago I didn't have one sex worker in place. Then we run into Jamal, et cetera, et cetera, and not only is he perfect material for the spa, he says he's got at least two friends who'd like to work there, too."

"Like I said, he's a sign."

"Whoa, Wanda, you still need to find a boat, spa staff, support staff—" I begin, but Wanda holds her hand up, palm open.

"I've already found the boat I want, a yacht that Ken Lay, the bum who stole all that money from Enron, commissioned a year or so before the company fell apart. Anyway, according to my yacht broker—don't ya love the sound of that?—even before he was indicted, Lay's lawyers told him to get rid of all the assets that 'evoke memories of robber barons and ostentatious conspicuous consumption at the expense of employees and shareholders.' Just my good luck that his custom-built yacht, which he planned to christen the *Lady Lay*—don't you love it!—went on the auction block. It's got twelve staterooms with private baths, a gym, three massage rooms, a sauna, whirlpool, and a fabulously equipped kitchen. And, for reasons I thought best not to delve into, every room is sound-proof. You'd think he'd built it just for me." Wanda smirks.

"How'd you find it? And how much?"

"Like I said, Odell, just like they have real estate brokers, they have yacht brokers. I found mine in the *Martha's Vineyard Gazette*, the local newspaper."

"How much do they want for it, Wanda?" I ask. "I know I've been living out here in landlocked Nevada for the last few years, but when last I looked, yachts weren't cheap."

"That's the beauty of it, Odell. The boat's going to cost me less than half a million."

"And that's because what's wrong with it . . ."

"Nothing. It's cheap because when Lay tried to sell it he couldn't find any buyers because people with the couple of million he was asking didn't want to be associated with anything having to do with him. I'm sure it was deeply painful for them to pass up a fantastic deal, but they knew it could hurt more if they appeared to be helping Kenny Boy out and prosecutors decided to scrutinize them and their companies. Hey, they're rats, and surely weren't going to *board* a sinking ship. To make a short story long, there were no takers. Lay's attorneys eventually advised him to donate the boat to a charity, take a tax deduction, and hope for some positive publicity."

"In short, get rid of it by any means necessary," Lydia interjects, standing by the side of the pool and lazily moving her big toe back and forth in the water.

"So Lay," Wanda continues, "who at that time had a house on Martha's Vineyard, which is why the *Lady Lay* was built and anchored there, donated the yacht to Island Affordable Housing, a group that builds and provides housing at affordable prices to year-round residents of the island. But the logistics, not to mention the potential liability and legality of housing families on a boat in the harbor, were really too much for the organization, so they decided better to sell it and use the money to construct housing on land. So that's how I found the perfect lust boat," she finishes triumphantly.

"You mentioned it was unfinished. What still needs to be done, and how much will it cost?" I ask.

"Lay was putting a pool in the belly of the boat when construction was halted. All that's there is the foundation for it. I figure we forget the pool and put the sex workers' rooms on that level."

"Let me get this straight, Wanda," I say, glancing down at the pad I always carry, its pages covered with notes taken during this morning's conversation.

"You want to franchise A Sister's Spa to the East Coast and open in eight weeks . . ."

"Yep. I want it to be a Memorial Day to remember." Wanda guffaws.

"You have a yacht that needs some work, possibly three sex workers, and no other personnel and—"

"Hold on, Odell. I've hired my cousin Sukey to do nail art. I've got a line on someone to do massage. I was going to ask if I could borrow Chef Marvini for a few months to help get the menu in order, and as for the sex workers, I was hoping we could borrow a few of them as well, just until we get situated."

"That sounds fine to me."

"What's fine with you, Odell?" Lydia asks, walking toward me from the pool, toweling what little hair she has with one hand and hopping on one leg, her right ear tilted toward the ground, to shake the water out.

"If Marvini goes east to help Wanda start up."

"Me, too," Lydia says.

"Me three," Acey chimes in.

"You three what, Ace?" Lydia laughs, slides into a chair beside her friend.

"That it's okay if Marvini helps Wanda get started. Wasn't that what we were talking about?"

"I meant me, too, as in I'm going east to help Wanda," Lydia says. "You all know my mom's best friend—my godmother, Ma Nicola— has a house on the Vineyard. She knows everyone on the island, and if she gives the spa her seal of approval, we're halfway there."

"Do we get to choose the sex workers we take east?" Wanda asks. "If so, I vote for the triplets, DeJuan, DeQuan, and DeMon, and Tree Man. They're tried, true, and we know they can deliver the client services we need, in addition to which they're each big enough to double as security if needed. Do you have any problems with us taking your baby brothers away for a few months, Odell?"

I can't help grinning at her description of the triplets as my baby brothers, since at six foot nine and two-hundred and fifty pounds each, it's almost impossible for me to remember that they were ever babies. Over the past few years they've matured and become valuable assets to A Sister's Spa.

"What do you think, Acey?"

"I think it's okay."

"So what's with the sad look?" Lydia asks, throwing an arm around Acey's shoulder and pulling her close.

"Yeah, this is going to be good for all of us," Wanda chimes in. "We'll soon be the twenty-first-century Madam C. J. Walkers of sex."

"Let's not get too far ahead of ourselves. When are you ladies planning to take your wagons east?"

"End of the week."

"Well, we'd better broach the subject to Marvini, the triplets, and Tree Man," I say. "Let's offer each of them a sizable bonus for helping out with the start-up."

"Not a problem. With the four from here and Jamal and his friends, that gives us seven sex workers, a good start. We've got eight working bedrooms, so we'll need one more worker; we're almost there," Wanda says. "Thanks. One more thing, for now. We'd like to take one of the white guys, too, for diversity. Mike, Ross, or one of the others."

I open my reservation book, flip through the pages of future bookings. "We can't spare Ross or Mike, they've got regulars, and Tino and Mark are still on probation. I guess that leaves Tollhouse. He hasn't been here long, but he's a good worker and we haven't had any complaints."

Wanda squints up at me, thinking. "Kinda cute, buffed, southern accent, and tattoos? Seems okay with me. Lyds?"

"Sure, fine, I broke him in. Quiet, nicely equipped, doesn't say much, but has a sexy drawl when he does."

"Sold. Done. Thanks, Odell," Wanda says.

"Fabulous." Lydia stands up, pushes up on her toes, arms in the air, and stretches toward the sky. "If that's all, I'm going back to bed. I swear, I'm still tired from that session with Jamal."

"I'm with you, girl." Wanda sighs, standing up and tightening her sarong around her hips. "I'm going to catch a few hours' sleep before the spa wakes up. Sayonara."

Acey and I remain on the patio. The sun is nearly fully risen and the desert is starting to hum with the sounds of insects, small animals, and heat, creating a strange, natural music all its own. I lean back in the chair, my mind on parallel tracks, thinking about managing the spa here and Wanda and Lydia's new venture. I'm so engrossed in my thoughts I'm momentarily startled when Acey asks, "What do you think, Odell?"

"About the franchise? It's a great idea. If we're cautious, discreet, and our success here is any barometer, it should do very well. Why? What do you think?"

"I think that everything is changing really fast," Acey says slowly.

"Remember what Karl Marx said, the only thing constant is change."

"I know, I know," Acey says, sighing again. "But that doesn't mean it's always a good thing."

CHAPTER 7

Lydia

I FIGURE THE SPA WILL BE RIGHT ABOUT here," Wanda says, standing and spreading her arms wide to encompass the dark blue-gray waters of the ocean that surrounds us, "in international waters." She plops down on the hard metal bench beside me, huddling close against the cold. We sit outside on the top deck of the ferry as it sails from Woods Hole to Martha's Vineyard. Wanda throws me a sideways glance, nods her head, and pulls the hood of her sweatshirt tight around her face. She mumbles something, but I have to strain to hear her, what with the churning of the ferry's engine, the howling of the wind, and the slapping sound the ocean makes as it splashes against the prow of the boat, plowing toward land. "What was that?" I yell.

"I said, cold as shit here!" Wanda says, pulling the neckline of her shirt away from her mouth. "Are you sure this place is a summer resort?"

"Absolutely positive. It's just the end of April, spring in New England. You can never be sure what the weather's going to be. You see me," I say, sweeping both hands from my head down the length of my body. I'm wearing a hooded Black Dog sweatshirt over DKNY cashmere sweats, under which I've got on silk thermal long johns and a T-shirt. My outfit is completed by a pair of wool socks from L.L. Bean, waterproof clogs, and an Oakland A's cap. The hat I wear not because I'm an A's fan—I prefer the San Francisco Giants—but as my sartorial way of giving props to sister Sharon Jones, the former A's executive who busted out owner Marge Schott for saying she'd "rather have a trained monkey working for me than a nigger." Trying to be cute, Wanda insisted on wearing chartreuse capri pants with a matching jacket and sandals, even though I told her the temperature differential between Reno, where it was eighty degrees when we departed, and Martha's Vineyard could be forty degrees. It's nearly sixty, but it's overcast, windy, and feels much colder on the water. Me, I grew up spending summers on this island and I'm happy to be back in New England with its sometimes turbulent winds and moisture-filled air. Wanda's been cold since we landed at Logan Airport in Boston and hopped into a rental car for the hour-and-a-half drive to the ferry. The best I could do was crank the heat up in the car, and when we stopped for gas and coffee at a Tedeschi Shop, Cape Cod's version of 7–Eleven, I helped Wanda find, among the Slim Jims, flavored coffees, and rapidly hardening donuts, the only XXL sweatshirt in the place. GIRLS ON THE CAPE DO IT BETTER, it says, but at least it's warm.

"Doesn't the calendar say spring?" Wanda mutters, shivering dramatically.

"It's one of those passing stormy days. You just have to get accli-mated," I reassure her.

"Either that, seasick, or pneumonia."

"Look over there," I say to distract her from the cold and com-plaints. "You'll see the island in a minute." I'm not quite sure if that's the island I think I see ahead or a mirage born of wishful thinking, but I pull Wanda to the railing at the front of the boat. We lean against it, our shoulders touching, the wind hard against our faces. Gulls surf above the boat on gusts of wind, looking for a chip, crust of bread, or other bit of food left behind. Not today. The gulls might actually have to dive into the water and work for food. Looking ahead, we both lean forward unconsciously, our ribs pressed hard against the ferry's railing, as if by straining we can hurry the boat along, quicken our arrival.

"It's cold, but it *is* beautiful," Wanda concedes.

"You know I love the weather and the desert in Nevada, but being here reminds me how much I miss the Atlantic Ocean and this New England weather. All this water and turbulence is good for my spirit. Just being here brings back so many memories."

Underneath my feet I feel the engine of the boat shift gears, slow-ing down.

As the boat turns into Nantucket Sound and the harbor in the town of Oak Bluffs, where my godmother, Ma Nicola Briscoe, the eighty-two-year-old best friend of my mother, Mavis Ransom Beau-coup, lives, the wind abruptly dies down. Wanda pushes back the hood of her sweatshirt. The smell and taste of ocean and salt fill my nostrils, and with it, I inhale the memories of childhood. My father holding me as he braces himself against the railing and I offer a piece of hot dog roll or cracker to one of the gulls that follow us across the ocean to this strange, small island, swooping down to snatch the food from my tiny fingers as I squeal with delight and pride and Daddy holds me even tighter. Ahead of us, I can see the outline of the harbor and, beyond it, the gray-shingled houses with their wide porches and intricately detailed, brightly painted wooden trim, looking not much different than they did when I was a child. The semicircle of Ocean Park spreads out right behind the dock, and I can see the green-and-white gazebo in its center, where the island band plays every other Sunday in summer and the adventurous get married. I turn to Wanda. "Look," she says, pointing upward. I follow her hand, and as seems to always happen when I cross the water to visit this place, the sun pushes its way through the clouds, enveloping the boat and the island in bright, warm light, welcoming us. "Now, that's what I'm talking about." Wanda grins, tossing her hair, unzipping her sweatshirt, and sitting back down. Her face, turned up to the sun, looks radiant and peaceful.

I can't help smiling and thinking, Good for her, enjoy it, since we'll be on the island in about fifteen minutes, and once we get there it'll be nonstop work if we're going to get the Floating Spa furnished, staffed, and open in three weeks. Marvini and Sukey, along with De-Juan, DeQuan, DeMon, and Sukey's equipment, are driving out and should be here in a week. Tree Man, Tollhouse, and Jamal's homeys Sekou and Isaac will arrive a few days later. Wanda's hard on Sukey, but so far not only has she been sober and not spaced out, she's been helpful. She found us a masseuse, a reflexologist, and a Reiki practitioner. Now if we can just find someone to run the water shuttle to and from the Floating Spa and a couple of maintenance people, we're good to go. Except, that is, for the essential ingredient: clients. We've already sent announcements to all the women in our database who've visited A Sister's Spa in Reno. We've asked them to pass the word, discreetly, to their friends. We've identified several organizations that we need to touch base with, paramount among them the Oak Bluffs Doyennes and the Island Mansioneers, women's organizations of island summer residents and homeowners who, in addition to raising money for local charities, can make or break a new visitor or business. I've arranged for Ma Nicola, a founding member and past president of the Doyennes and honorary member of the Mansioneers, to help us connect with them. I've convinced my almost eighty-year-old mother to leave her eighty-five-year-old boyfriend, Mr. Blanchard, in Oakland for two weeks, the most time she can take, she says, "before one of these old biddies tries to snatch him up," and come to the Vineyard and help me politic with Ma Nicola and her cronies.

Maybe if I hadn't been so deep in thought I would have caught a glimpse of the ratlike critter sniffing around the railing to my right. If I had, I would have made some noise or gesture to run it off and that would have been that. I'm not even close to being a dog lover, but I've got nothing against them as long as they stay in their place, preferably away from me and definitely on a leash. My beef with dog people is that for the most part they seem incapable of comprehending that some folks don't love canines. Their reassurances that "She won't bite," "He's just being friendly," or my favorite, "He just looks mean," don't say squat. Not only that but there's always a small but radical cadre of dog lovers who either assume everyone loves dogs like they do or just don't give a damn and feel entitled to ignore the rules. Even though there're signs all around the ferry about dogs being restrained and the purser makes an announcement several times during the forty-five-minute trip, I should have known better. Still, I can't help shrieking in revulsion and clutching Wanda's arm when I feel something grip my leg and look down to see a Yorkshire terrier humping my leg.

"Shit, Wanda. Help." I'm shaking my right leg as hard as possible without toppling over, but the little sucker clings tenaciously. In fact, it seems as if my shaking, stomping, and kicking to make it release my calf has the opposite effect. I feel the tiny nails of its hairy little paws press deeper into my leg and the motion of its body accelerate.

"Wanda!" I shriek; my leg now off the deck, I'm damn near doing high kicks in an effort to dislodge the horny canine. As for providing assistance, Wanda's useless, too busy backing away out of range of my flying foot, clutching her stomach, and convulsing with laughter to help a sister out. In my peripheral vision I see that a small crowd has gathered to watch the show, coffee cups clutched in hand as if they're popcorn at the movies, and one man's actually scarfing mouthfuls of steaming soup as he observes the spectacle.

One hand on the boat's railing to steady myself as I pound my heel against the deck, I look down in horror at the dog clinging to my leg, still pumping away. Its back is arched and its beady eyes glitter as if they're about to roll back in its tiny head in orgasm. Frankly, the spectacle of a Yorkie creaming on my leg, not to mention my cashmere sweats, takes me past disgust, fear, and anger to homicidal rage and self-preservation. I prepare to lift my leg, clinging pooch and all, swivel around, and rest the back of my knee over the railing so that the mutt hangs over the side of the boat. Then I'll beat the little pooch's paws with my pocketbook until it lets go and topples into the ocean, hopefully to die an unnatural death being ground into shark chow by the rotors of the ferry.

I glance toward Wanda, desperate for assistance, support, something, but she's sprawled on the bench laughing so hard tears are running down her cheeks, worthless. Obviously the attack by doggie dick and my misery have taken her mind off the cold and vanquished her grumpy spirit; she's laughing so hard she's sweating. I take a deep breath, pull in my stomach muscles, and prepare for action. But before I can undertake this acrobatic motion to dislodge, the loud bass bleat of the ferry's horn sounds, momentarily stopping me as it always does, a response apparently shared by the humping canine, who abruptly releases my leg, falls to the deck, and lies there panting and quivering, its tiny pink penis erect and wet.

"Mr. Boule! There you are," a man's voice calls, moving closer. I look up as a small, wiry man approaches, his body, just slightly bigger than an eleven-year-old boy's, offset by a disproportionately large head. He holds a leather leash in one hand and looks down at the canine leg rapist lying at my feet as though he's found the pot of gold at the end of the rainbow, reciting a mixture of admonishments and terms of endearment as he advances. He wears cream-colored flannel slacks, a classic white V-neck tennis sweater banded in red and blue, underneath it a starched white business shirt. His child-size feet are clad in new Docksiders, sans socks, and the watch on his wrist is a Rolex. Not only is his head too big for his body, but his face looks too vast for his features. His nose, not dissimilar to Michael Jackson's, seems isolated in the midst of his face and does not match his full lips or wide-set, heavily lashed, artificially induced green eyes. With his oversize cranium and diminutive stature, he almost looks like Jiminy Cricket, or maybe Mr. Potato Head. He squats down in front of me, scratching the terrier's stomach.

"Here you are, Mr. Boule, here you are. You ran away, didn't you? Did you make friends with the nice ladies? Did you, did you?" Mr. Boule doesn't say anything, although the glint in his moist eyes suggests he's trying to figure out how to grab on to his owner's forearm and continue getting his hump on. Hey, it'd serve his leash-law-breaking owner right.

"We're not nice ladies, and your damn dog tried to screw my leg." The boy-man looks up, finally acknowledging my presence.

"Mr. Boule did that? Naughty, naughty boy." As he speaks he reaches down and scratches behind Mr. Boule's ears. For his part, Mr. Boule is now sitting up and licking his miniature balls.

"You can say that again," Wanda chimes in, wiping the last of the tears from her cheeks and leaving behind a trail of melted mascara. "I thought I was about to witness my first dogasm," she adds, bursting into laughter yet again. I throw her a dirty look and glance down at my leg in horror. No wet spot, I note with relief, although the cashmere looks slightly mauled where Mr. Boule latched on.

The elfin man stands up, pulls a small leather notepad and a Montblanc pen from his pocket. "Dogasm, very clever, let me make a note. Perhaps I can use it in my next book." He finishes writing, turns to me. "Allow me to introduce myself and apologize for Mr. Boule's misplaced ardor. Aaron Semple Stone, at your service." Does he really make a slight bow, or does the pompous tenor of his voice simply suggest one? "And you lovely ladies are?"

"Lydia Beaucoup. And that useless chick who can't stop laughing at my misfortune is my ex–close friend LaShaWanda P. Marshall."

Aaron Semple Stone perks up, extends his hand toward Wanda. "Of *the* Thurgood Marshalls? I wasn't aware they had a home on the island," he says, reaching into his notebook pocket. Being a Beaucoup obviously doesn't rate; I'm nothing but old chum on the water.

Wanda shakes his hand, shrugs. "I wasn't aware of it, either, and as far as I know, we're not related, although with black folks you never know."

"True, true, which is precisely the subject of the book I'm working on, *I'm Rich and I'm Proud: The Real Black Aristocracy Revealed.* I'll be on the island for the summer conducting interviews."

"Catchy title," Wanda says.

"I thought I recognized your name. I read your first book, *White Like Me,* and I've got your most recent one, *Not My People: Why the Negro Elite Must Reject the Black Underclass.*" Of course, I don't bother to tell him where I've got his book I never finished reading, which is propping up the uneven leg of an end table. One thing I've learned as I've gotten older is there's no point in making enemies gratuitously.

"Guilty as charged," he responds, grinning and oblivious. For him, as for most people in postmodern America, it's not the quality of people's recognition that matters, it's simply being recognizable. How else to explain the legions of citizens eager to humiliate themselves on *Jerry Springer* and *American Idol* or voluntarily admit to their participation in the latest sex scandal? A few weeks ago a woman proudly came forward to confess that she'd regularly screwed a married congressman at the local Days Inn, the low-rent location, to my mind, nearly worse than the adultery. "Beaucoup, Beaucoup. That name's not familiar. Does your family have a home on the Vineyard?" Before I can respond, Mr. Boule, now leashed, begins barking and lunging toward an enormous golden retriever, no doubt the proverbial bitch in heat, a horny glint in his bulging eye. Aaron Semple Stone gives him a stern glance and a yank on the leash. Mr. Boule, chastened, goes back to licking his balls.

"Nope. We're going to visit my godmother."

"Who is?" I can almost feel Wanda roll her eyes.

"Ma Nicola." Before I can say "Briscoe," her last name, he gasps, looks up at me with a gaze full of newfound interest. My connection to Ma Nicola, who, like Prince or Madonna, needs no surname to identify her, has immediately added value. His eyes open even wider and he looks at me as if he's an appraiser on *Antiques Roadshow* who almost missed an authentic Grecian urn buried underneath centuries of tarnish.

"*The* Ma Nicola, but of course, there is no other," he coos, placing a hand on my forearm and turning toward me. Now it's Wanda who's fish bait, but I doubt she gives a damn. She's busy trying to get the mascara marks off her face and fix her lipstick. Me, I smile enigmatically. "We've never met, but I've read and heard so much about her, I feel as if we are old friends. She is on my list. An essential source for my new book . . ."

"Do you have a home on the island?" After all, turnabout is fair play.

"Sadly, no. But I shall be staying with my cousins."

"Who are?" I ask condescendingly. Hey, this is what he gets for letting his mutt masturbate my leg.

"No one important, really, distant cousins and owners of a quaint cottage in Oak Bluffs, the Mitchells of Medford, Massachusetts." His voice is apologetic and slightly embarrassed, but that's on him.

"Stevie and Chubby Mitchell?" He looks relieved.

"Do you know them?"

"Absolutely. Stevie was the best fast dancer on the island when we were young, and as for Chubby, aka Muscle Thighs, girls used to line up to grind with him when a slow record came on. I haven't seen either one of them for years."

"Yes, well, perhaps we can all have a drink. With Ma Nicola, of course."

"Wow. Stevie and Chubby. What're they doing now?" I ignore Semple Stone's dismissive tone and obsequious focus on Ma Nicola. My mind and the space between my thighs have time-traveled back thirty years, Marvin Gaye's pleading to "Let's Get It On," and me and Chubby are furiously dry-humping as only virgins can, getting our grind on. Semple Stone shrugs indifferently.

"Our paths diverged, and I have not stayed in close touch. Stevie does something in Medford, and I believe Chubby runs a charter fishing boat on the island. Now, shall we set a date for that drink with your godmother?" I know what's coming, so before he can pull out his little notebook and pen, I interrupt.

"I can't really set a date without checking with Ma Nicola, but give a call. Ma Nicola's number is four-two-eight-two." I give the last four digits, a small island conceit. Semple Stone is so close to slobbering, you'd think I've given him that week's winning Power Ball numbers.

"No doubt with the oldest prefix, six-nine-three. Let me write that down." He reaches for that damn notebook.

"Don't bother, she's in the book."

"Ah, of course. Isn't it only the nouveaux riches who feel the need to pay for privacy? The true aristocracy hides in plain sight," he gushes conspiratorially.

"Whatever."

"Speaking of plain sight, we're almost there," Wanda who-is-not-of-the–Thurgood Marshalls interjects, standing up and stretching. "I'm going to find the bathroom, take off this damn sweatshirt, and fix my face. Didn't Jamal say he was going to get a hot drink half an hour ago? Hope the brother didn't get confused and fall overboard, 'cause if he did, we're screwed. Nice meeting you, Aaron. Lydia, I'll meet you at the car." She saunters away. Aaron Semple Stone bends down and picks up his dog.

"Let me apologize once again for Mr. Boule, although I must say he has excellent taste."

"Yeah, all's forgiven, though you need to teach him to pick on someone his own size. Not to mention breed."

"Please give Ma Nicola my fondest regards, and I look forward to seeing you on the island."

"Ditto Mr. and Mrs. Mitchell."

"Ciao."

I make a mental note to track down Chubby Mitchell and see if he can help with our shuttle boat as I make my way across the rolling deck of the ferry, weaving around excited children, exhausted parents, and the ubiquitous hyped-out golden retriever determined to entangle in his leash and take down as many humans as possible. I keep an eye out for Jamal, but there's no sign of him on deck. I step over the threshold into the snack bar, where the attendant is restocking shelves with sandwiches, donuts, and bottles of water, preparing for the return trip. I'm so busy looking for Jamal I nearly trip over the long, crossed legs of a man intently reading the *Boston Globe*, but luckily the only thing that goes down are the pages of his newspaper. "Sorry," I mutter, squatting to help collect the loose sheets. I've been so busy these last few weeks I haven't had much chance to read the paper, which is just as well. I catch a glimpse of a photograph of the president on the front page, next to the headline PREZ PUSHES NEW INITIATIVE: NO CHILD, NO BEHIND and groan involuntarily. I thrust the recovered newspaper into the hands of its owner and move away in search of Afrodonis. I scan the tables around the room, but no Jamal, only a cluster of women gathered around a booth tucked against the wall. As I approach I hear a familiar voice.

"Yes, ladies, I will be working at the Floating Spa all summer. We offer a wide variety of services, and I am sure there will be something that appeals to each and every one of your tastes. Take one of these cards and please come and visit us."

"Who's this 'us' you're talking about? I'm interested in visiting you," a husky voice declares. As I get closer I see it is attached to a woman who looks to be in her late forties or early fifties dressed in white pants, a blue blazer with gold buttons, and a captain's cap, complete with gold braid. Her nautical attire telegraphs that she's a first-time visitor to the island, since she's dressed as if she's Shirley Temple on the Good Ship *Lollipop*. Clearly she doesn't yet know that the Vineyard's summer residents are masters of ostentatious understatement, the fine art of dressing down to project an image of being "just folks" even though everyone knows that regular folks have a hard time spending a weekend on the Vineyard, much less the season. First-timer or not, I can tell by her Anne Klein duds, Ferragamo flats, and interest in Jamal that she's got disposable income and is probably looking for a good time, our perfect customer.

"Of course you may request my services, and if I am available, I will be most happy to see you," Jamal responds.

"And exactly what kind of services do you provide?" asks a voice with a mixture of curiosity and flirtation.

"Massage, Reiki, reflexology, manicure and pedicure, and some very special surprise international spa services as well."

"What exactly are international spa services?" someone asks.

"Ah, if I told you that, the grand opening of the Floating Spa on Memorial Day weekend would not be a surprise, would it?" Jamal responds.

"Oh, Jamal, you are such a tease." Another voice giggles.

"Not at all. Just a man who is able to keep a secret. That is good, is it not?" By this time I've pushed my way through the crowd to the booth where Jamal's enthroned, a woman beside him, two across the table, and five or six crowding around the periphery. The bottle of water he went to get an hour ago sits unopened on the table in front of him.

"Absolutely," I say firmly, reaching over and tapping Jamal on the shoulder. He turns his head to look up at me.

"Ah, Lydia. Let me introduce you to my friends." He grins, taking my hand from his shoulder and pulling me toward him. The women around him turn to look at me, and their glances aren't welcoming. Instead, they're the mixture of disappointment, mild anger, and envy that I've seen on the faces of women much of my adult life. Quiet as it's kept, it's an expression I used to have when I thought I'd found the elusive "Good Brother" and then found out—sometimes under traumatic circumstances—that he was already engaged. It's a glance born out of the feeling that most of the good men are married, hooked up, or not the least bit interested in monogamy. Then there are the legions of others who are in prison, unemployed and basically unemployable, substance abusers, or loaded with so much baggage that even your standard multitasking, all-suffering black woman can't or won't help carry the load, which is seriously saying something. Factor in those who are out and gay, who you've got to respect, and the creeps creeping around on the down low who get no respect or, hopefully, pussy, and that leaves black women with not enough men to go around.

In that landscape, finding a heterosexual, working, unattached brother is about as rare as finding government assistance in a hurricane. I completely understand why the expressions on my sisters' faces aren't very sisterly, because now here I come, probably to claim my man and spoil the fantasies already unraveling in their heads. The good news is that nothing could be further from the truth. Not only is Jamal not my man, I don't want him to be, or anyone else. Frankly, I'm happy with life just the way it is, flying solo, having sensational sex not only when I want it but how I want it, no heartstrings attached. Occasionally, Acey tells me that I'm into "avoidance," some term she undoubtedly got from her therapist, and that between losing my father when I was twelve and ten years of marriage to Lorenzo the Insane, I have issues with men that I need to resolve. I can't say for sure that she's wrong, but right through here I don't have either the time or inclination to "deal with my issues," as Acey puts it. Anyway, if she rags on me about that shit too much, I bring up her history with her sexist Bible-thumping father, her wonderful but long-dead husband, Earl, and her last serious relationship with a self-involved, pontificating, no-sex-having attorney named Matthew. Once we go there, we do what best friends do, agree to disagree and go on about our business, at least until the next time.

"Hey, how you all doing? I see you met my friend and employee Jamal." I put the emphasis on the words *friend* and *employee* to make it clear that I've got no tire tracks across Jamal's back and they can ride him to their hearts' delight, for a price. The faces of the women around me relax slightly, although Nautical Woman continues to look at me quizzically, but short of shrieking, "He's not mine, but he can be yours—if the price is right!" there's nothing for me to say.

"Have we arrived on the island?" Jamal stands up and stretches. I notice the members of Jamal's fan club trying to be discreet as they do the crotch search for a glimpse of Jamal's package. I don't bother. I already know from experience they will not be disappointed. As a former copywriter at an ad agency, I sold women a lot of crap in my day. No longer. "Where is Wanda?"

"Waiting for us at the car; the ferry's about to dock and we'd better go. I hope we'll see you all at the Floating Spa in a few weeks," I say, smiling at my sisters.

"How do we get out there, swim?" a woman asks.

"Nope. We'll be running a shuttle boat from the harbor. Just call us, make a reservation for services, and we'll pick you up. Jamal, you gave each of the ladies a card, right?" In response, every woman in the group holds up the Floating Spa business card. "Great. Come spend a day on the sea being pampered by Jamal and the rest of our staff. I guarantee you won't regret it."

"You mean there's more where he came from?" someone asks.

"Many. The Floating Spa offers full-body services delivered by superbly trained, er, massage therapists," I say. "We also offer a variety of wraps, massage, and, after intense negotiation, we've succeeded in luring Sukey, an extraordinary nail artist formerly based in New Orleans and San Francisco, to work at the spa." When I say this shit about Sukey I lower my voice, as if confiding information that only those in the know will understand and appreciate, like getting advance notice of the time, date, and location of the St. John's sample sale. The women exchange quick glances and tuck the Floating Spa cards in their pockets or handbags for safekeeping. But enough already. Underneath my feet I feel the stillness as the rumble of the ferry's engine cuts off. We're docked.

"Don't forget. We open the Saturday of Memorial Day weekend. Jamal and I look forward to welcoming you to the Floating Spa." It's no surprise or skin off my back that my words are ignored, lost in enthusiastic cries of "Bye, Jamal!" "See you in a few weeks!" and, from Nautical Woman, "You can row, row, row my boat anytime, honey!" Jamal eases himself from the booth, but not without rubbing up against a few of our future clients. It's impossible for me to tell if he does this consciously or it's just a tight squeeze, but who cares? It works for me. After all, business is business, and sex is how I make my living.

CHAPTER 8

Odell

W HAT A WEEK. I DON'T THINK I COULD have made it without you, Odell." Acey drops into the leather chair beside my desk, looking every bit the corporate professional in a lavender lightweight summer suit, Brooks Brothers shirt, and subtle silver Elsa Peretti earrings, necklace, and bracelet. Her only concession to the hot, dry climate is the absence of stockings. Putting her feet up on one corner of the desk, she uses the toe of one of her Manolo Blahniks to push off one shoe, shrugs her foot out of the other, and crosses her ankles. Without moving my head, I glance up with hooded eyes at Acey from behind the desk where I'm sitting, leaning forward on my elbows as I go over the weekly doctor's report on our sex workers. Starting at her toes, I surreptitiously let my eyes run along the length of her manicured feet and up her shapely calves to the place above the knee where the hem of her skirt begins. I can't help grinning as I look back down at the pile of medical reports in front of me.

"What's funny?"

"I was just thinking that I'm sure you could have taken care of business without me, but it wouldn't have been as much fun."

"Fun? That's not exactly the word I'd use to describe the last few weeks. Getting five new workers settled in and up to speed to replace five of our most popular workers, who are off on what darn well better be temporary loan to the Floating Spa. How about hosting Evangeline Worthington's eighty-fifth birthday bash? Six women in their eighties for the weekend. I was worried about the celebration being too strenuous and one of those octogenarians having a heart attack, then darned if those sweet old gals didn't send one of our thirtysomething workers to the infirmary with heart palpitations. And as much as I like Marvini's replacement, José, and as delicious as his Latin fusion food can be, do you think he's finally got it through his head that he can't serve frijoles and rice in the workers' dining room every day? I mean, we've run through a few hundred Tums and almost a crate of Jo Malone scented candles." Acey shakes her head, her expression someplace between amused and chagrined. Even though I've lived through the same drama with her, the images she's conjured up—overconfident studs abruptly humbled by the demands of being professional sex workers, sexually voracious grannies, the devastating possibility of out-of-control flatulence, not exactly appealing in a brothel—are so vivid I have to laugh. After a moment Acey joins me and laughs until I push the box of tissues on my desk toward her so she can wipe her eyes.

"See. I told you even the difficult stuff is fun when you have a partner," I tease when she's caught her breath.

"Maybe . . ."

"Maybe? Since Lydia and Wanda have been gone, we've run things without a hitch."

"I guess so . . ." Her voice drifts off, as if in search of contradiction or a problem.

"Hey. A woman's got to give a man his props."

"What'd you say?" Acey's voice is startled.

"A woman's got to give a man his props."

"Funny, Earl used to use those same words."

"And did they work?"

"What work?"

"Did you give Earl his props?"

"Oh yes, and I'm giving you yours, too. I apologize, Odell. It's just been a long time since I heard that phrase. Or had a man who felt like a partner. I guess I've gotten used to being alone."

"Did it ever occur to you that you feel that way because that's what you expect?"

"Which means what?"

"Which means that if you expect to do it all alone, maybe that's what you get."

"I don't expect anything," Acey snaps.

"And that's what you'll get. You've made my point."

"So, now you're a philosopher?"

"Me? No. I'm just trying to figure out my own life and sharing a bit of what I've learned."

"Which is?"

"That it's easy to get stuck in your head, and where your head goes, your life will follow."

"What does that mean, Odell?"

"I'm still working on the meaning of life. What I'm trying to say is try and live in the moment and imagine the future. The past is what was."

"What's that, a quote from the latest bestseller in the self-help aisle?"

"Could be, I've been checking out a few of those books lately." I shrug, a bit defensively. Much as I like to think of myself as an atypical male, I have to admit my testosterone flares when Acey casually exposes my forays into the self-help aisle. It's not easy to let go of years of machismo; I'm a man, I help, I'm not helped, conditioning. "I'm just trying to figure out where I want to go in the next third of my life, you know? 'Imagine the future' is how one of those spiritual writers puts it."

"Imagine the future?"

"Or maybe *actualize* is a better word. Visualize what I want."

"What do you want, Odell?" I hesitate, surprised, because it's the first time in years that anyone, especially a woman I love, other than my moms, has asked me that question. I put my response together carefully, because unlike with my mother, who's always supported the dreams of her three sons, there's risk involved here.

"I want to be known, really known. Not for who I appear to be. Or think I am. Or who someone else thinks I am or wants me to be, but for who I really am underneath. The good, bad, and ugly, including those parts of myself I might not even know are there."

"Tall order."

"And I want intimacy."

"Does it always come back to sex?"

"Hey, I might have sounded like Marianne Williamson a minute ago, but now you're sounding like a man, equating intimacy with sex. I'm talking about intimacy, being so close to a woman in mind, body, and soul that we'll each know what the other is feeling just from seeing, smelling, touching one another. Intimacy where you can be your worst self, or your best self, or plain old average and still be loved."

"Small order."

"No, it's not. But as the writer Shay Youngblood once said, 'Get one who adores you and who you adore.' Although maybe not always in that order."

"Wow. That's asking for a lot."

"Yes, it is. But isn't that what you and Earl had?" Not that I don't already know the answer, I just want to keep Acey in the conversation. I've heard the ballad of Acey and Earl so many times the CD's almost worn out: met at college, married when Acey was nineteen, ten years of bliss, Earl goes windsurfing off Alcatraz Island one day, body washes up two weeks later, Acey dates sporadically but never finds another living, breathing superhero. For the first year I knew her, she'd insisted Earl's ghost visited her in the pantry of the spa. She doesn't talk about that much anymore, although I've caught her sitting in the dark alongside the shelves of food enough times to make me worry.

"Uh-huh, we did, but that part of my life is past, over."

"I don't agree. I think the past is always with us, it just can't be where we live."

"Be here now, huh?"

"Yep, and keep an open mind and an eye out for the good stuff up ahead."

"Sometimes I feel that the good old days are all behind me."

"Yeah, well, that's the safe way to look at life."

"Which means?"

"Which means that hope and expectation and desire are risky."

"Aren't they?"

"Hell, yeah, but what's the alternative? And sometimes risk pays off. It did for me when I met you and Lydia a couple years ago. I thought

Lydia was nuts when she told me you all were opening a brothel and offered me a job. Then, after you and I went to church and made love in the bell tower . . ." Acey looks embarrassed and I look away, walk to the window, and stare out at the dark desert. Remembering, I can almost feel her wetness and warmth gripping me as I stroke her from behind and she clings to the stone of the tower, feel the cool air against my face, hear her muffled cries as she comes into the wind high over San Francisco. I feel myself begin to harden, summon an image of my mother's face in a successful effort to deflate.

"So what, Odell? Risk works, guaranteed?"

"Nothing's guaranteed, but taking risks, living life, is the only game in town. Whether the risk is me quitting a good job at UPS, or you and Lydia opening A Sister's Spa, or now Wanda starting a franchise, or even you letting go of the good old days, living in this moment, and taking the risk that the future holds something just as good. Maybe even better."

"You sound like Marvini."

"Maybe that's not a bad thing. Underneath that cloud of weed smoke, Chef Marvini is a deeply spiritual brother."

"As opposed to religious?"

"I don't think being spiritual and being religious are opposites, more like two sides of the same consciousness. You know what Marvini said to me right before he headed east?"

"What?"

"'Lighten up, Odell, man, enjoy. These are the best days of our lives. They're the only days we have.'"

Acey smiles. "I like that. I'm going to add that thought to my prayers."

"It's already part of my daily mantra, I'm willing to share it."

Acey grins. "Thanks for being so magnanimous, Odell."

"See, like I said, everything's easier when you have a partner." Acey nods her agreement, closes her eyes, and shifts her feet. Seeing the movement, I reflexively reach out as if to catch something of great value before it skitters away. I cup her bare toes, still propped on a corner of my desk, in my hands and massage them gently. It is all I can do to refrain from bending over and kissing slowly from toe to calf to thigh to . . . Maybe she can read my mind, because just as in my imagination I'm about to kiss that place between her thighs, Acey rouses herself and swings her legs onto the floor.

"That's enough philosophizing for one day. How about a little mindless television, then it's off to the hot tub and bed for me."

I press the power button on the remote, the television in the armoire across from my desk sputters to life, and the president's face fills the screen. He stands behind a podium in the White House while in front of him dozens of reporters call out and wave, vying for his attention. As always, the leader of the free world's expression is vacuous. The look in his squinty, crinkled eyes is nervous and predatory, not unlike that of a slick, complacent nutria, although I'd bet that animal looks more intelligent.

"Turn please," Acey says, but I can't. Like drivers on the highway slowing down to rubberneck as they pass an accident, I can't turn away, especially since for the last seven years it's been the U.S.A. crashed and mangled on the side of the road.

"Mr. President," a voice rises above the others. "Rita Rankin, *Detroit Free Chronicle*. Isn't this new No Child, No Behind initiative an undemocratic invasion of privacy?" The president tilts his head to the side quizzically and pokes the side of his right ear with a finger.

"Do you think it's true that his handlers are telling him what to do through an earpiece?" Acey asks.

"Probably."

The president abruptly stops looking confused, straightens his head, begins speaking. "Good question, Rita, and the answer is no. It's impossible for the president of a democracy to be undemocratic. That's just a plain misnumber. I believe No Child, No Behind will only make our country stronger." He fiddles with his ear. "I mean misnomer."

"Mr. President, a follow-up for clarifi—" a furiously scribbling Rita begins. The president cuts her off with a downward chop of his hand.

"No follow-ups, Rita, you know the rules. Try asking a better question next time." He smirks.

"But, Mr. Presi—" Rita begins, but before she can finish, two large men in suits with wires in their ears approach from either side, grasp her elbows, lift her off her feet, and carry her, clutching her reporter's notebook, from the room. None of her colleagues in the media says a word. In fact, the two national television reporters sitting on either side of her lean obediently away, clearing a path. Once she is removed, like the Red Sea behind Moses they return to their seats, moving seamlessly into the chair recently vacated by their colleague, hands waving to get the president's attention, shameless brownnosers vying for the teacher's attention. "There's no reason to strip-search me, I just asked a question. Please . . . no . . . stop!" Rita Rankin's muffled protestations can be faintly heard from outside the room. Her colleagues, and the president they serve, ignore them.

"Bob O'Lechery, Fox News, Mr. President. First, let me apologize for my colleague's behavior. Would you give us a few details of No Child, No Behind?"

The president gives his trademark smirk. "Hullo, Bob. First, let me say, great golf game Thursday. Here's the way I see it, and to my mind, it's simple."

"Well, that goes without saying," I mutter.

"Odell, why are we watching this?" Acey moans. "I've learned to restrict my viewing to the Food Network or HGTV after dark, otherwise I have nightmares. No politicians or news after eight o'clock, just food and furnishings."

"Give me a minute. I'm always hoping this'll be the time when he implodes on national television, kinda like the Wicked Witch of the West."

"Our great country is at war abroad and at home. First we got the war on terror, and now we're gonna have No Child, No Behind. What I like to call the war on terrible people." He pauses, laughs at his own words. As if on cue—maybe there's a sign out of camera range that lights up and says LAUGH—the assembled members of the free press chuckle obediently.

"War demands two things—sacrifice and soldiers. Contrary to popular belief, it's not all fun and games. No Child, No Behind asks Americans to do their part, just like the infidels, and procreate."

"Procreate?"

The president nods. "Yep, Bob, make love to make war. Create the next generations of little soldiers for the long war on terror ahead."

"Mr. President, exactly how do you intend to accomplish this worthy goal?"

"Good follow-up, Bob. In the next months I will present a bill to both houses of Congress outlawing all forms of birth control. That bill will mandate that all American men, and women in their reproductive years, can legally fornicate only for the purpose of procreation." The room begins buzzing before the president has finished speaking as reporters with barely veiled expressions of incredulity on their faces turn to talk to one another, hands go into the air, and urgent and shrill shouts of "Mr. President! Mr. President!" fill the room.

"Are you mandating unprotected sex and out-of-wedlock births?"

"Righto."

"Why not just reinstate the draft?"

"Because then the children of the middle class and wealthy would have to serve in the military, and that wouldn't be fair, would it? You know my motto, 'To whom much is given, less is expected.'"

"What about menopausal or postmenopausal women?"

"What about them? As we say in Texas, a gelding who can't foal is fodder for the dog-food factory."

"Where does that leave lesbians, gays, and transgendered Americans?"

"Exactly where they belong: out."

"Forcing the sexually active to procreate? A ban on recreational sex? Isn't that unenforceable?" A voice rises over the chaotic din. Not to mention absurd and unconstitutional, I can't help thinking to myself, but when did that stop these folks?

"Not according to the vice president, the attorney general, and other experts on my team. We are at war. War calls for extreme measures."

"Mr. President, are you proposing outlawing sex?" a woman's voice full of skepticism calls out. The camera swings around to the questioner, Tonya Poteat of WFLP radio, San Francisco.

"I'm glad you asked that question. Our intention is to put sex back where Almighty God intended it to be, in the bedrooms of heterosexual, married couples, for the purpose for which it was intended, procreation. My bill will offer a cash bonus to all couples who marry and procreate. Heterosexual couples. So if any of you with your hands raised want to ask a question in support of the gay lobby, don't bother," he finishes, a belligerent look on his face.

"How can this possibly be enforced? Are you going to put sex police in every American's bedroom?"

"No, we're not going to put the sex police in every bedroom," the president responds, mimicking the questioner's voice. "We are going to implement a broad campaign through government organizations and our churches to encourage marriage and procreation. Starting tomorrow, we will be sending a letter to every household in America asking them to voluntarily cease and desist."

"How will No Child, No Behind be enforced?"

"I've briefed the directors of the Central Intelligence Agency, the Federal Bureau of Investigation, and the National Security Agency, and all have agreed to make their surveillance apparatus available in this domestic war."

"Sir, isn't government spying on citizens illegal?" a young reporter asks nervously.

The president laughs gaily. "Girlie, you must be new around here. There is a power greater than the Constitution, the power of God. That is the law I obey. Next question."

"What about the perception that this No Child, No Behind program is racist and discriminatory?"

"Oh, boohoo, boohoo, the president's picking on the poor minorities." He pantomimes rubbing tears from his eyes with his fists. "So, sue me and my Supreme Court. Alito good it'll do you. Alito, alotta, get it?"

"Do you anticipate a critical response to No Child, No Behind?" a familiar voice calls out. I catch a glimpse of Barbaralee Edison sporting a camouflage-patterned cat suit and matching flak jacket that ends just where her not insubstantial rump begins.

"I never anticipate negative responses. But if they do come, we've got to ask ourselves: whose rights are they really protecting, the American people's, or the terrorists' who are so jealous of our freedoms that they want to kill us all?"

"So I take it that's a yes," a voice calls out.

"That's Jacques Westin from the *National Chronicle*," Acey says, sitting up. "Maybe there are a few voices of sanity left in the press corps." The camera pans from the president to a tall, barrel-chested man standing in the crowd. The president taps frantically at his right ear.

"Mr. President?" Westin repeats. The room falls silent as reporters await the president's response.

"I heard your question, Jacques. I'm just waiting for . . . waiting for . . . waiting . . ." He digs in his ear canal with an index finger as if trying to dislodge a mosquito that's buzzed in.

"You say No Child, No Behind is a part of the war on terror. How so?" Westin's voice is insistent. "Mr. President, who are the experts who helped formulate No Child, No Behind?" he adds.

"I, well, er, some of . . ." The president cocks his head to one side. "No, I will not tell you their names, only that they are selfless Americans from the political, religious, and business communities who— well, that's all, folks, I've got a country to run." The president suddenly turns on his heel and walks away from the podium, leaving Jacques Westin and the rest of the press corps in the lurch.

"We're doomed." Acey groans. "Please turn it off."

I laugh bitterly, pointing the remote at the screen. "So, what'll it be, *Spice Up My Kitchen* or *Deserving Design?*"

Acey rubs a hand across her forehead. "Odell, did you hear the commander in chief? It's not enough that he's got us in an endless war on terror, now he's declaring war on sex. You know where that leaves us, our clients, and workers? Out in the cold. Maybe we'd better call Lydia and Wanda and tell them to forget the Floating Spa."

"No way."

"No way? What do you suggest we do?"

"What we've been doing, business as usual, discreetly, and wait and see."

"Wait for what? To see what? The sex police rolling up the driveway in Humvees?"

"That's a ways off. No Child, No Behind has got to go through the legislative process, get through Congress. It's hard for me to believe that the American people will actually go for this . . ."

"Really, Odell? If there's one thing the last seven years have taught us, it's that our fellow Americans will go for anything if they're scared enough."

"Can't argue with you, except to say, like they do in Alcoholics Anonymous, everyone has their bottom. Maybe as a country we haven't reached ours yet. Besides, with all the crap the government's into globally and nationally, statistically the odds are against them stumbling onto either of our business ventures as long as we stay calm, cool, and quiet."

"Your plan is?"

"Do nothing till we hear from them, to paraphrase Billie Holiday. And watch their asses."

"So, what's your pleasure? Food Network? HGTV? Reruns of *Curb Your Enthusiasm*?"

"Oblivion. As usual, our president took my last bit of energy and gave me a headache. I think I'll take a quick shower and climb into bed with Pearl Cleage's new novel." Acey pushes herself out of the chair.

"Let me give you a quick shoulder rub," I offer, walking behind her and gently pulling her backward. I place my hands on her shoulders, rub my fingers gently along either side of her neck, over her collarbone, and massage the knots of tension at the base of her neck.

"That feels fabulous, Odell."

"Happy to be of service," I say with a chuckle. The phone on my desk rings. I glance over at the caller ID and ignore it.

"Do you need to get that?" Acey asks, eyes still closed.

"Nope. It can wait. It's the fifth call in the last few days from some-one named Sollozzo, a 401 area code. I have no idea who or where that is. I'll get to them when I have time. For now, sit back, relax, and let me work my magic, partner."

Acey sighs, wiggles under my hands as if shaking off tension. The deepness of her breathing tells me she is relaxing. The lines on her forehead and around her mouth begin to ease. Her full lips, painted a creamy orange red, open slightly and she sighs, shifts again under my fingers. My chest tightens, and I feel the rhythm of my heartbeat speed up.

Involuntarily, I bend down toward her lips. I can feel her warm breath on my face, smell its slightly minty aroma. I close my eyes as I lower myself those last few inches to kiss her. The next thing I know, I've been head butted like a sumo wrestler on a bad day, my hand's gone involuntarily to my aching nose, and Acey's sprung out of the chair.

"Odell, I can't do this. We can't do this. We're friends." She backs away as if I've suddenly turned into the Big Bad Wolf.

"Okay, I hear you. No problem." I gingerly squeeze either side of my nose with three fingers to make sure nothing's broken. "Sorry I of-fended you."

"I'm not offended, Odell, just confused. And overwhelmed."

"Sorry."

"Don't be. You've given me a lot to think about. It's just been a long day."

"Isn't this where our conversation started?"

"Anyway, if our idiot president has his way, soon you and I making love will be illegal. Unless we're making babies."

"Which may be all the more reason, as our sisters and brothers in the Black Panther Party would put it, to seize the time."

"Maybe," she says, and slips out the door. I'm left standing in my office confused and rejected, wondering if it's significant that she used the phrase *making love* and contemplating what my next move will be.

CHAPTER 9

Wanda

I WATCH AS THE MAN CROUCHES BETWEEN my spread thighs. His long arms reach behind him and he takes my toes—nails painted in blue waves and whitecaps by Sukey a few days earlier to celebrate her arrival on the island—in his hand. His hands massage the muscles of my calves, then my thighs, work their way to the spot where my thighs join my pelvis. He slips four fingers beneath my thighs, caresses the abundant, warm flesh with his fingertips. His thumb brushes my clit, teasing open the fold of flesh that protects it. I feel the blood move to between my legs, the walls of my labia get hot, the head of my little man in a boat begins to rise, the flesh around it begins to pull back. I close my eyes, lie back to enjoy the action. I feel his warm breath between my legs, feel his soft hair on my thighs before his warm, moist tongue touches my clit. He moves his tongue slowly, without rhythm, across me, and I lift my hips to meet him, pushing the moment. Enough of this teasing and tempting, I'm ready to grind my bush against his mouth and come. He pulls away, slows the motion of his tongue until I fall back against the sheets. His hands reach up and he takes each nipple between two fingers. Rolling them back and forth, he opens his mouth and takes my love spot between his lips.

I lie there, saying "Om" over and over in my head in an attempt to distract myself and slow my body down. I try not to thrust upward, not to rush, will myself to surrender to the slow pace of this man's lovemaking and enjoy the trip. But shit, it's not as if I've got all the time in the world. The Floating Spa opens in a week, and while the man now fucking me is the last sex worker I've got to audition, we've still got to find someone to run the water shuttle, someone to pick up the curtains on the island, and someone to bolt down the equipment in Sukey's salon.

I surreptitiously glance at my watch for what I am certain is the first time in life I've checked the time in the midst of making lust. Catching myself, I grimace, wondering at the significance of not being able to lose myself in this soon-to-be-orgasmic moment. Maybe it's a sign of maturity, of being grown-up in ways I never suspected, when even the promise of sexual ecstasy no longer serves to fully distract me from the demands of worlds other than the ones in the bedroom and between my legs. It's like the first time I cavalierly pulled out my BlackBerry to make a lunch date with a friend and was startled to discover that the soonest I could find a free afternoon was two months away. In that moment I became aware of a shift that had until then gone unacknowledged, that I was a busy grown-up and that certain levels of freedom and spontaneity were no longer a part of my program. This secretive glance at my watch must be a similar pivotal moment, because it's sure not any reflection on the skills of Isaac, the man between my legs. I haven't reached orgasm yet, but it's clear he's up to the job, we're good to go, and clients are sure to come.

The Floating Spa is almost ready for business. Still, I sure would like it if Odell were here, would love to have his male eyes and read on the new workers, the decor, the ambience of this new venture. But business at A Sister's Spa in Reno is booming and we'll be lucky if Odell and Acey can make it out here for the long Fourth of July weekend as planned. That'll be their first chance to see the East Coast setup, and Lydia and I are hoping that by then the spa will be running smoothly and the four of us can enjoy the fruits of our labors and some R&R.

July Fourth is also the weekend the Oak Bluffs Doyennes host their annual fund-raising clambake, undisputedly the biggest social event of the season here on the island among high-siddity black folks. Not only is the clambake the Doyennes' major fund-raiser, it also marks the official start of the social season, an opportunity to publicly announce that you're on island, let people know you've survived another winter, or that you've finally arrived and purchased your piece of the rock. The clambake is an intense, accelerated version of Negro Geography played by three hundred people standing ankle-deep in sand on a small stretch of beach alongside the Atlantic Ocean. The game is played while simultaneously clutching a full glass in one hand and a plate laden with corn on the cob, steamers, new potatoes, and a lobster in the other, all the while carrying on a coherent conversation and not splattering the front of a definitely expensive outfit with a sure-to-stain combination of hot lobster juice and melted butter. The game consists of meeting, greeting, and connecting with people based on the understanding that if there are six degrees of separation between white folks, there are no more than two or three between the elite of color. The object of the game is to traverse these separations as quickly as possible without discomfort or screechingly crass social climbing, an effort that takes more than a little skill. Making other players feel as if they have been rounded up in a police sweep and are being interrogated is not a winning strategy. Questions begin with queries as simple as where are you from, where did you go to school, do you play tennis or golf, will you be on the island all summer, and progress from there. The object is to find that place where the lives of those who are black and successful collide, the common ground of the upwardly mobile. As in "We were in the same class at Howard, Harvard, Spelman," or "You're wait-listed for membership at Farm Neck? I've been a member for years, let me know when you want to tee off," or "Yes, I'm a Polar Bear, we swim every morning at seven thirty. Come join us any day." Possible prizes and rewards from a game of Negro Geography are myriad—a golf date, poker buddy, new client, job, source of gossip or funding, beach buddy—depending on what you are looking for. Best of all, there are usually more winners than losers, since simply by virtue of being in the position to play means that at the very least you've figured out when and where the right time and right place are. For the most part, people leave the clambake happy, as the game of Negro Geography ends with admittance into the land of commonality, connection, and belonging. What one chooses to do once they've crossed over into that rarefied country is up to them.

A luncheon at Ma Nicola's is the first step in our two-pronged strategy. The first move is to meet and gain acceptance from the Doyennes, Mansioneers, and unaffiliated-but-no-less-influential women on the island and invite them to the Floating Spa. With their help, encouraged by the backing of and not insignificant leverage of Ma Nicola, Lydia's godmother, we're hoping to make the opening day of the spa a must-attend event. Ideally, by the time the Doyennes' clambake rolls around on Independence Day, every one of the women at the lunch will have visited and been serviced at least once, and the hot question in the game of Negro Geography will be, "Have you been to the new Floating Spa? No? But you must."

The weeks on the Vineyard have been a real initiation into the lifestyles of the black and bourgie for this sister from the Bronx, nothing like the idyllic photo spreads in *Ebony* or *Essence*, you know, the ones where everyone's sitting on a porch or boat or beach looking fabulous, holding a drink in a bejeweled hand, and laughing so hard you'd think Chris Rock was doing a stand-up routine just out of camera range. Call me naive, but during all those years on the outside working my ass off to get through school and earn enough money to get to Martha's Vineyard, I figured once someone made it here, everything was everything. When you don't have money it seems like people who do are a well-oiled, cohesive monolith with their own agreed-upon customs and values. United in the shared desire to enjoy the life they've worked so hard to achieve and protect their exclusivity from the riffraff who might bring down property values or social standing, or interfere with the feeling of entitlement that goes along with being among the privileged few. Kinda like nirvana for the financially successful, one great unitary black upper-middle-class consciousness.

The weeks I've been here with Lydia have been a crash course in the truth behind the lifestyles of the rich, famous, and infamous. Don't get me wrong, the island is beautiful and so are many of the people, but if this is nirvana, it's a lot more complex than it seemed when my nose was pressed against the window. I guess I wanted to believe that all that tribalism was solely the result of the imperative to fight over scarce resources and that when people have enough they lay down their swords and shields and live happily ever after. In the short time I've been on the Vineyard, I've learned that having money and being on this beautiful island doesn't eliminate tribes, it just upgrades them. But like my granny always said, class don't have nothing to do with money. In the Bronx, we fought for the basics: food, elevators that worked, and safety. The well-heeled and well-fed folks on the Vineyard fight for social, economic, or intellectual turf. Different goals, still tribes. The socialites, the rich folks, the pseudo vs. the real intellectuals. The Republicans vs. the Democrats vs. a sprinkling of left-wing radicals. The Oak Bluffs Doyennes vs. the Island Mansioneers, the Afrocentrics vs. the assimilationists vs. the indifferent. The high yellow against the brown against the blacks. The people who go to the beach vs. those for whom sand and salt water are anathema. There's even a tribe of people who are a tribe simply because they're too cool, or socially inept, or maybe plain tired, to join any of the other tribes. There are only a few people, and lucky for us, our hostess Ma Nicola is one of them, who, as a result of a combination of having been summering on the island for nearly eighty years, wealth, intellect, being a superb and egalitarian hostess, a shrewd poker player, and a superb raconteur, can move fluidly among tribes. When she puts her indomitable will to the task, she can also bring them together, albeit temporarily.

"LaShaWanda, would you please be on your hands and knees?" Isaac asks softly, yanking me away from contemplation of black American tribes back to my straight-out-of-Africa warrior, the real thing. Dutifully, I flip over, push myself up, catch a glimpse of my plus-size body in the mirror, and give my reflection a quick wink. I'm a big girl, happy with it, and haven't gotten any complaints. As one of my lovers told me early on in response to my asking that question damn near every woman has asked at least once in her life, "Do I look fat?" . . . That man gave me a look so full of lust that all these years later I can get wet just remembering it, and said, "Wanda, flesh is best." I've never

forgotten those words. Don't get me wrong, I'm no Mo'Nique, hatin'
my skinny sisters or anybody else. I'm just happy where I am and it's
all good.

On hands and knees, I look past my swaying, pendulous breasts,
the curve of my stomach, and the bush of my pubic hair and watch
Isaac squat behind me. Reaching forward, he places his hands on either side of my waist, just above the hips, steadies himself. His pecan
skin glows with a light sheen of sweat. He places the head of his penis
against the opening of my pussy, at the same time straightening his
legs slightly, so he is angled forty-five degrees above me. Easily, he
pushes the head inside me and I moan, feel myself wrap around him
in welcoming. I close my eyes and let my head hang down, anticipate
the rest of him sliding in. Opening my eyes, I see us in the mirror. He
is poised above me, all angles, his face intent, his large nose almost
beaklike, a prehistoric bird of prey, a raptor about to feed.

Thoughts of tribes are banished as he moves inside me, and once
again the wonder and magic of being well fucked take over, and there
are no distinctions, no Bronx or Kenya or tribes, no him or me, us or
them, just good sex that takes you to that place where there is nothing
other than surrendering to the feeling. The skin of my inner thighs
starts to tingle and little sparks bounce from legs to arms to neck, elec-
trifying my body. I pass it on to him until we are nothing but a conduit
for energy and I slide down, now holding myself up by my elbows,
my fingers in front of me, knit together as if in prayer to accentuate
the angle of penetration. Isaac takes low, easy strokes and I feel the
heat, the clenching everywhere, and I come again and again on hands
and knees, each orgasm so good it sparks another, a worshipper in the
temple of sexual satisfaction.

"So, I take it the sex was good?" Lydia asks the next morning.
"We're ready to roll." We're sitting in the reception area/living room of

the Floating Spa, cradling steaming mugs of Chef Marvini's fabulous cappuccino. In the background Cassandra Wilson's now-mournful voice sings "If Loving You Is Wrong," polished teak wainscoting reaches three feet up each wall, and we've painted the space above it a pale peach. The furniture is antique rattan, chairs with matching ottomans, a couple of deep couches, a coffee table and pair of end tables topped with beveled leaded glass. I can see my reflection in the mahogany floor, and scattered around are colorful hooked rugs duplicating the designs of the quilts a group of sisters from Gee's Bend, Alabama, have been making for a hundred years.

"Yeah . . ." I draw the word out slowly.

"But?"

"But I never thought I'd say it, but I'm whipped."

"Who you telling? That's why we call them sex *workers*." Lydia laughs.

"It's not the sex, it's the whole thing."

"What whole thing?"

"The move. Getting the yacht furnished and ready for business. Dealing with these crazy folks on the island. Shit, it's more than a notion."

"In what way?"

"Every way, girl. I feel like I'm trapped in a combination of that movie *Groundhog Day*, and *West Side Story*, like I wake up every morning and have to fight the same gang war over and over again, but different."

"How so?"

"How not? Everyone here's got an agenda, and trying to navigate between them is like walking in a minefield. You name it, there's an argument over it and a faction representing it. Lydia, these folks even have different names for the same damn beach. Doyennes call it the

Inkwell. Mansioneers prefer the Getwell. The unaffiliated hipsters in-
sist upon Town Beach. The nouveaux use all the names interchange-
ably, depending upon which faction they're trying to cozy up to, and
half the time they've got it wrong. A few days ago a woman asked me
the way to the Ink Spot, then got huffy when I asked her if she meant
the deceased singing group." Lydia laughs.

"Yeah, people can get a little territorial."

"A little? Yesterday I heard two women in the grocery arguing
about whether authentic lobster rolls were served on toasted Bunny-
brand hot dog buns or brioche."

"Hey, they've just got too much time on their hands. Once the spa
is running, we'll take care of all that excess tension."

"Yeah, well, I hope so. Otherwise, it'll be murder and mayhem on
the high seas."

"They'll be so tired, there won't be any energy to think about
agendas."

"I hope you're right."

"So do I."

"Anyway, what's *our* agenda for today?"

"Take the boat into town and have lunch with Ma Nicola and some
of her friends."

"What's the skinny, old money?"

"I don't know how old it is, but yeah, probably money. Or mouth.
Hopefully both."

"Married?"

"Mostly, but there are probably some widows, weekday or full
time, in the group. Divorcées, too. Some of them work, or did. Quite
a few have school-age children, so they arrange to spend the summer
here with the kiddies. The husbands who are alive work, which is why
their wives are here alone most of the summer."

"Manless by divorce, death, or other circumstances. So, we're going to luncheon and convince a bunch of high-siddity babes with absentee husbands and lots of money to come to the Floating Spa for a day of pampering and, if they so desire, some superlative dick?" I laugh. "No problem."

"It shouldn't be, as long as we present the more, uh, intimate aspects of the services we offer in a tasteful way."

"But of course," I say in my most pompous voice. "We shan't have it any other way."

"The politics are kinda complex. About half the women who'll be there are members of the Oak Bluffs Doyennes, a group of women who own homes on the island that started around sixty years ago. Ma Nicola is one of the few surviving founding members. Back then, there weren't more than twenty or thirty Negro homeowners on the island, and most everyone was a member, although rumor has it that it wasn't until the riots in the sixties that those of a more pronounced hue were welcomed into the Doyennes with alacrity."

"Pronounced hue? Alacrity? You mean brown-skinned sisters and darker need not apply?"

"First off, Wanda, you don't apply to join the Doyennes, one must be invited by a member in good standing."

"Good standing? That means what?"

"Dues kept up to date and you've held the deed for your house more than twenty-five years."

"Girl, you must be kidding."

"I wish I were, Wanda, but it's the truth."

"So what, you gotta carry your deed around in your beach bag and show it on demand? Kinda like those pass laws in South Africa?"

"Not exactly that crass, but you get the gist."

"Damn, I thought you bourgie Negroes were all for one and one for all, the talented tenth and whatnot."

"Please. Anyway, another group of women there will be members of the Island Mansioneers, another homeowners association."

"They need two?"

"The Mansioneers were started by a different generation. Lawyers, businesswomen, producers, doctors who started coming to the island in the nineties and couldn't get into the Doyennes because they hadn't owned property here long enough. There was an effort to amend the deed requirement, led, I'm proud to say, by my godmother—"

"Right on, Ma Nicola, all power to the new people," I interrupt.

"That, too, but I suspect her motives were more pragmatic. Ma Nicola's a realist. She saw right off that these newer arrivals were not only younger, better educated, and more energetic than the aging Doyennes but they had more resources."

"Is that a euphemism for money?"

"Money and contacts. Remember, in spite of all the bickering, sniping, and interminable meetings, the official purpose of the Doyennes is to raise money for island charities. Ma Nicola saw that these newcomers brought some serious added value. However, her efforts at inclusion were defeated. The women who were rejected formed the Island Mansioneers, a name that offends many of the Doyennes, a reminder as it is that serious new money scoffs at quaint cottages and builds sprawling trophy houses, not only in Oak Bluffs, but all over the island."

"Please tell me the Mansioneers aren't our darker sisters," I plead.

Lydia laughs. "Nope, they're all colors. By the early nineteen nineties, land and houses had gotten so expensive, not to mention the costs of ferry, gas, food, and a pair of AA batteries, the only color that mattered here, at least for the most part, was green."

"This lunch should be fascinating."

"Oh, it will be. There's one more group that'll be there. Sisters who don't belong to either the Doyennes or the Mansioneers."

"Losers?"

"Not at all. Free spirits. Single women. Sisters without the excess income to spend on dues. Women who don't want to go to meetings in July and August but do want the freedom to participate in the activities of both groups. Or not."

"Wow. And I thought y'all Vineyarders were one big happy family."

"Get real, Wanda. There's no such thing. What's important is that these biddies have a network. Collectively and individually, they are the major social arbiters on the island. Damn near every spook who comes to the Vineyard comes through one of these women, if not directly, then through a friend of a friend of a . . . you get the idea. If we can figure out a way to get the women at lunch on board the Floating Spa, and our workers take it from there, we're golden."

Lydia falls quiet, sipping her coffee. I slide off my high stool, cup in hand, and walk into the spacious reception area. In one corner is a small desk where guests will register, sign up, and pay for services. Beside it is a dressing room with lockers for clothes and personal belongings, and a stack of thick, fluffy robes, each one embroidered with the words THE FLOATING SPA in our signature orange.

The Floating Spa will offer day services only. The boat's too small, the ocean's too big, and the logistics of ferrying women to the boat and back are too dangerous for anything but a twelve-hour stay, max. We've tailored our services and our prices accordingly. Unlike in Reno, where our clientele runs the gamut from wealthy women looking for four days of hedonism to hospital union workers in Reno for their annual convention, we're gambling that parked off the number one vacation destination of bourgeois black folks—not to mention white ones—we'll be servicing an affluent clientele. While their stay with us here on the bounding main won't be as long, we've tailored our services to give them as much bang for the buck as possible.

"Lydia, let's go over those packages we cooked up one more time, okay? Then on the way to lunch we can drop them off at DaRosa's Stationery Store to get printed," I say, looking out the window at the polished teak and brass railing, the blue-green ocean beyond it.

"Okay." Lydia pulls the papers on the granite counter toward her, flips through them. "Right. First we've got the 'Quick Dip.' That's an early-morning pickup, massage, two hours with a sex worker, and back on land by eleven o'clock."

"Let's throw in breakfast, too. We can get Marvini to cook up something healthy and delicious and they can eat it on the deck while they wait for the shuttle to take them back." Lydia nods, scribbles on the pad. "Next?"

"We've got the 'Float On.' Massage, choice of full-body salt scrub or authentic indigenous seaweed wrap, nail art by Sukey, and three fabulous hours with one of our international sex workers, guaranteed to make her feel as if she's weightless, adrift on her own personal sea of pampering and passion."

"What the hell is an 'authentic indigenous seaweed wrap'?"

"An artsy way of saying that the seaweed comes from the beaches around the island," I say, smiling. "It sounds good, the clients will love it, and it won't cost us anything."

"Yeah, I guess seaweed's seaweed."

"Amen. Now, we still haven't decided if the next package is going to be called the 'Ship Ahoy' or 'Caribbean Queen.'"

"What is it again?"

"Everything that's in the Float On, except you get the seaweed wrap *and* the salt scrub and a massage and your sexual delights will be delivered by not one but two of our finest."

"Ship Ahoy makes me think of those crappy cookies." Lydia shakes her head. "I vote for Caribbean Queen 'cause it sounds good, even though we're in the Atlantic. Let's put DeJuan and DeMon in that package. With their buffed, bronze bodies and locks, they look like they should be in the Caribbean. Anyway, once two-thirds of the triplets start working their magic, a woman won't give a damn where she is."

"Fine with me. Last but not least, our longest and most luxurious package. A full day on the boat, her choice of any or all of the services we offer, and as many sex workers as she can handle."

"And back on land by nightfall."

"What about 'Lost at Sea,'" I suggest, grinning. "That name says total escape and it will definitely be that. After a full day here, a woman'll be lucky if she can find her way home after we drop her off."

"Sounds great." Lydia stands up and stretches. "We done?"

"Almost. Since we're going with the theme of a menu of services, I'll have the printer put the nails, massage, various scrubs and rubs under appetizers, and divide the other packages between entrées and desserts."

"Good idea."

"Even better, let's call them 'Your Just Desserts.'"

"Just desserts, just desserts." Lydia repeats the words as if they're a mantra and she's searching for enlightenment.

"Did I hear someone mention dessert?" Chef Marvini emerges from the circular staircase leading to the staterooms and, below them, the employees' quarters, a fat spliff emitting a cloud of pungent marijuana smoke in one hand and a stick of fragrant Nag Champa incense in the other. He's wearing a multicolored woven cap from Guatemala tilted ace-deuce on his short-cropped hair, an original T-shirt from Bob Marley's 1979 concert at New York's Apollo Theatre, and a pair of damp, baggy swimming trunks.

"Good morning, Marvini. How you doing?"

"Always good," Marvini says, pulling on the joint. "Breakfast time. I dreamed of half a grapefruit with honey, blueberry sour-cream muffins, an egg-white omelet with goat cheese, mushrooms, and scallions, salmon croquettes, and a pot of vanilla-bean coffee to wash it all down."

"Not to mention swimming three miles to shore to work it off." I laugh. "Sounds great, but I gotta pass. Captain Chubby will be here any minute to run us to the island."

"Your loss. Lydia?"

"Huh?"

"Something wrong about the one with the tattoo."

"You mean Tollhouse?"

Marvini shrugs. "That could be his name. Only name I got for him is Tattoo."

"Tollhouse. He's the only worker with a tattoo," Lydia says.

"Yeah, whatever, why're we talking about him?"

"Could be trouble."

"How? He's still asleep."

"Nope. Been up since before dawn. Swimming laps around the boat."

"You're kidding."

"Wish I was. Dude's strange."

"Strange how?"

Vini shrugs, tokes. "Too quiet. Unsettling. Told me he didn't like water. What's he doing getting up at the crack of dawn swimming laps around the boat, training for the Olympics?"

"The sex Olympics, I hope."

"You're tripping, Vini. When I interviewed him he said he grew up down south around boats."

"Yeah, maybe you'd better cut back on the reefer."

"Nothing wrong with the smoke or me."

"What's your point, Marvini?"

"Not sure yet."

"Well then, thanks for sharing, but no thanks. We got a brothel to open and clients to woo. Honestly, I don't give a damn what he does on his own time as long as he's attractive, disease-free, and can bone."

"Which he is, I can testify."

"I got too much to do to worry about what some eccentric does on his free time. I'm sure he is strange, but he's a sex worker. Ya think men who do this kind of work are normal? Talented, yes, but not normal."

"You got a point," Chef Marvini says, backing down the steps to the galley, a stream of smoke in his wake.

I walk over to the entertainment center, slip in Anthony Hamilton's CD, fast-forward to my current theme song, "Sista Big Bones." Hamilton's voice, a mixture of down-home innocent and city slicker, fills the room.

"Well, at least we finally found someone to run the water shuttle."

"Yeah. You'd think on an island, finding a man with a boat would be easy."

"Apparently it's more lucrative to take a few dozen inept fisherman out half a mile, drop anchor, and let them swill beer, roast in the sun, and fish for porgies all day."

"Or stay on land and join the building boom. Judging from the number of former boatmen I've met who abandoned ship for dry land, apparently the skills needed to operate a boat are about the same as for being a carpenter, plumber, or electrician."

"Thank goodness you reconnected with Chubby Mitchell. I had visions of our clients paddling their way to the spa on boogie boards."

"Yep, we're good to go in his whaler, at least for our first season."

The rich chime of a ship's bell, brass against brass, interrupts our conversation, underneath it Bob Marley's voice singing "Satisfy My Soul" rides on the ocean breeze, announcing the arrival of our water shuttle. I walk out on deck and look over the railing into Cap'n Chubby's upturned face, resembling some weird sea creature, tendrils of kinky hair in randomly alternating shades of reddish brown and silver cover his face. The only skin visible is on his fat, round cheeks, littered with so many moles, they look like freckles. His hazel eyes, ringed in that odd sky blue that sometimes comes with age, peer out from under brows so thick they look like awnings. His body is hard and compact, the muscles in his legs, arms, and back bulge from years of working on his boat, *Phish Tales*. On his ring finger he wears a gold wedding band, and on a silver chain around his neck hangs a necklace of what looks like a dozen multicolored coins the size of half-dollars, anniversary talismans to mark two decades of sobriety. His standard uniform is a plaid lumberjack-type shirt from L.L. Bean from which he's ripped the sleeves, khaki pants rolled up at the cuff, a crumpled and fading New York Knicks baseball cap, and whatever shoes have rubber soles and dry rapidly.

Lydia describes Cap'n Chubby as one of the tribe of sweet lost souls who woke up one day in a demanding job in a crowded city near burnout and opted out before they totally crashed and burned, retreating to one of the thousands of islands around the world to live a simpler life. Chubby Mitchell quit his job, came to the island, bought a boat, dropped his surname, and got sane. Stopped drinking and drugging, started going to meetings of Alcoholics Anonymous, Narcotics Anonymous, and any other group that helped him figure out how to live one day at a time and sober. He met and married a half–Wampanoag Indian island woman, settled down, had four children, built a new life, and prospered. He could smell where the schools of big fish were, feel their presence under the waves, see through the depths of the dark ocean to where they swam and fed on the small fish. Because of this, the year-round fishermen respected him and the summer fishermen loved him, chartered his boat months in advance, confident that after a day at sea with Cap'n Chubby, they'd return to shore heavy with bluefish, striped bass, and the elusive, delicately delicious bonito. He'd taken the job driving the water shuttle for the Floating Spa because he was bored with running charters and as a favor to Lydia, whom he'd had a crush on since they were teenagers grinding away in a corner at a blue-light house party. He'd confided to me that being around Lydia reminded him of the old days and he could hear Marvin Gaye singing 'Let your love come down,' remember the feel of her thigh pushing between his and the way her once-long, pressed hair smelled and felt against his sweaty, once-hairless cheek.

CHAPTER 10

Lydia

W HAT'S NEXT?" WANDA AND I
meander up Circuit Avenue, the main
drag in the town of Oak Bluffs. We've just
dropped off the stuff that needs to be printed at
DaRosa's and been assured it'll be ready before
the holiday weekend.

"That's it on my list. You?" I raise my empty
hands in a gesture of surrender.

"I'm just along for the ride."

"We aren't due at Ma Nicola's for another
forty-five minutes, either."

"Damn, I'm starving. I should have told you
and Cap'n Chubby to hold your horses and at least
grabbed a muffin."

"Amen. I've eaten so many Altoids in the last

hour I can feel them burning a hole in the lining of my stomach. I'd slap anyone who stood between me and a piece of food or a Tums."

"Let's walk up to Post Office Square. There's a bakery. We can grab a donut and chill until it's luncheon time."

It's eleven thirty on a gorgeous May morning just a few days before Memorial Day, and the small town of Oak Bluffs is alive in anticipation of the summer season. The sidewalks are not crowded and there are still a few empty angled parking spaces, although in a few hours parking in town will be impossible. The narrow sidewalk on either side of the street will be crowded with meandering people in search of lunch, desultory window-shoppers, parents with baby carriages and demanding children, day-trippers over just for the afternoon frantically searching for a reasonably priced lobster roll (there are none), a piece of clothing with the Black Dog logo on it—no problem, a few years ago the only drugstore in town that filled prescriptions closed over the winter, replaced by the latest outpost for Black Dog–abilia—and something to take home to commemorate their trip to Martha's Vineyard. From July Fourth until after Labor Day, the streets will be packed from sunup until long after the bars close, the sidewalks nearly impassable. In a few weeks, walking down the street will entail hopping on and off the walkway to avoid hordes of oblivious window-shoppers, careening strollers, runaway toddlers, grumpy year-rounders resentful of the summer crush and their dependence on it to make a living, and teenagers with nothing to do but loiter and preen for one another. Ma Nicola refuses to venture into town after ten thirty in the morning during the summer months and insists upon dismissively calling Circuit Avenue "Circus Avenue," an accurate description.

"Lydia. Across the street. Do you know him?" Wanda hisses, jerking her head toward the other side of the street. "I thought you told me there were no fine men here." I look across the street at a

Tupelo-honey-colored man in shorts, a sleeveless T-shirt, and shoulder-length dreads pulled back in a ponytail. He's energetically washing the windows of a gift shop named Encore!, the muscles of his legs and calves bulging as he reaches and rubs. Maybe he feels us eyeballing him because he turns, flashes a 150-watt grin, and waves a soapy rag in our direction.

"Bonjour, ladies!"

"Well, bonjour back at you," Wanda calls, turning as if to cross the street and pulling me with her.

"Down, girl. No, Wanda, what I said was there were no *available* men here, fine, ugly, or in between." I wave and keep on stepping. "That's Jean-Claude, he's French, lives here year round, is very much married, and his wife plans to keep him that way."

"Smart woman." Wanda shrugs agreeably. "Never thought I'd say it, but I'm beginning to suspect there's something to settling down, if you can find the right person."

"Hello? Hello? Has a member of the president's sex police taken over the body of LaShaWanda P. Marshall?"

"Nothing that extreme and I didn't say anything about having children, requisite in the commander in chief's eyes. I guess running the spa has made me think about sex and men in different ways."

"Like what?"

"Like once you can have sex all day, every day, any way you want, and gratis, what's next?"

"What's next? More of the same, methinks."

"I know, but even that can get stale. Didn't Aldous Huxley say something about LSD losing its mind-expanding qualities if tripping became a habit?"

"I don't know what he said, Wanda. Anyway, he was probably tripping when he said it. In my world, good sex is always mind-blowing."

"I'm not saying it isn't, I just sometimes wonder if it's enough."

"Wanda, we're opening a brothel for women in a few days. We'd better hope it's enough, because that's what we're selling. If not, we've wasted a ton of time and money."

"Yeah, you're right," Wanda says absently, stopping in front of a tiny cottage decorated with ornate wooden gingerbread trim painted in three shades of gold that give it so much definition, depth, and dimension it seems to glitter in the bright sunlight. Through two large, arched windows I can see paintings, drawings, and photographs, most of them of places on the island, artfully hung on the walls. Above the door hangs a sign, AUNT CAMILLE'S GALLERY.

"Look." Wanda pulls me forward, pokes the glass of the window with her finger. Inside on a display case a sign reads JOIN US FOR A RECEPTION AND BOOK SIGNING, AND MEET THE AUTHOR OF *JUSTICE, NOT JUST US: CIVIL RIGHTS AND UNCIVIL WRONGS.* Propped beside it is a book, its cover a photograph of the scales of justice, a man standing on either side of them so it is perfectly balanced, his arms raised in protest, triumph, or both. On an easel beside the book is a glossy eight-by-ten photograph of the handsome face, penetrating eyes, and vaguely predatory grin of none other than Judge C. Virgil Susquehanna.

"I wasn't expecting to see Judge Susquehanna here."

"This is the Vineyard, Wanda, everyone who's anyone passes through here sooner or later."

"We've got to go. I didn't get a chance to thank him after the trial."

"Definitely, it'll be fun. Aunt Camille's is famous for great openings: music, champagne, great art, and crowded. Even on perfect beach days, folks stop by, they're a must-go, and if it's raining there'll be a line to get in." I grab a flyer from the little wooden box attached to the gallery's porch railing, stuff it into my bag, and linking my arm through hers, pull Wanda away from Judge Susquehanna's visage and toward the post office.

Is it my imagination, or do I really hear a faint but growing din of voices as we near the drugstore on the corner next to Post Office Square? Ever since I was a child visiting the island, even before the street in front of the post office was closed to cars, it was at Post Office Square that all the communities, tribes, and personalities of Oak Bluffs met, greeted, and sometimes collided. Now landscaped with planters and occasional benches, bordered on one side by a bakery and a bank, on the other by a restaurant and several shops, the square in front of the post office has become a destination in itself, the collection of mail secondary to the socializing. Gym rats stop to drink a bottle of water and linger to chat. News junkies arrive early to purchase the *New York Times* or *Boston Globe*. People in pursuit of breakfast wait here for a table at Linda Jean's restaurant, seeing who's on the island and what's going on while they kill time. Homeowners recently arrived come to open their mail boxes for the season and newcomers gravitate here to see, be seen, and connect. A much-resisted-but-often-irresistible rite of summer on the island requires the purchase of an apple fritter, a two-inch-thick wad of dough the diameter of an average adult's head, into which pieces of apple have been kneaded before it was deep-fried and drenched in a sugary glaze, an edible harbinger of summer. With the possible exception of the Polar Bears, a group that meets every morning from the Fourth of July through Labor Day to swim, wade, exercise, and some Sundays sing spirituals at the town beach known as the Inkwell, Post Office Square may host the most democratic and egalitarian gathering on the island.

"Lydia! Lydia!" I hear my name the moment we turn into the crowded square. A tall woman wearing a stained trench coat, her gray shoulder-length hair matted and disheveled, and a wide, sincere smile on her face separates from the crowd and lumbers toward me, arms outstretched. Wanda disengages, heads into the bakery.

"Lydia. When'd you get down? How was your winter? How long will you be here? How's your family?" Her questions come rapidly and without pause for response, a soothing incantation in a childlike voice hidden inside the body of an adult woman.

"Arbela, I'm glad to see you. It's been a long time. How have you been?" I say, reaching into my pocket. The mentally disabled sister of a childhood friend, Arbela lives in a group home on the island, a safe place where she can roam out of harm's way. She spends a part of each day in the square, repeating her familiar litany: "When'd you get down? How was your winter? How long will you be here? How's your family?"

She stands in front of me, grinning happily, asks the final question in her familiar inquisition, "Do you have a quarter?"—an amount never adjusted for inflation. I pull a dollar from my pocket, press it into her hand. She mutters her thanks, stuffs it into the pocket of her coat, and smoothly turns to pursue a man walking by. "Ralph. When'd you get down? How was your winter? How long will you be here? How's your family?"

"Who was that?" Wanda offers me a piece of fritter.

"Sister of an old friend."

A woman pushing a bicycle interrupts. "Lydia Beaucoup. How long has it been? How was your winter? When'd you get down? Will you be here all summer? We've got to catch up?" She stops briefly, kisses the air beside my cheek, and moves on before I can open my mouth to respond.

"Lydia. Long time? How long you down for? Let's have drinks?" A tall man in workout clothes manages to give me a hug without breaking his stride.

"Hey. Haven't seen you in ages? When'd you arrive? You're at Ma Nicola's? See you at lunch?" A tiny freckled woman in her eighties wearing pink shorts, a matching shirt with a sequined lobster over the pocket, and a gold sun visor grabs my hand and squeezes it as she eases by.

"Damn. Is it my hearing or is there a question mark on the end of every sentence?" Wanda asks, popping a hunk of dough into her mouth.

"Welcome to the Vineyard."

"The slow sister was the only person who seemed to have time for you."

"Could be, since she's one of the few people who doesn't have some sort of agenda. Except getting that quarter, and that's easy."

"Nothing personal, Lyds, but did you notice no one stays still long enough for you to answer?"

"That'd be too much information, Wanda. This is a social ritual, not friendship."

"Where I come from, if you're not interested, you don't say shit."

"Yeah, well, here you speak to everyone and keep on moving. You never know who might be important, so why risk offending anyone? Friendship takes place in more private spaces."

"Ah, the bullshit of how the talented tenth live."

"Maybe it's bullshit, maybe not. It's easy to be cordial in this safe little place where the price of airfare or getting your car on the ferry ostensibly weeds out the riffraff. Most of the year folks here live isolated in suburbs or in cities where speaking or making eye contact can be construed as an act of aggression. It's kind of a relief to be able to let your guard down and be friendly, even superficially. It beats a blank and there's a sort of comfort in seeing the same people every summer for twenty or thirty years. Even if they're not exactly friends, they're friendly."

"I don't know if it'll offer other than cold comfort, but there's Aaron Semple Stone." I look in the direction Wanda's head is tilting. Dressed in tennis whites so immaculate they may never see a racquet or court, Aaron Semple Stone stands in a circle of men, talking animatedly. Mr. Boule snuffles around his feet, apparently searching for either a place to pee or fallen pieces of fritter.

"That's ridiculous, Aaron. You cannot believe that No Child, No Behind is legitimate government policy. Or legal," a man in a fishing hat scoffs. I recognize him from several television talk shows as James Winbush of Harvard Law School.

"I know you have to maintain your standing with the extreme left, James, but even you would agree that fornication has gotten out of hand."

"I really haven't given it that much thought, though apparently you have," Winbush responds. "Even if you believe people are having too much sex—which may in fact be a contradiction in terms—surely it's not the job of the government to regulate sexual activity."

"Nigger, I hope not, 'cause if it is, I'm in deep shit!" a voice roars, followed by a boisterous laugh.

"Isn't that . . ." Wanda begins.

"Yep, B. T. Lincoln from Harvard."

"What time are we fishing?" a quiet voice interjects.

"The boat leaves from the pier at Menemsha at one o'clock."

"See you there." The quiet man walks away.

"Aaron, do you seriously support No Child, No Behind or are you being perverse?" asks the only woman in the group, tall, thin, with a long, intense face.

"I do think the program has merits."

"Perverse? Shit, niggah, the president has lost his mind. It ain't my job to make babies for the crusades," B. T. Lincoln yells. "I already spent two hundred grand putting the one child I have through college." Aaron Semple Stone laughs, but the woman ignores B. T. Lincoln.

"Aaron? Perverse or sincere, which is it?"

"That's Lulu Langlais, isn't it? Didn't she sue a right-wing radio station for calling her a 'lesbian affirmative-action, academic nutcase'?" Wanda whispers.

"Yep, and won."

"Neither perverse nor sincere, Lulu. I think of myself as open-minded, unlike some people who prefer to remain safely in the left wing." Semple Stone sniffs.

"The only wing I'm in is the sane and thoughtful, Aaron. Perhaps you've heard of it?"

"It doesn't seem very thoughtful to dismiss No Child, No Behind out of hand, Lulu."

"Are you questioning my intellectual rigor, Aaron?" I can hear the bristling in Lulu's voice.

"Fight! Fight! Fight!" Wanda whispers, snickering.

"You niggahs gonna take it to the beach, not the streets!" B. T. Lincoln screams, nearly jumping up and down in excitement, his eyes darting around as he takes in his growing audience. "You can take a niggah to the Vineyard, but you can't take the niggah out of a niggah, that's what I'm sayin'."

"Which isn't much, and makes no sense," I whisper to Wanda.

"Who you telling? I'm from the Bronx."

"I'm not questioning your anything, Lulu. After all, we're both Harvard alums."

"I'm relieved to hear that, Aaron. Especially since I'm a member of the committee reviewing complaints about your scholarship in *Not My People*." Semple Stone looks chastened. Mr. Boule lifts his leg and prepares to urinate on one of B. T. Lincoln's impeccable summer sandals. B.T.'s foot darts out and lands a solid blow to the dog's midsection. Whimpering, Mr. Boule retreats to safe ground between his master's feet.

"I am confident my name and scholarship will be vindicated. Frivolous complaints from disgruntled Negroes who weren't included in the book. Or pretenders who were and exposed as such," Aaron says huffily.

"According to the complaint, you interviewed several people posthumously."

Aaron waves his hand as if swatting a gnat. "A dating error by my transcription service."

"A mistake they say is impossible, since their documents are automatically dated and linked to NASA's clock."

"I got to go talk some white folks out of a million bucks over breakfast," B. T. Lincoln announces, holding up a flashing, vibrating beeper from Linda Jeans. "But we need to come up with a topic for this year's event at Union Chapel. Talk some shit, entertain the folks, sell some books, it'll be a blast. What do you say, Lulu, Aaron?"

"I'd be honored to be included, B.T.," Aaron simpers. For her part, Lulu Langlais looks as if she wants to run away, retch, or both.

"Come on, Lulu, say yes. We need someone to represent the sisters," B.T. cajoles.

"I'm not the only black woman with a brain on the island."

"Maybe not, but you're one of the few with name recognition. We're trying to draw a crowd, Lulu."

"We should invite Dr. Angelique Shorter Crawford, then. She's been summering here for eighty years, knows everyone, and my mother tells me her forthcoming book about insurgent white racist groups will be groundbreaking."

"Really?" B.T. asks intently.

"Really. Apparently she's discovered direct links between Confederate groups involved in Abraham Lincoln's assassination and organizations that still exist today."

"Fascinating. That would probably draw a crowd and sell out Union Chapel. And lots of books."

"Not save the race?"

"And save the race," B.T. hurriedly agrees. "But we can't do that if no one hears us, can we? Lulu, can you arrange a lunch with Dr. Crawford? We can get more information about her new work and, if it looks good, invite her to speak at our annual event July fifth."

"I guess I can call Auntie Angelique . . ."

"Auntie Angelique? I didn't know you were related," Aaron simpers. "I do so want to interview her for my new book, *I'm Rich and I'm Proud: The Real Black Aristocracy Revealed.* Perhaps . . ."

Lulu reaches into her pocket and removes a beeper.

"My table's ready. Gotta go." She rushes away, a look of extreme distaste on her face.

"Let me know, Lulu. It'll be fun," B.T. calls after her. "I've got brunch with my matching-grant white folks from up island. Later, niggah." He gives Aaron Semple Stone five so hard it sounds like a thunderclap, scurries around the corner and out of Post Office Square. People move away, going about their business now that the black intelligentsia show is over.

I grab Wanda's arm and pull her along before Mr. Boule gets a whiff of my scent and either he or his master can make their move.

CHAPTER 11

Odell

THIS IS ODELL OVERTON RETURNING
Mr. Sollozzo's call . . . No, I didn't know
his name is pronounced so-LOT-zo. Thank you
for the clarification . . .

"No, I don't know to what this call is pertaining. I'm returning his call . . .

"Thank you, I'll hold while you see if Mr.
Sollozzo is in his office," I say, struggling to keep
the impatience out of my voice. As I wait I sort
through the stack of folders on my desk, planning
the day ahead. I need to go over the last month's
bills to make sure our condom, lubricating gel, vibrator, and other suppliers aren't cheating us, review applications, find substitutes for four workers
going on vacation, touch base with Wanda about

FICA and other withholding, do my daily walk-through of the spa to make sure everything's top-notch, then meet with Acey to report on all of the above and anything else that might turn up.

As I cradle the receiver between my ear and shoulder, my mind drifts to my encounter with Acey a few days earlier. Well, not exactly drifts, more like zooms to the place where her rejection is like a new scab I just can't help picking. My mind keeps reviewing what happened, as if it's a scene in a movie I keep rewinding and replaying, in search of some essential detail I've missed. Simultaneously, I'm trying to sort out my feelings, too, why I can't simply let go of what didn't happen. What part is injured male ego? How much of what I felt and did is pure lust? Then there's the question of what my true feelings for Acey really are. I like her, respect her, and have felt lust for her since we met, but there's something else going on. If it's love, I sure wasn't looking for it and what do I do about it? We've all made a pact that we'll be friends and business partners, that's it. "Overton! Eddie Sollozzo here!" a voice, rough from years of smoke and yelling, barks into my ear, pulling me, unwillingly, back to the business at hand.

"Good morning, Mr. Sollozzo. I'm returning your call."

"Damn straight you're returning my call, and about fucking time. I've called you, what? Six, seven times."

"Mr. Sollozzo, I won't tolerate obscenities. Now, how can I help you?"

"Yeah, right," he responds, his voice heavy with sarcasm. "It's about my nephew."

"Your nephew?" I ask, turning my attention to the to-do list on my desk. I figure he's yet another concerned relative trying to track down a male family member who came to one of the numerous brothels for men in Nevada and didn't return home on time. His isn't the first such call I've received, and probably won't be the last, since there's no way to determine the nature of our services from our listing in the Reno yellow pages.

"Yeah, my nephew. What's the matter, your ears don't hear?"

"Mr. Sollozzo, we don't service men here. Did you try Canyon Ranch or the Pussy Cat Corral? If you'd like, I can give you their numbers."

"Don't bother, I got the numbers. What's the matter, you deaf? I didn't say I was looking for any goddamn snatch, did I?" he says, his voice rising. I consider hanging up or going street on his ass, but take a deep breath instead.

"Then how can I help you?"

"Cut the crap. I can help you."

"How is that?" I keep my voice level and glance at my watch. This guy's got three more minutes to cut to the chase or I'm gone. Given his attitude, he'd have to offer me a sweet deal—say one hundred leopard-print vibrators for the night table in each room at below cost—before I'll do any business with him.

"Like I said, it's about my nephew, Little Anthony."

"Who?" The only Little Anthony I know used to head up a singing group, Little Anthony and the Imperials, and that was before my time. I wouldn't even know that much if my parents, married forty years, didn't still occasionally play his 1964 hit, "I'm on the Outside (Looking In)," and dance around their living room and down memory lane.

"My nephew Anthony Sanucci. He worked at your place until you fired him a few weeks ago." Ah, the kid who insisted on playing R. Kelly and 50 Cent and couldn't distinguish between pain and pleasure. Tony.

"I remember him," I say slowly, hoping that his uncle doesn't want a detailed account of why we let his nephew go. For some reason, men often think that being a cocksman is hereditary. I'm not interested in getting into a fruitless, macho conversation around "insult my nephew's dick, insult all the dicks in the family," although I make a note never to consider an application from anyone named Sanucci or Sollozzo.

"Yeah, I bet you do. But even if you don't, he remembers you. Kid got back to Providence broken up, said he felt like a failure. His mother, my sister, says he's still moping around the house, says he's depressed. Depressed? What the fuck is it with these fucking kids today? When I was coming up we didn't have time to get depressed—what is that shit?" When he says this, I figure Sollozzo's pushing seventy and, like my parents, from the generation that believes depression is a modern-day indulgence that means you have too much time on your hands.

"Mr. Sollozzo, I'm sorry your nephew didn't have a successful tenure at A Sister's Spa and that he is depressed. But why are you calling me?"

"Why am I calling you," he repeats in a high-pitched, mocking voice. "Why am I calling you? I'll tell you why. I had a long talk with my nephew about what goes on at that spa of yours, and I got a way to make him and me feel better."

"What would that be?" As much as I'd like to believe Eddie Sollozzo's simply a concerned uncle hoping to talk his screwed-up nephew out of depression and back into a job, it's clear from the tone of his voice and the tenor of our conversation that this is not his objective. A hollow feeling passes through my stomach, reminding me that I've had nothing but coffee all morning. I reach over and shake three Tums from the jar I've found myself keeping on the desk in the last few weeks, chomping them like they're popcorn. Fleetingly, I wish I'd never called Sollozzo back, that I could simply rewind life to before I'd punched in those eleven digits.

"You go to church, Overton?"

"Not often. I consider myself more spiritual than religious—"

"Cut the New Age crapola, that's a no, right?" Sollozzo interrupts. "Except for weddings, funerals, and christenings, me either. The point

I'm making is that I run an organization kinda like a church. Ya know, we help our members out in times of need, we're there for them and all that shit, but in order to do that, we need our members to tithe so that if a problem comes up, we got the resources to help out."

"Tithe?"

"Damn straight again, *T-I-T-H-E*. The going rate is ten percent of your annual income, but for you, I'll reduce that to nine and a half."

"Let me get this straight. You want me to pay nine and a half percent of A Sister's Spa's annual gross—"

"Net."

"Annual net, in exchange for what? That's extortion."

"Ow. That word hurts, it really does. Why you have to talk like that? This is a family business, started by my dear departed father, Vincente. We prefer to call it tithing for protection."

"Mr. Sollozzo, we don't need your protection. In fact, we're doing just fine for ourselves."

"Yeah, today, but that could change in a heartbeat. Say those delivery trucks bringing food, water, liquor, rubbers, whatever the fuck you can't do without, say they get delayed, break down on the road, forget your address? Ya never know what can happen, what with the desert heat, fucking hophead truckers zonked out on methamphetamine or maybe distracted by the smell of all that pussy wafting through the window. Better safe than sorry, ya understand what I'm saying? I got another call coming in. Lemme put you on hold and you can think about it."

Before I can say anything, I hear the electronic beep as he switches over to the other line, which is just as well, since I'm speechless and struggling to clear my head and order my thoughts. The truth is, all I can hear is the theme to *The Godfather* building to a crescendo in my brain while visions of the Corleone family and their associates brandishing weapons dance in my head. I swivel my chair and look out the big window at the flat desert beyond the manicured lawn of the spa, shimmering in the heat.

"Overton, you there?" Sollozzo barks into the receiver.

"I'm here."

"As I was saying, then there's the cops who could crack down on you, hassle you out of business, the husbands and boyfriends who go berserk when they find out the little woman ain't at Rancho La Puerto with the girls. These are the problems you don't have yet. And won't once we work it out. So, whadda ya think?"

Since it doesn't seem wise to tell him I'd like to jump through the phone and break his neck, I say, "Not much. I need time to do that. And to talk with my partners."

"Yeah, sure, time. How much?"

"Where are you?"

"In my fucking office, where do you think I am, in a phone booth or sleazy storefront? It doesn't work like that. This is the new millennium."

"I mean, are you on the East Coast?"

"Yep, Providence, Rhode Island."

"Listen, the four owners of A Sister's Spa will be on Martha's Vineyard in three or four weeks. Why don't we settle this there and then?"

"A sit-down in three or four weeks. That's a long time," he says, hints of both suspicion and threat in his voice.

"So is a lifetime of tithing."

Sollozzo's laugh, thick with smoke and phlegm, erupts through the telephone with such force I can almost feel the slimy spray on my face. "You know, I've lived my whole life in Providence and never been to Martha's Vineyards—that's saying something since my wife nags me about it every summer. 'Take me to Martha's Vineyards, Eddie, all my friends are going, I wanna see the ocean, have a nice lobster dinner with one of those cute bibs, go shopping,' on and on and on. Me, I'm happy spending two weeks in Florida in January, any more than that is a fucking bore. So yeah, maybe I'll bring the wife over, send her shopping, and the five of us can have a meet. Shit, maybe even a lobster dinner, huh?" The thought of having a "meet" with Eddie Sollozzo is unappetizing enough; I have no intention of watching him dismember and consume either a lobster or A Sister's Spa.

"Maybe. Why don't I get back to you in a week or so with some dates?"

"Yeah, do that. But between then and now I need a sign of good faith."

"A what?"

"A little something to let me know you're not trying to fuck me, although you can bet your ass that wouldn't be very intelligent."

"Such as?"

"Such as you pay my nephew Tony his salary until we have a face-to-face." I rapidly calculate the cost in my head, $5,000 for five weeks, not cheap when you're getting no work in exchange, but worth it to buy some time to figure out how to deal with this creep. Maybe Eddie takes my pause as hesitation, because he quickly says, "Listen, I know the little prick's a pain in the ass. I can believe the selfish mama's boy's shit in the sack. But it'll get my sister off my back, and you can bet your ass he'll get over his depression when he starts getting a grand a week for not doing squat. Kids," he wheezes conspiratorially. "What can you do?"

Suddenly exhaustion comes down on me like a thunderstorm in August. I want nothing more than to get off the phone and focus on the work I can handle, manage, and control.

"I'll put Tony back on payroll today and he'll have a check by the end of the week. As soon as we have some dates, I'll call you and let you know."

"Good man, Overton, that's thinking smart." Sollozzo gives a rheumy chuckle. "Pleasure doing business with you," he adds, his voice growing fainter with each word, as if this bit of politeness is an afterthought that came while he was already replacing the receiver. Then the line goes dead.

I don't realize I haven't hung up the phone until I'm startled by the disembodied voice of an operator droning, "If you'd like to make a call, please hang up and try again." I replace the receiver and sit at my desk staring at the piles of paperwork that need my attention. Right now I don't have any to spare. The words *We're being extorted by the Mob* keep looping through my brain, along with an endless reel of unsolicited and unwanted flashbacks to the most violent scenes of every book, television show, movie, or newspaper article about the Mafia I've ever seen. And enjoyed. The truth is, I own the deluxe edition of *The Godfather* trilogy and after I first saw *The Godfather,* I took to scratching my face like Don Corleone: curling all but the thumb of my hand against my cheek and slowly rubbing the fingers upward. Never again.

It's been great running things with just Acey and for the most part smooth sailing since Lydia and Wanda went east, but I damn sure wish they were here now. I'd welcome a dose of their "kick ass and take no prisoners" attitude, combined with Acey and my opposite tendency to negotiate first and confront only as a last resort. Not that there'd be a good time for Eddie Sollozzo and his Church of the Mob to step to A Sister's Spa with a shakedown scheme, but right now couldn't be worse. We're about to open the first franchise and half the team's three thousand miles away. Not only did we fire Tony but with the summer-vacation season about to begin, we need to replace him and hire at least two more workers to deal with the crush. Then there's the president's No Child, No Behind initiative, which could seriously fuck with—make that ruin—our businesses. Talk about feast or famine.

A man doesn't ever want to feel powerless. The belief that I can influence most situations is crucial to the way I define myself in the world and in my head. Having power has a lot more to do with my sense of manhood than how much pussy I get, or children I father, or money I make. For the first time since I brushed my teeth this morning, I smile, imagining how Lydia would pounce right on that statement if she were here, try to convince me, and maybe herself, that my little head calls the shots, Wanda chiming in her agreement and cackling as she offers anecdotes from her life to support Lydia's position, me getting caught up in the argument even though I know I shouldn't, Acey not saying much, just listening intently, legs crossed and head slightly tilted.

Thinking of Acey, bad as things are, I can't help grinning. There's a knock on the door and Wil, one of our original and best sex workers, sticks his head in.

"Sorry to bother you, Odell, but the woman I was servicing, Mrs. Irving, refuses to check out. Says it's part of her karmic debt to remain here indefinitely. I need some help, bro. Hope I'm not interrupting something critical, but I've tried everything I know and the woman ain't budging."

"No problem. I got this." I stand up, shake my legs out, put my hand on my crotch, and adjust Johnson. He falls into place exactly where I want him. If only putting Eddie Sollozzo where he belongs were as easy.

CHAPTER 12

Lydia

THE HOUSE MA NICOLA INSISTS UPON calling her summer cottage is a sprawling two-story, seven-bedroom affair with wraparound porches and the modest, weathered-gray shingles and white trim characteristic of New England homes. The shingles and white trim give the houses a WASPy uniformity and create the appearance of a coherent and understated community—an external facade, inside which residents can do as they please. You could be eating Cheez Whiz and crackers to survive, or have a two-lane bowling alley in the basement, but the exterior of the house will never tell. Recent arrivals to the island eschew white for periwinkle blue, Pernod yellow, Nottingham green, or bolder colors and invite a glimpse into their personality and temperament via their trim. However, many older residents view such colorful paint as exhibitionism inappropriate for closeted New England.

For the most part it is the plants and flowers surrounding the houses that offer information about the occupants. The yard around Ma Nicola's cottage is riotous with color, as the reds, oranges, yellows, and purples of summer flowers tumble over one another in the seeming disarray that she had perfected. "One's garden is either a reflection of one's inner soul or not, but whichever it is, it cannot be left to chance," Ma Nicola would lecture as I tagged along with her in the early mornings as a child, sent downstairs by parents determined to sleep late. "A garden is like a smile—the first impression passersby or visitors have of you. It is important to determine what impression you would like to make, and then implement it." I can remember working in the yard with my godmother from childhood through young womanhood, wearing the miniature garden gloves she'd bought me and listening to what at the time seemed to me occasionally interesting or funny, but always too-long, discourses on gardening as we pulled weeds, fertilized, mulched, and cut a rainbow of flowers for the enormous bouquets that always graced her public rooms. It was not until years later that I figured out that Ma Nicola wasn't just talking about gardening; she was talking about life. The lessons she taught me have come in handy even though I've never planted another seed.

Her house sits on one of the bluffs dotted with oak trees across from the ocean that give this town its name, Oak Bluffs, and it looks out over Nantucket Sound. Built in 1898, her home is in the town's historic Copeland District, named after Robert Morris Copeland, who in 1866 drew the first plans for the town that became Oak Bluffs. Like Ma Nicola's, all the houses on her street and the surrounding ones are protected by the Historic Commission, which requires that all exterior changes be approved. Because of this, the houses, churches, and even the shops look just about as they always did. I can almost see my father and mother thirty years earlier standing in the porch doorway watching Ma Nicola and me on our knees in the garden. Or long before that, in the 1800s, women in long skirts and bonnets, men in jackets and stiff collars coming for the Methodist camp meeting at the wrought-iron tabernacle that still stands in the campgrounds a half mile away, enjoying a stroll by the ocean during a break in the sermons and revival meetings. It's as if this place is frozen in time.

As we approach, the mullioned windows glitter in the sunlight. On the beach across the street, gulls call and dive, scoop unlucky crabs and mussels from the shallow water, and drop them on the two-lane road to shatter the shells. Between passing cars they swoop down and pick out the meat, shaking it loose with their sharp beaks. Once Memorial Day arrives, the roads will be filled with cars until fall. The gulls will return to scavenging food left on the beach or stealing it off grills and picnic tables when vacationers go for a dip, fall asleep, or turn their heads for the scantest second. As we near the house, I can see activity on the two porches facing the ocean, as the Oak Bluffs Doyennes, Island Mansioneers, and assorted other women of means, discretion, and I hope prodigious sexual appetites arrive. Marcia de Costa, Ma Nicola's secretary, house manager, and indispensable assistant, instructs the two Brazilian women who were brought in to help with the event as they carry plates and other paraphernalia to the tables set up on the big screened porch facing the ocean. Seven or eight women in bright colors and hats mingle in the sunlight of the open porch next to it, glasses in hand. The wind shifts toward us and brings with it a warm breeze and the sound of women's laughter, muffled voices, and the creamy tones of Dinah Washington singing, incongruously but probably as a result of Ma Nicola's obscure and perverse sense of humor, "Cottage for Sale."

"Dag, I don't know if I'm properly dressed to attend a garden party with a bunch of bourgie Negro women," Wanda says, pulling at the top of her scoop-neck shirt in a futile attempt to minimize cleavage.

"Chill, Wanda. You look great," I say. Wanda had heard about the Black Dog Bakery for years and insisted we visit it soon after we arrived on the Vineyard. She'd left not only with a large sack filled with muffins and cookies, much to Marvini's feigned dismay, but two enormous shopping bags stuffed with Black Dog sweatshirts, T-shirts, hats, mugs, and even a fanny pack—although I can't imagine her wearing it under any circumstances. Today she's decked out in full Black Dog regalia: cap, scoop-neck baby tee, zip-front sweatshirt—all bearing the familiar profile of a black Labrador-Boxer mix with a red collar—and a pair of red linen cropped pants. "Black Dog wear is always appropriate on the Vineyard; it's damn near the local dress code. At least you thought to wear a hat. Besides, who are you to call other people bourgie, Miss Millionaire?" I tease.

"I'm not bourgie yet; I'm nouveau riche. And my money's so new I'm barely that."

"Whatever, relax. This'll be fun. And don't forget that we're not selling snake oil but something every woman needs and wants, even if she doesn't know it yet."

"Aye-aye, Captain." Wanda sticks her headphones in her bag, gives me a quick salute, and takes a deep breath. "Here we go."

As we step onto the fieldstone walkway to the porch, a woman stands in the open doorway waiting at the top of the six steps, a huge smile of welcome on her face. Her once jet-black hair, now mostly silver, is cut in a cropped, wavy style that flatters her face and is topped by a black golf visor. As we approach the house, Ma Nicola grins so hard her plump cheeks, baked brown from working in her garden, rise up and nearly conceal her eyes. As always, she wears an enormous pair of designer prescription sunglasses, of which she has dozens in colors and shapes to match every occasion, mood, and outfit. Just under five foot five, she carries substantial girth around her stomach and hips, and as she has aged, her breasts have become so full that they resemble one enormous mammary. I know from photographs of Ma Nicola and my mother when they were young college students at Talladega College in Alabama in the late 1930s that Ma Nicola once had an enviable figure, the vestiges of which, visible beneath her short mud-cloth dress and matching jacket, are a gorgeous pair of gams. Her round body is falling slightly forward as her hands hold her weight against the porch railing. Heavy gold earrings in the shape of a bunch of grapes, each fruit marked by a small diamond, sway from her ears as if waiting to be plucked. Every one of her fingers glitters with at least one ring set with precious and semiprecious stones. She resembles nothing so much as a small, fierce but friendly bull, fitting for this classic Taurean.

"Lydio, my darling, how wonderful to see you." She calls me by the name she gave me as a child. "This has got to be the infamous LaSha-Wanda. I hope I can call you Wanda, and do call me Ma Nicola or Nicks. Everyone does," she commands, reaching out to embrace both of us in a warm hug. I press myself against her and kiss her cheek, soft, papery, and welcoming in the way that only old cheeks are, and smell the familiar scent of Joy, the perfume she has worn for a lifetime.

"Ma Nicola. It's wonderful to see you. The house looks great."

We step onto the porch. Two tables for six are beautifully set with linen cloths, china, enough glasses and silverware at each place to give Amy Vanderbilt pause, and sterling silver place-card holders. I catch the look on Wanda's face and Ma Nicola does, too.

"Don't take this hullabaloo seriously," she says, gesturing toward the tables with one hand and hugging Wanda closer with the other. "When you get to be eighty-two, if you have any sense, you've realized there's no saving stuff for a special occasion. Every day I don't wake up dead is special. That goes for silverware, dishes, dresses, hats, shoes, and energy," she continues. "I live every day to the fullest. Everything I own is for every day, and I try to use it. I've learned that some things in life are meant to be lost or broken, so I use everything I've got and don't mourn it when it's gone. Well, that's not exactly true; there is some very special stuff I haven't used in the ten years since my husband died, but I think you ladies may have the remedy for that, if what Mavis has told me is true." She finishes with a quick wink.

"Did Mom get here yet?"

"I asked Cap'n Chubby to go to the airport to pick her up. She should be here in a few minutes. Let's get you two a drink. I'll introduce you to the ladies, and we can chat until she arrives. Ah, here are the guests of honor!" she says, pushing open the door to the porch, where the ladies are gathered, and thrusting me and Wanda ahead of her. I hadn't even realized we'd moved at all, what with Ma Nicola chattering away, but that's her, steel hand, velvet glove. No wonder my mother's nickname for her is La Directress.

"FYI," she whispers as she steers us to the center of the porch. "I have told the assembled ladies that you are simply opening a luxury spa at sea, would appreciate their patronage and support, and will give a brief presentation today. I left the more, er, compelling details to you.

"Ladies, I'd like you to meet my goddaughter, Lydia Beaucoup, whom some of you may remember from when she's visited over the years, and her friend and business partner LaShaWanda P. Marshall. Introduce yourselves while I greet Mavis, and we'll talk more over lunch." Conversation stops at Ma Nicola's announcement and the dozen assembled women turn toward us. They are a rainbow of ages, colors, and sizes. Perhaps as protection from the bright sun, but more likely at Ma Nicola's instruction, they all wear hats: straw caps, hats with wide brims in pastel shades, and a few elaborate creations by New York's famous Mr. Bunn. One woman wears a bright green floppy straw number that looks as if it got caught in the rain and lost its shape, the brim flopping down and obscuring her face, but maybe she's going for that Alicia Keys style. All I can see is bright red lips and a champagne glass pressed against them. Three short, plump women, looking like nothing as much as a gaggle of fluttering, nervous hens in matching baseball caps, big grins, and a delicate waggling of plump fingers, greet us. Some of the women turn to us with appraising looks and polite smiles, not unfriendly, just curious and reserving judgment. A few look wary and indifferent, a not unfamiliar reception from those who see themselves as self-appointed guardians of exclusivity. Their glances seem to say, "You're nobody until you've proved you're somebody by pedigree, job, class, or bank account, and I don't have any energy to spend on you until you do."

On my last visit here more than a decade earlier, I was over thirty, worked every day for a living, wasn't wealthy, and didn't have a man. Some of the biddies on the island made me feel as if I had about as much to offer them as Monica Lewinsky let loose near the Oval Office—not a feeling I am eager to revisit. But as Dinah is singing in the background, "What a Difference a Day Makes." One of the any wonderful aspects of getting older is that most of the things that used to bother me I now see as humorous or stupid. Or even better, I simply can't remember them. I'm not copping to senility or early-onset Alzheimer's, but I am convinced we're born with a fixed number of memory cells, and as time goes on, old memories are pushed out to make room for new ones. That's cool with me. Besides, once you figure out that your time on the planet is incredibly short and that battles should be few, far between, and carefully chosen, both life and the quality of your new memories improve.

Before I can do more than say hello, my cell phone rings. I murmur excuses and ease outside. As I go I hear Wanda saying, "Good afternoon, I'm LaShaWanda. How are you ladies doing on this gorgeous day God has blessed us with?"

"Hello?" I whisper, sotto voce.

"Lydia, what's going on? Why are you whispering?"

"Hey, Acey. I'm whispering because Wanda and I just arrived at the luncheon Ma Nicola's giving to introduce us to the influential ladies of the island."

"I thought that wasn't until the week before the spa opens."

"Ace, where've you been? It's a few days before the spa opens and we've got to get these biddies on board. Anyway, what's up?"

"I guess everything's okay, but we may have a little problem out here . . ."

"Are you okay? Odell? No nonperforming sex workers or obsessed clients who've convinced themselves that great sex means happily ever after, I hope?"

Acey laughs. "Nope. We had to hire a few summer fill-ins, but business is great."

"But?"

"A month or so ago this guy started calling Odell, leaving kind of hostile messages demanding Odell call him back, like he's a collection agency—although one of the things I admire about O is that he doesn't have any debt."

"Yeah, yeah, Odell's a model of fiscal responsibility, but lunch is about to be served. Can you cut to the chase?"

"We've been so busy that at first Odell didn't return his calls, figuring he was selling something and would get the message, but he started calling four or five times a day at the weirdest times. Odell finally called him back."

"And?" I say impatiently.

"And he said his name is Eddie Sollozzo. He works for a company based in Providence, Rhode Island, and he wants to set up a meet."

"Tell him you don't run track."

"Nice try, but not funny. This is serious. He wants a meet."

"A what?"

"Lyds, that's exactly what he called it, 'a meet,' and he's not talking about the summer Olympics. Odell's been putting him off, gambling he'll go away, but there's something creepy about the whole deal."

"What's he want? A job?"

"Remember Tony Sanucci, the sex worker I told you we fired last month?"

"Vaguely. And?"

"And apparently the kid went home and told his uncle, this Sollozzo guy, that we'd ruined his life, and Uncle Eddie's in the Mob and wants us to pay his nephew one thousand dollars a week starting now and meet with him."

"Wait. Slow down. You're joking, right?" I interrupt.

"I wish I could laugh, but I'm scared."

"Hello? Hello? This must be a bad connection, because the shit you just said sounds like an awful pitch for a B—no, make that a D movie."

"I wish. Odell and I both believe he's for real enough that Odell agreed to pay Tony and to meet Uncle Eddie. Can you hear me now?"

"Yeah, unfortunately."

"I called your mother to ask if she'd dig up some info on Sollozzo, but Mr. Blanchard told me she'd gone to the Vineyard for two weeks."

"Cap'n Chubby's picking her up from the airport; she'll be here any minute. I'll ask her to look into this Sollozzo guy. You know my mother, the research queen. She might leave her man behind, but never her laptop." I hear Acey's relieved exhalation.

"You okay, Ace?"

"Yeah, I guess . . ."

"What?"

"I know you don't believe in signs, but . . ."

"I don't mean to be cold," I interrupt, "but can we talk later? I think I see Ma Nicola's car coming up the street, which means that my dear mother, Mavis Ransom Beaucoup, has arrived. I don't want to begin our time together with her berating me about the cell phone as an anti-social defensive device used by people who are afraid to interact with others or be alone in their heads."

Acey laughs. She's heard that lecture more than once, too. "Okay, but we need to talk. Soon. About Sollozzo and No Child, No Behind. The Justice Department's sent letters to all the businesses in Nevada since prostitution is legal here. I'm sure your mother the news junkie knows about it. Talk to her, and don't forget to ask her to find out what she can about this Sollozzo guy."

"Absolutely. Gotta go. Don't worry, it'll all work out. Love to you and Odell." I flip my phone shut as Ma Nicola's heavy black diesel Mercedes pulls into her driveway. I head toward the car and watch as Cap'n Chubby jumps out of the driver's seat and opens the passenger door. The sound of Bob Marley's "Jammin'" is the first thing out of the car. I have to smile, knowing that my mother, determined to stay current, instructed Chubby to play whatever music he enjoys on the way from the airport. Appropriate choice. "Hi, Mom," I call as I wait for her to emerge.

"Lydia! How are you? How's the Floating Spa going? Come down and help me with this box. I have carried Nicola's favorite, my home-made red velvet cake with cream cheese frosting and walnuts, across the continent without mishap although there were a few times I thought that tiny Cape Air plane might plunge into the sea, taking me and my cake along with it, but we both made it intact, where's Nicola and a cold drink anyway?" Did I mention my mother doesn't breathe when she speaks? "Cap'n Chubby, thank you for that fascinating abbreviated history of reggae, to be continued. Now, please take my things up to the aqua room left at the top of the stairs to the end of the hall that is always my room in this house," my mother continues, bending down to check her lipstick in the car's rearview mirror and shaking her head. "Not bad for an old lady. Where's Nicks and the ladies and I am famished the truth is a half hour more and I might have eaten the cake myself but no need for that now although what I do need is a Jack Daniel's and soda lead the way." She slips her arm through mine and propels both of us up the stairs. "I haven't missed anything, have I?"

"Nope, we're just about to get started."

"Perfect, but first I need a drink," she says, stopping at the small table laden with bottles. Before she can say anything, the bartender, no doubt briefed by Ma Nicola, hands her a drink. She takes a long sip and then, with a smack of her lips and a wink, dispensing air kisses to the women she knows, warm hellos to those she doesn't, and all the while declaring, "Nicola, my darling Nicola! Let the games begin!" she makes her way with outstretched arms toward her hostess and oldest friend.

"Just to keep things moving and relatively honest, I'll introduce everyone briefly, Lydia and Wanda will make an equally brief presentation, and then we shall discuss," Ma Nicola says ten minutes later, after herding us to the tables to be seated. "To my left, Ellen Canning of Aquinnah, who has lived on the island most of her life and is an elder of the Wampanoag tribe." Almost six feet tall, Canning has dark hair shot with silver and pulled back in a ponytail, emphasizing her large, dancing black eyes. She's dressed in a casually chic purple linen pantsuit, which is accentuated by a gorgeous, clunky wampum and silver necklace and bracelets. She smiles and nods to me and Wanda, and her dangling wampum earrings in the shape of the island sway alongside both cheeks. "So wonderful to meet you both. Welcome to Noepe," she says, using the native name for Martha's Vineyard.

"Occupying the three seats next to Ellen are the sisters Faith, Hope, and Charity Conover, better known as the Hydra. Schoolteachers. Retired. Philadelphia. They never miss a social event and know everyone and everything." Nicola laughs. Three women who look to be in their early seventies giggle and murmur warm words of welcome.

"I guess you ladies like to party." Wanda grins.

"We do, we do," Hope agrees. "Who doesn't?"

"You party animals can bond later." Ma Nicola shushes them. "Next to Charity is Audreen Bishop, former member of the Katherine Dunham dance company, public-relations maven extraordinaire, and the well-fixed widow of not one but two wealthy men." Audreen, a sharp-featured woman in her seventies with tightly coiffed steel gray hair and a Marlboro Light 100 between two fingers, bows her head regally in acknowledgment. When she looks up, her eyes are hard and appraising.

"Next to her is Bea Fulton, attorney, D.C., mother of quite appealing twelve-year-old twins." Ma Nicola nods toward a woman in her late thirties or early forties. Bea looks across the table at us with a broad smile. "Welcome to Martha's Vineyard. I visited A Sister's Spa in Reno last year and had an absolutely fabulous time, so I am really looking forward to hearing what you sisters have up your sleeves."

"And beside Bea is Jeanette Howell Tiger." Ma Nicola gestures toward the woman with the floppy hat I'd noticed when I came in. "Somewhat late in life, Jeanette and her husband, my contemporary, the retired Reverend T. Terry Tiger, became parents of now three-year-old twins. They've recently bought a home on the island in search of a place where their children can meet other similarly situated black children."

"She means other bourgie brats," Audreen Bishop says in her cigarette voice, and everyone at the table laughs.

Jeanette, who's been intently studying either her lobster salad appetizer or her nearly empty martini glass, slowly lifts her head, at the same time sweeping off her hat. She looks at me and Wanda full faced, a broad smile on her lips and her hazel eyes dancing. "And to assist my husband in finishing his memoir, don't forget," the woman growls in a voice that's pure Eartha Kitt. "Welcome to this lovely island. What a surprise to see you both again." She gestures toward the woman sitting beside her. "I believe you already met my best friend and houseguest, Lorrie Jonestone, on the ferry."

"We met, but I didn't pay them any mind; I was too busy trying to get the four-one-one on Jamal, I'm not embarrassed to admit." The woman laughs, leaning over the table to shake hands and looking over our shoulders at the same time. It's the sister from the ferry, no longer clad in newcomer's nautical wear but a taupe silk blouse and pants and high-heeled slides. Her captain's hat has been replaced by one of island artist Myrna Morris's signature "Sisters in the Bluffs" baseball caps, an embroidered gaggle of multicolored women dancing across the brim. "When Jeanette mentioned the luncheon, I canceled my golf game, secretly hoping that handsome man would be with you, but I can see it is, yet again, just us girls. Still, I intend to be there with bells on when the spa opens, ready for my massage." She plops down in her chair and reaches for her drink.

I give Lorrie Jonestone what I hope is a sincere smile and nod, not wanting to reveal my shock at seeing Jeanette Howell Tiger. Ma Nicola continues with her introductions, but I'm too busy trying to hold on to my game face and escape the stiletto heel of Wanda's shoe, which she's using to viciously kick me under the long linen tablecloth, to hear the rest of the introductions. Jeanette Howell Tiger is the second wife of the Reverend T. Terry Tiger, who tried desperately to destroy A Sister's Spa as part of his Crusade to Resurrect Morality a few years ago. We'd beaten him back, in no small part thanks to Jeanette. The last time I saw Jeanette was in the parking lot of A Sister's Spa, where she'd just told T. Terry she was pregnant. That was the last I'd heard of either one of them. The introductions finished, the guests dig into their salads, chatting easily among themselves.

"Jeanette Tiger, still with old Terry. With twins, no less. And on Martha's Vineyard," Wanda whispers to me between bites of salad. "Make that one degree of separation."

"I'm surprised, too, but Jeanette's cool. Don't forget the last time we saw her."

"And herself."

"Yep. As I recall, even though she was technically spying for Terry, she enthusiastically availed herself of the spa's services."

"She's probably thankful we're here. T. Terry's no spring chicken, and even if he can still get it up without pharmaceutical assistance, he's probably too whipped to want to, after chasing twins all day."

"That's what I'm thinking. This works for us, Wanda. We've got someone at the table who's experienced the joys the Floating Spa will bring to the island."

"I hope you're right," she whispers, forking up a last hunk of lobster meat as the help begins to replace salad plates with our entrée of grilled bass, haricots verts, and fingerling potatoes roasted with garlic and rosemary. Ma Nicola taps her butter knife gently against her crystal wineglass for silence.

"Thank you. I have gathered you women here because you are members of the Doyennes, the Mansioneers, and are otherwise influential women on the Vineyard. Your formal and informal affiliations encompass this small island and beyond. At this table we have representatives of the most important black women's organizations in the country. Links, National Council of Negro Women, the Bright Set, Gay Timers, Association of Black Women Attorneys, Black Women in Business, Coalition of One Hundred Black Women, Ladies of Leisure, and every significant sorority on the East Coast. Each of you represents a community far greater than yourselves, and your influence and address books are extensive. Without your imprimatur and goodwill, any venture which asks for the support of women of color on this island faces an uphill battle to succeed. I have invited my goddaughter Lydia and her business associate Wanda here today to tell you a bit about the spa they will open next week. Need I say they come seeking both your blessing and business? Lydia . . ."

"Thanks, Ma Nicola, and thanks to all of you for taking time out from your busy schedules to meet with us," I say. "A week from today, we will open the Floating Spa on a yacht anchored three miles from the island. We believe that the serenity we all seek from the spa experience will be deeply enhanced by enjoying the services we offer while floating in a sea of tranquillity, miles away from land and the demands of everyday life. The Floating Spa will offer massage, Reiki, reflexology, a variety of wraps and scrubs. Delicious, healthy, gourmet snacks and meals prepared by the fabulous Chef Marvini. We will also offer the services of Sukey, nail artist extraordinaire, who will pamper your nails, not merely polish them. Wanda?" Wanda thrusts her hands forward, nail side up. A tiny image of the ferry to the island rests on whitecapped waves that seem to crest when she wiggles her fingers. The ladies around the table lean in, oohing and ahhing appreciatively.

"We have created a menu of services that we hope will appeal to each of you. Or you can design your own day of pampering," Wanda chimes in. "We also have some discreet specialized services available to the adventurous. Whatever your tastes, we are confident we can guarantee that you'll return to land profoundly rested, relaxed, and with your next visit already booked."

"We'd like to invite each of you and a friend to be our guests for a complimentary service at the Floating Spa on opening day. We will do everything possible to make sure you enjoy yourselves—"

"And tell all your friends!" Wanda interrupts.

"That, too, of course. Now, we'd be happy to entertain any questions."

"How will we get there?" one of the women asks.

"We'll have a shuttle service that will pick you up and deliver you back to the dock."

"My grandchildren are coming for the Fourth. Do you think Susan can paint their pictures on my nails?"

"It's Sukey, and I'm sure she can. She's marvelous."

"Frankly, I don't get it," Audreen Bishop says, flipping open a gold lighter and firing up another cigarette. "We already have a perfectly sufficient spa in town that offers, with the exception of 'nail art'"—she arches an eyebrow skeptically as she says this—"the same services."

"And it's on dry land. I can't swim," one of the Conover sisters chimes in.

"They said there's going to be a shuttle boat," her sister says.

"Why bother when we can walk over to Rub-A-Doll?"

"Who're they?" Wanda asks.

"That's the day spa on Circus Avenue." Ma Nicola sniffs.

"I don't know about anyone else, but I haven't been that happy with their services," Bea Fulton says.

Another woman chimes in. "Neither have I, but they're the only spa in town."

"We tried to support their venture, or at least I did," Bea continues. "I had a hot rock massage at Rub-A-Doll and ended up with a burn the size of a fist on my back that took all summer to heal."

"They burnt me, too. I was so embarrassed I didn't mention it to anyone." Hetty Foster Wilson pipes up. Medium height and slim, her eyebrows are perpetually arched in a look of either mild astonishment or inquiry. "Just above my breast. I couldn't wear any of my low-cut clothes for the remainder of the season."

"Honestly, I can do my own nails better than their nail technician and that's not saying much," Charity Conover confides. "Two days after my session with her my cuticles looked like shag carpet."

"I hate to lead the rebellion, but I'd be happy to check out the services of the Floating Spa."

"I've never understood the fascination with spas. Come to Aquinnah for one of our Native ceremonies and spend time in the sweat lodge. I guarantee you will be rejuvenated and spiritually elevated—for free." Ellen Canning chuckles. Audreen responds by exhaling an enormous cloud of smoke. It floats over the table like a storm cloud.

"Let's not forget that the owners of Rub-A-Doll are longtime island residents, not—and please excuse my language, Nicola—carpetbaggers. That should count for something," Audreen declares. It's as if she's thrown a bomb into the middle of the room. I mean, if all spa services are equal, who wants to side with the money-grubbing West Coast carpetbaggers against the perhaps inept but hardworking and good-intentioned locals?

"Tell them about the discreet specialized services," Jeanette Howell Tiger says, breaking the uncomfortable silence and replacing it with another one.

"We love surprises, don't we?" Faith Conover coos, turning toward her sisters, who nod affirmatively.

"Oh, you are definitely going to be surprised," Jeanette assures them.

"Does Jamal perform these discreet services, because if he does, sign me up," Lorrie Jonestone says with a whoop.

"Are you affiliated with that spa outside Reno? If so, tell me more." Besides saying, "Hello," this is the first time Olga Alexander has spoken. Around thirty-five, she has a body like Naomi Campbell, strawberry-colored hair in one of those fabulous tousled styles that cost plenty to achieve, arms even I might be willing to work out for, three gorgeous children, and a husband who's rumored to be, as Ma Nicola put it, and as only a woman of her generation would dare, "queer as a three-dollar bill."

"Yes, tell us." Suddenly we've got the undivided attention of the sixteen sisters in the room, no easy feat when you're competing with my mother's red velvet cake. Wanda gives me a glance, takes a sip of wine, and smiles demurely.

"Sex," she says.

"What about it?"

"We're selling sex. Along with the usual spa services, we're offering a menu of fabulous, safe sex with men trained in the art of pleasuring women."

"Oh, my lord." Faith Conover falls back in her seat, fanning herself with her napkin.

"Don't mind her." Charity laughs. "It's been so long since she's had any, the word alone gets her hot and bothered."

"How fabulous," Olga asserts.

"Now, that's what I'm talking about," Lorrie declares.

"You're selling sex?" Hope asks.

"Well, I take it back; we don't offer that at the sweat lodge." Ellen Canning chuckles, her eyes dancing.

"Oh, my lord," Faith, still fanning, murmurs again.

"Thank you, Jesus, my prayers are answered," Lorrie exclaims with a smile.

"Perhaps you might elaborate," Ma Nicola suggests.

"We believe that sex is, if you will, the missing link in the usual spa experience," I say. "We are committed to taking the intimacy of the spa experience to the next level. What could be better than fabulous, multiorgasmic sex after being massaged and pampered?"

"On the real side, what's better than great sex, before, after, or even during a day of pampering?" Wanda asks.

"Great sex is pampering," Jeanette says.

"When did you say you're opening?" Olga asks.

"Are you booking appointments today?" Bea turns on her Black-Berry as she speaks, fingers poised above the keyboard.

The expressions on the faces of the other women are a familiar combination of surprise, curiosity, giggling embarrassment, and desire. They look shell-shocked. At least our strategy of sex and awe is having an impact.

"What about disease?" Faith asks softly.

"All of our sex workers have been extensively tested, are healthy, and receive a weekly physical. Condoms are mandatory."

"So what you're saying, dear, is that you're selling sex. Is that right?" Faith asks, having caught her breath.

"Quietly, discreetly, and to a select, upscale clientele. That's why we asked Ma Nicola to host this luncheon. We would like to invite each of you to visit the spa on opening day, bring a friend, and enjoy the complimentary service of your choice."

"Is this legal?" Audreen Bishop asks skeptically. Before I can say anything, my mother, previously silent and intent on communing with her main man, Jack Daniel's, puts both glass and fork down and turns to Audreen.

"As chief of research for A Sister's Spa," my mother begins, instantly conferring a title on herself, "a brothel for women isn't exactly legal or illegal; it exists in that gray zone where legal opinion has not yet ventured. There are, as you may know, numerous legal whorehouses in the state of Nevada, the only state where prostitution is legal. Two years ago my daughter, Lydia, her best friend, Acey Allen, and LaSha-Wanda opened A Sister's Spa outside Reno, catering to the sexual desires of women—an overwhelming success. This expansion to the East Coast is our effort to spread the joy. The Floating Spa, situated three miles offshore in international waters, floats, to my mind, in that gray area I referred to earlier, where discretion is key and anything is possible . . ."

"I visited A Sister's Spa once and had a glorious time," Jeanette pipes up. "If not for my marriage and pregnancy, I would have visited again, and given that Terry recently celebrated his seventy-fourth birthday and isn't interested in much besides Little Terry, Little Jeanette, and completing his memoir, I intend to visit the Floating Spa as soon as it opens."

"Well, I'd certainly like to see it." Faith Conover giggles. "I don't know about those other services, but I did read an article in Oprah's magazine about reflexology. I'd love to try it," she says coyly. Like bobblehead dolls, her sisters nod their agreement.

"That's cool," Wanda says smoothly. "Whatever turns you on."

"Count me in," Bea Fulton declares. "I've been on the island alone with the kids for almost a month and my husband won't be back until Fourth of July weekend. I could use some male hands rubbing my body, even if it's just a massage. As for the other services, well, as Billie was just singing, ' 'Tain't Nobody's Bizness If I Do.' "

"I'm with Bea. It's a free country, or at least it still was when I read the paper this morning."

"Let's all remember that discretion is the better part of valor," Ellen Canning says.

"Exactly," I add. "The Floating Spa's like Vegas: what happens there stays there."

"I propose that we take a voice vote to take advantage of the offer to visit the Floating Spa opening weekend and, barring any unforeseen circumstance, throw our full support behind Lydio and Wanda's endeavor," Ma Nicola says.

"It's a goddamn mistake," Audreen says, her voice slightly slurred but her eyes alert and darting from face to face. "We have a reputation to uphold."

"Exactly what would that be?" Bea asks.

"Dried-up and sexless, apparently," Jeanette says.

"Upstanding and decent women committed to charitable endeavors."

"Audreen, exactly how does visiting the Floating Spa interfere with our charitable mission?" Ma Nicola asks gently. "It's not as if we'll be holding our meeting there."

"Although, so many of us will probably be there, we could." Olga Alexander snickers.

"Besides the moral issues?" Audreen asks sarcastically. "It is a time-consuming distraction from working to meet our annual fund-raising goal. The island depends on our charitable contributions."

"How much?" Wanda interrupts.

"How much what?"

"Is this year's fund-raising goal?"

"Charity, you're treasurer. What did we decide last fall?"

"Twenty-five thousand dollars."

"The Floating Spa would like to donate five thousand dollars as a show of support, respect, and good faith." Wanda's announcement is greeted by gasps, smiles, and a smattering of applause. Perhaps realizing that our offer of pampering, sex, and a big-ass donation trumps her complaints, Audreen simply shakes her head and drains her glass.

"In favor?" Ma Nicola asks. All of the women around the table except Audreen nod affirmatively.

"Opposed?" Audreen remains motionless. "Abstain?" Still nothing. "Audreen, my old friend, let's you and I go together and see what the Floating Spa has to offer," Ma Nicola says warmly. "If we find services to our liking, that's all to the good. If not, we two old ladies will have enjoyed a pleasant boat ride and tour of the yacht. What do you say, dear friend?"

"If you say so, Nicks. I guess it can't hurt." Audreen shrugs.

"It might even help." Ma Nicola smiles, leans over, and pats Audreen's shoulder. "I for one look forward to my visit with great alacrity. Now, business finished, who'd like another piece of Mavis's splendid red velvet cake?"

CHAPTER 13

Lydia

"I DON'T BELIEVE THIS SHIT. THE DAMN fog stalked us from San Francisco." Wanda, Sukey, and I stand on the deck of the *Lady Lay* expectantly looking toward land, from whence our clients will come. Or more accurately, looking in the direction we think land is, since in the heavy fog we've lost our bearings.

It's almost eleven o'clock on Memorial Day, opening day of the Floating Spa, and everything's ready but the weather. We're in constant cell-phone touch with Cap'n Chubby, who's at the dock in Oak Bluffs waiting to shuttle clients, among them several of our invited guests from Ma Nicola's luncheon, out to the boat, but like us, he's waiting for the fog to lift. Call me crazy, but even though I know that among the few things I can't control Mother Nature is one, I'm doing everything I can to make the fog disappear. I'm trying not to whine aloud, but in my head I'm begging, pleading, demanding, and even though I'm not a prayerful sister, throwing in an occasional prayer just in case.

"Hey, I think it's lifting," Sukey says, peering into the mist in front of her. She's wearing orange shorts and a tight T-shirt of the same color embroidered with A Sister's Spa's logo, a black woman with her eyes closed and a blissful smile on her face. There's a tiny boat to the left of the woman's lips, like a beauty mark, an added touch for the Floating Spa. The sex workers wear the same uniform, although their shirts are tight enough to show off their pecs and abs, their shorts skimpy enough to make sure the package they're waiting to deliver to our clients won't be a surprise or a disappointment.

"What makes you think that?"

"The gray's changing colors," she says, pointing. "See, it's not so solid anymore, you know what I mean?"

"No, I don't know."

Beside me, Wanda turns a slow 360 degrees, examining the fog from all angles. "You know, I been up watching the fog for hours. I think it is lifting."

"Yep. I prayed for a successful day. That's what we're gonna have, Wanda-babe."

"I hope you're right, Suks. What I'm going to have right now is one of those sour-cream strawberry muffins Marvini baked this morning. Between too little sleep, too much coffee, and trying to bend the weather to my will, my stomach feels as if it's trying to digest rusty nails. A delicious muffin is definitely called for," Wanda says, walking toward the stairs to the galley and food. "Call me the moment the sun gets here," she tosses over her shoulder, leaving me and Sukey alone on deck.

"Lydia, you haven't seen the salon yet; come on and let me show you around," Sukey suggests, grabbing my arm as I pace by. "It'll take your mind off the fog, and I bet that after your tour, it'll be gone."

"Okay." I check my phone for the twentieth time, making sure it's on and that I haven't missed a call from the Cap'n. "Lead the way." I can't resist glancing behind me as I step over the sill and inside the lounge. Maybe it's a hallucination, but the impenetrable gray does seem to be dissipating, the sky now dotted in places with hints of blue.

On the floor beneath the common rooms, we've divided the boat into two sections. Aft is the larger one, with eight luxurious staterooms for sex; forward a smaller section with rooms for massage, Reiki, reflexology, and Sukey's nail salon. Besides okaying invoices and writing checks, Wanda and I had pretty much left Sukey on her own in deciding how to decorate and set up the salon. We'd decided that Sukey could stay through the summer. If she didn't bring in some serious revenue, we'd let her go, turn the salon into a bedroom, and hire another sex worker to man it. Me, I wasn't too tough on the whole nail-art idea from jump, but Wanda wanted to give Sukey a chance, which is fine with me.

"Ready?" Sukey stands in front of a wooden door with a brass plaque announcing SUKEY'S SEA SALON, her hand on the knob and her voice excited.

"Yep." I try to put some enthusiasm in my tone, but really, do I give a damn? Seen one nail salon, seen 'em all. I'm still worrying about the fog.

Sukey pushes the door open, flicks the light switch, and we step inside not a nail salon or a room but a glowing jewel. The walls and ceiling are covered in a deep orange fabric imported from India, embroidered in paler shades of orange, red, and gold in a swirling pattern, the delicate cloth inlaid every four or five inches with mirrors the size and shape of dimes. The lighting comes from several Moroccan oilskin lamps whose conical shades are painted with colorful, intricate designs, the light they shed soft and flattering. The mirrors woven into the fabric on the walls catch and refract the light, and the small room glows and shimmers. The floors are covered with a patchwork of small kilim rugs, each design different but all the colors playing off the orange, red, and gold wall covering. In the background, the music of the string quartet Sojourner floats seductively from unseen speakers. The room smells faintly of sandalwood and nearly overripe fruit, sexy and good for you at the same time. Against one wall a long, wide wicker chaise is covered in a deep orange fabric and piled with pillows. Next to the chaise is a small table, beside it a small refrigerator. Against another wall is a long, narrow table covered with a silk cloth, a small chair on wheels in front of it.

"This is my equipment," Sukey says, pulling the fabric up. Underneath are neatly organized shelves and drawers holding polish, brushes, fake nails, acrylic, sanding tools, all the paraphernalia necessary for nail art. "Once the client is settled in the chair, I can just roll my stuff over and get to work," she explains. "Look at this." She walks over to the chaise, pulls a handle at the foot of it, and the chaise slides easily apart, becoming a chair and an ottoman. In the space between is a basin for the feet. She turns it on and jets of water begin pulsing. "Cool, huh? Once she sits down, she's in, whaddyacallit, a total environment, I do everything for her." Sukey grins at the stunned look on my face. "Nice, huh? Cousin Wanda was really surprised, too. I guess she didn't take me seriously, either." She shrugs. "See, Lydia? I told you I could handle my business."

I nod my wonder and agreement. Gazing around the gorgeous, lush cocoon Sukey has created, even though I don't give a damn about my nails, I wish I had the time for a session of her nail art, if only for an excuse to lie back in that beckoning chair and let this space envelop me.

The sound of a boat horn shakes me out of my reverie. Spa. Opening day. Mother Nature not cooperating. The spell broken by reality.

"It's really beautiful, Sukey," I say, giving her a long, sincere hug that ends only when my cell rings. I flip it open and listen for a few moments. "That was Chubby from the dock. He says the weather's clear enough for him to bring the first clients out. He says only three showed. Let's hope once he drops them off and heads back to the dock, the fog'll have burned off and more will be waiting."

"I'm sure they will be."

"Go on upstairs, tell Wanda the shuttle's on the way; Marvini, too. I'm going to make sure the sex workers are ready."

I pause outside the door to the men's dormitory, knock softly, and announce myself before I enter. The sex workers stand at attention in front of their beds, visions in snugly fitting orange shorts and T-shirts.

"Lydia. It is time, am I correct?" Jamal asks, flashing that smile.

"Almost. Everyone and everything ready?" I look slowly into the eyes of each worker, holding his gaze. Each man returns my stare, their eyes filled with variations of confidence, anticipation, and a smoky, sexy look that has me remembering each man's sexual prowess. Jamal's amazing tongue; Issac's acrobatic, aerobic, and orgasmic positioning; Tree Man, who likes to carry a woman in his arms while he fucks her; the triplets, DeJuan, DeQuan, and DeMon, whose youth and enthusiasm make a woman forget her name; Sekou whose thick penis actually makes you forget—temporarily—the clitoral orgasm; Tollhouse, who can find a woman's G-spot like a hound to the foxes. Looking at them, I can't keep a great big grin off my face.

"Ready, willing, and, as you know very well, able," Jamal responds. "Since early morning we have meditated and prayed to the gods to bless and endow us with their power, to help us serve and satisfy the goddesses. We are eager to please."

"I know you've all heard it before, but bear with me; I'll be brief. Pleasure. You have all been chosen because of your superlative abilities to give women sexual pleasure. That is why women come to the Floating Spa, and that's why they'll be back. Wanda and I have done everything we can to make a woman's time here relaxing and luxurious. Chef Marvini will make sure that the food is delicious. But the spa's success is in your hands. Each of you has the power to make a woman's visit here the ultimate in pleasure. Don't let us down." It's always been Odell's job to inspire new sex workers with a rousing pep talk, tapping into that man thing that's a combination of a love for women, physical prowess, ego, and humility that characterizes the best lovers. I'm doing my best, but without Odell, I've come to depend on Jamal to take care of the brother-bonding stuff that only those with a penis, balls, and a full load of testosterone can truly fathom.

"We will not," Jamal says firmly, and the men nod.

"Well then, all hands on deck, the shuttle is about to arrive and the first thing I want our guests to see is you gorgeous men." The workers file out of the room, Jamal in the rear. "They all look great, Jamal, thanks." I turn to him after I watch the last pair of tight buns, muscles rippling, ascend the stairs.

"Lydia, you are welcome, but we may have a problem."

"Please, no." I groan, glancing at my watch. "There's no time for problems, Jamal. The shuttle will be here in minutes."

"Tollhouse."

"What about him?" I'm trying to keep the sharpness out of my voice, but it ain't easy.

"He missed morning exercise and meditation."

"Maybe he was tired and overslept."

"My thought also. Yet when I came upstairs to find him, he was not in his bed."

"Maybe he was in the galley getting something to eat, in the lounge, on deck. Did you look?"

"There was no time."

"Jamal, what's your point?" I don't even try to keep the impatience out of my voice. It's opening day, the boat looks fantastic, Sukey's delivered, the fog has finally lifted, and the shuttle's about to arrive. I don't have either the time or the inclination to worry about what Tollhouse was up to as long as he's now present and accounted for.

"I am not sure why he is here. My concern is that he is not fully committed to the Floating Spa," Jamal says, a frown on his face, definitely not the look we want when he greets our clients shortly. I give him a quick hug.

"I hear you, but let's talk later. Right now it's showtime, so upstairs and let's take care of business."

"Lydia! Come up here! You are not going to believe this!" Wanda shouts when I'm halfway up the steps. She stands on the deck pointing toward land, Sukey and Marvini beside her, flanked by sex workers. I hear the motor of the shuttle as it nears the Floating Spa. I walk to the railing, squeeze myself in between Wanda and Marvini, look in the direction of land.

"Do you see this?" Wanda asks incredulously.

"Well, I'll be damned." Our official water taxi with Cap'n Chubby at the helm is in the lead and Ma Nicola, Audreen, and a woman I don't know stand beside him. A small fleet of vessels follows in his wake. A cat boat, several small sailboats, two of what look like rowboats with outboard motors attached, one of those bright yellow inflatable dinghies used to ferry passengers or supplies from land to ship, and bringing up the rear a forest-green two-seater kayak. Jeanette, the Conover sisters, Lorrie Jonestone, other faces I do not recognize. Like pilgrims or penitents in search of deliverance, healing, and the laying on of hands, they advance toward us, a ragtag armada delivering acolytes to the Floating Spa. They come not to make war but love, not in search of plunder but to be lustfully and lovingly plundered. The women stand in the prow of their boat, tilted forward, living figureheads. Their faces are lit with expectant grins and they wave enthusiastically.

"Smile. Wave back," I tell the sex workers, lifting my arm and gesturing as if I'm trying to get a taxi on Market Street during a rush-hour downpour. "Wanda, my love, we are about to get paid," I whisper. Wanda grins, tosses her hair, daps me five.

"Thank goodness for my sisters." Wanda laughs. "I couldn't sleep I was so worried, then when I saw the fog this morning . . . I guess when it comes to women and great sex, we're like postal workers, 'Neither rain nor hail nor fog—'"

"Will keep a sister from good dick and multiple orgasms," I finish. "Lower the lift and haul 'em up," I instruct, hearing Chubby's motor slow almost to idling. "Let the games begin."

CHAPTER 14

Odell

T HEN, ODELL, MY PRAYERS, LATE AND sporadic as they are, were answered. It was magic, pure Hollywood. Out of the fog came all these boats; it was like they were storming the beach at Normandy in reverse, although this time they weren't after Germans, but sex. And they've just kept on coming, in both senses of the word. If this keeps up, the Floating Spa will do better than we ever expected or dreamed. You should have been here, Odell."

"She's not exaggerating, either; it was a regatta of women in search of satiation. Thank goodness we actually have some traditional spa services available to send the clients to while they wait for their sex worker to become available. Not only were the bedrooms fully occupied but the masseuses gave so many deep-tissue massages they had to soak their hands in ice, ditto for the reflexologist. If business keeps up like this, we're going to have to think about expanding."

I lie on the couch in my office, head against the armrest at one end and feet propped up on the other, and enjoy the flood of good news flowing from East to West Coast. It does a brother proud to hear how well the opening day and first weeks of the Floating Spa have been going, and good news is always welcome, particularly right through here.

"They're hungry, too, brother." Chef Marvini's deep voice joins those of Lydia and Wanda coming through the speakerphone. "A few assumed I was a sex worker, but once I told them I was the chef and my gig was to satisfy a different kind of hunger, they were on it. I chopped up so much fruit and whipped up so many energy shakes and mango frappés I had to break out my auxiliary blender. I may need an assistant." Laughter floods the speakerphone, and I take advantage of Marvini's, Lydia's, and Wanda's chuckling to finally get a word in edgewise and change the subject.

"Sounds great. Now, there are a few issues to talk about. Acey's on her way to my office. When she gets here the five of us need to put our heads together about some serious business."

"While we're waiting on Acey, forget serious," Wanda says, laughing. "Let me read you a few excerpts from the exit questionnaires. 'An absolutely superlative spa experience, especially my time with Jamal. Rebook me for the same time next week!' And listen to this one: 'It's been twenty years since I was with a man, and my experience with Tree Man suggests it's been even longer than that, with apologies to my departed husband. Long live the G-spot and the clitoral orgasm!' Check this one, Odell: 'What a workout! First a relaxing massage, then some

internal stroking, and finally a fabulous session with Sukey. I leave relaxed, spent, and without an arthritic bone in my body. See you again
in a few days.' How about that?"

"Congratulations, Wanda and company. I like to think of myself
as cautious, but I'm happy to be proven wrong," I say easily, and mean
it. "What are the receipts like?"

"Fifty percent above expectations," Lydia crows. "We have more
women coming for shorter stays, so a much faster turnover. Income is
at or above expectations for the sex workers and every other category,
except nail art, not surprisingly."

"What's the problem there? Clients not interested in getting their
nails done?"

"Nope, Sukey's bookings are strong, but the sessions take too damn
long," Wanda says. "We'd figured forty-five minutes a session, max,
but with almost half of the clients Sukey takes more than twice that
amount of time, which cuts our profit roughly in half."

"Not that any of the clients are complaining, Odell. In fact, they
seem extremely pleased. I'm just saying that at the speed Sukey works,
we'll be lucky if we break even on the nails."

"Any way to speed her up?"

"We're working on it," Lydia responds. "But it ain't easy, O. You
have to understand that what's just a manicure, pedicure, and a quick
polish to us is art to Sukey. Seriously, she sees herself as the Kara
Walker or Romare Bearden of nails. The last time I tried to talk to her
about speeding it up, she gave me a lecture about great art taking time,
with references to the Pyramids, Sistine Chapel, and Statue of Liberty.
Go figure." I laugh.

"Any resolution?"

"Not really. She looked like she was going to break into tears, kick
my ass, or both, so I asked her to consider what I'd said and scrammed."

"Wanda, any chance you can talk to your cousin?"

"I've tried, and I'll go at her again, but I know Sukey. She has her own way of doing things, and it's hard to shake her. Plus, the clients she does do are all pleased and rebook. It's not her product that's a problem, she just needs to hustle. I'll give it another try."

The door of my office opens and Acey walks in. Seeing I'm on speaker, she calls out, "Hey, everyone. Sorry I'm late," and slips into a chair.

"Hey, Ace, we all miss you. How's everything at A Sister's Spa? Y'all still coming out here for the Fourth, right?" Lydia, Wanda, and Marvini greet Acey all at once.

"Hello, all. Miss you, too, and yes, Odell and I are coming for the holiday," Acey responds, looking over at me, her eyebrows raised in questioning. "Everything going all right out there?"

"Fabulously. Can't wait until you get here."

"No problems with Jamal and the workers?"

"Problems? Only if you think it's a problem that our clients love them, we're solidly booked, and if we had the room, could use another half dozen of them," Wanda says.

"I was kinda worried about Audreen, one of Ma Nicola's cronies who was negative as hell about the spa at the luncheon. Honey, I shouldn't have wasted the brain cells. She arrived opening day with her nose in the air and a skeptical expression on her face. A few hours later, she stumbled out of here looking like somebody'd rode her hard and put her away wet, and did I say she had a slap-happy grin on her face?" Lydia cackles delightedly.

"Seriously, everything's going fabulously with the exception of my slow-ass cousin, and I'll figure out how to light some fire under her or she's out of here and Sukey's Sea Salon will become a revenue-generating boudoir."

"Marvini, brother. You aren't saying much. Does that mean you agree with the ladies?" I ask.

"Mostly, O. Don't feel right about Tollhouse. Can't put my finger on it."

I know Marvini's intuition isn't something to ignore. "You're keeping an eye on him?"

"You know that."

"Good. Keep me posted. Okay, now, how're my knucklehead brothers doing?"

"They're great, Odell. I think you're gonna have to drop the term *knucklehead* when referring to them."

"Anyway, Odell, what's the serious business you want to talk to us about?" Lydia asks. I clear my throat, look at Acey, who's making a hurry-up gesture with one hand.

"You all are doing a great job out there, congratulations. Unfortunately, we're having a couple of problems on this end. Remember the guy we fired, Tony? Apparently he went home slinging his dick around to prove we were wrong and whining about being fired."

"So what?" Wanda grumbles.

"'So what' is that it turns out his uncle Eddie's a big-time mobster in Providence, Rhode Island, who wasn't happy to see his fuckup nephew back in town. Now Uncle Eddie's looking to get paid."

"I thought Acey was exaggerating or being paranoid," Lydia says faintly.

"Extortion is his business," I say. "Although he quaintly and euphemistically calls it 'tithing' to his church. I had an extremely unpleasant conversation with him a few weeks ago and he's serious. He wants nine and a half percent of our net. If we won't do it, he says he'll make it impossible for us to do business." The only sound coming through the phone now is grim silence.

"Damn," Marvini finally says slowly. "How's he planning to do that?"

"It wouldn't be hard. We're in the middle of the desert. We depend on truckers to deliver everything from food to condoms to water, on limousines to deliver customers. If he intimidates the truckers and drivers we already have, and makes the roads dangerous for any new ones we hire, we're out of business. The last thing we need is the tires blown out on a limo filled with women who've paid to be pampered, not shot."

"You didn't agree, did you?"

"We didn't agree to anything. Yet. Said we had partners on the East Coast and couldn't make any decision without them. We told him we'd be out that way in July and could meet then, face-to-face."

"Who's got a plan?" Marvini asks.

"That's one reason we're calling."

"I think it's all bullshit," Wanda says. "Some jive motherfucker's trying to hold us up for our hard-earned money, probably got nothing to do with the Mob. Saw what they thought was an easy mark and decided to go for it. I say fuck 'em."

"We hoped that, too, Wanda. But I asked Mavis to do some research on Uncle Eddie Sollozzo. Unfortunately, he's for very real. I'll fax you her report on him when we finish, but let me say that his nickname is 'Burns' and he didn't get it because he can cook.

"At least not food," I add, hoping for a chuckle or two, but no one's laughing. "Listen, we have a few weeks before the meeting to try and figure something out. If we don't, I say we plead poor, offer him five percent for a few months, and then consider our options."

"Which at this point are either pay up or be destroyed," Acey says glumly.

"Ain't this a bitch, sister can't get a damn break. Here we are minding our own business, trying to do our thing and deliver a much-needed service, build our little black capitalist empire, ain't hurting nobody. Now the Mob's on our ass? Only in America," Wanda snarls.

"I hear you, Mrs. Don King, but that's where we are, like it or not."

"And that's not the only problem," Acey says. "There's your president's No Child, No Behind initiative."

"He ain't my president, and we've been too busy to read anything except assembly instructions since we got here. Remember, there are no televisions on board, and the only radio is the battery-powered one Marvini has in the galley."

"No Child, No Behind? I heard something about it the other day, but I turned to the reggae station," Marvini says.

"Briefly, he's trying to push a law through Congress to make sex for purposes other than procreation illegal. Today we received a letter from the Justice Department instructing us to cease all purely recreational sexual activity."

"They're after A Sister's Spa?"

"Not specifically. Yet. First they're writing all businesses in Nevada counties, where prostitution is legal, and asking for voluntary cooperation."

"What's he smoking, and where did he cop?" Marvini asks.

"Would that he were stoned, he'd be a kinder, gentler leader of the free world, but no such luck, bro," I say.

"This shit is serious?"

"Not only that, Congress will probably go along with it," Acey chimes in. "The Republicans are looking for an issue to distract people from the war and the economy. They've already tried flag burning, phony terrorism alerts, and a constitutional amendment outlawing gay marriage, without success. As for the Democrats, the president's already suggesting that anyone against No Child, No Behind is not only soft on terror but an amoral recreational fornicator. Remember, there's an election in November. I know No Child, No Behind sounds absurd, but it's no joke."

"What's the time frame?"

"Yeah, when do they vote?"

"The president is calling for a special session of both houses right after the Fourth of July holiday."

"That's less than a month."

"Dag, I thought the Providence Mob was a problem. Now we gotta contend with the D.C. mob as well," Marvini says, his voice high-pitched and tight from simultaneously talking and holding in smoke. "Mr. Charlie's a bitch."

CHAPTER 15

To: Acey Allen, A Sister's Spa
From: Mavis Ransom Beaucoup,
    Director of Research

A BRIEF REPORT ON EDDIE
"BURNS" SOLLOZZO

With the exception of a few minor
traffic violations, Eddie Sollozzo, 73, has
never been convicted of a crime. Federal
and state law enforcement officials are
convinced that for the last thirty years
Sollozzo has been head of the Mafia in
Providence, Rhode Island, a position it
is said he inherited from his father, Vincente, who arrived in Providence in the
early 1940s, soon after the breakup of his
New York crime family. He brought with
him his seven children, five of whom are
currently alive; Eddie is a middle child.
Reports are that the Sollozzos traffic in

heroin and handguns. In the last ten years, twelve members of his organization have been convicted of extortion, assault, and murder. Eddie began working alongside his father before he was a teenager and took over the business in the late 1950s, after his father was killed by a load of wet cement accidentally dumped on him while he was urinating down a small incline on the side of Interstate 195 outside Providence. Within a year, the driver of the cement truck burned to death inside the headquarters of his employer, Fratiani Construction, and 75 percent of their fleet was destroyed. Eddie Sollozzo is suspected of having ordered or carried out numerous murders, and earned his nickname, Burns, because of his fondness for using fire on his victims. In summary, there can be no question that Eddie Sollozzo is a bad cat, if I may say so, but perhaps not completely. Oddly enough, besides the Italian civic and charitable organizations he is a member of, he's also a lifetime member of Racial Solidarity Now!, a status conferred only on those who consistently make large donations. This is not exactly an organization you'd think he be attracted to, but there's supposed to be some good in everyone. Who knows? Perhaps he has a bit of black in him—remember Hannibal and the Moors conquered Italy—but that is purely speculative on my part. That said, while I find his organizational membership intriguing, it's clear that, all things considered, never meeting or having anything to do with Eddie Sollozzo puts one in the plus column.

Respectfully Submitted,
Mavis Ransom Beaucoup

CHAPTER 16

Wanda

"TERRY SAYS THE TWINS LOOK JUST LIKE me and I guess that's good enough for both of us," Jeanette Tiger says, walking across the green and assuming the position on the ninth hole as she prepares to tee off. "While I was pregnant, I thought about having DNA testing after the babies were born to establish paternity, but once they arrived, it seemed irrelevant." She shrugs. "Not to mention if it turned out he wasn't the twins' daddy, it would break Terry's heart." She swings and the golf ball arches into the sky. Jeanette squints in its direction, holding one hand over her brow.

"Yeah, well, I guess everything worked out for the best, huh?" I say, walking to my golf bag and staring at it blankly, trying to remember which club is for what and coming up empty. This is only the second time I've played golf. The first time was yesterday, when I had a one-hour lesson with the club's resident golf pro, and that was only because Lydia insisted that we should do some outreach to the golf and tennis set. Hey, I love to watch Venus and Serena Williams pounding the court but can't see myself exerting myself to chase a tennis ball, so I'd chosen golf, a game I know nothing about except I've never seen Tiger Woods run or sweat. I'd bumped into Jeanette in the restaurant at the clubhouse after my lesson and she'd invited me to play with her today, although if I had my druthers, I'd be sitting in the clubhouse sipping an iced tea. My idea of a good time does not include being out here before noon trying to figure out which club to use, where to aim, and that most elusive question of all, why.

"Absolutely. Since the twins were born, all Terry does is play with them and work on his memoir. Says he's dedicated to the two *p*'s, paternity and posterity. Frankly, although he won't admit it, a third *p*, pussy, is no longer on his list."

"That's what the Floating Spa's for."

"Amen. That's why I've got my regular weekly appointment." Jeanette grins, tossing her shoulder-length, honey-colored, blond-streaked hair and smoothing her lavender pleated golf skirt. "You going to tee off or just stand there and pose, Wanda?"

Did the pro say arm straight or bent? Are my toes supposed to be turned in or out? Am I using the right club? I stand on the green under a blue sky in which the few scattered clouds look like white cotton candy, simultaneously trying to recall the basics of Golf 101 and scheme about how to get off the course and into the clubhouse to a cold drink ASAP. I pull back the arm with the club in it, swing downward toward the ball, and miss. The only thing that flies into the air is a clod of grassy dirt. Jeanette laughs.

"I get the impression that golf's not your game, Wanda."

"Or tennis, volleyball, in-line skating, or any other outdoor sport," I admit happily, bending down and trying to smooth the part of the green I'd dislodged and recovered—without difficulty, since it landed six feet away—back into the fairway.

"There's an indoor racquetball court at the club," Jeanette suggests.

"Let me make myself perfectly clear: I've promised myself I'll start working out when I'm forty, but until then I'm planning to enjoy the next five years, you know?" Jeanette nods her head, laughing.

"I hear you, Wanda," she says, sliding her club into her bag. "Since you're not feeling golf, let's have a cold drink."

"Sounds perfect." We stroll easily toward the clubhouse, and now that I'm not pretending to play golf, I find myself enjoying the beauty of the setting. The only thing constant is the perfectly manicured, even grass. The shape and views from each hole are different. One leads down into a hollow shaded by ancient oak trees, another takes us up onto a hill from which, looking east, we can see the ocean, yet another offers a vista of forest, ocean, and woods. Sometimes groups of golfers talking in whispers pass, but for the most part, the course seems empty and hushed, the smell of wild honeysuckle and the salty ocean occasionally wafting by. On a hill just past the fourth hole, Jeanette stops, points toward a group of six women, each wearing a maroon T-shirt with a powder-blue B9 on the back, preparing to play the third hole.

"What a treat," she whispers. "I heard the Back Nine were coming to play here. What great luck to stumble upon them in action."

"The Back Nine?"

"They're an organization of women golfers, founded more than fifty years ago."

"Professionals?"

"Nope, though many of them are so good they could be. It's more of a social, fun thing. They spend three weeks every summer traveling together and playing different courses. I read in the *Martha's Vineyard Times* and the *Gazette* that they were playing the Vineyard this year, but there were no dates mentioned. The ladies are very private and not looking to draw spectators. We're blessed."

"You ever play with them?"

"I wish I were that good, but not in this lifetime."

"How many of them are there?"

"Maybe two hundred, I think, but they don't all travel together. I think it's thirty to each course during the summer, then they vote on the most challenging course and all meet there for their annual meeting."

"They bring their families with them?"

"It's my understanding that the Back Nine is not a family affair," Jeanette says vaguely.

"Which means?"

"Which means it's an all-girls event."

"Bingo. Let's stroll by and introduce ourselves," I say, patting the pocket of my golf skirt to make sure I've got business cards easily accessible. "If there're thirty women, I bet more than a few of them'll be interested in visiting the Floating Spa."

"Somehow, Wanda, I doubt it."

"Jeanette, you're married, living with your husband, who's on island twenty-four/seven, and you're a steady customer," I tease. "You telling me that a woman spending six weeks away from home with twenty-nine other chicks isn't hungry for some TLC? Get real." I start walking toward the third hole, gesture with my hand for Jeanette to come on.

"Slow down, Wanda, you're not hearing me. These chicks ain't into dicks."

"Excuse me?"

"They're lesbians, Wanda. The Back Nine is a lesbian organization."

"You lie."

"Nope."

"You sure?"

Jeanette raises her hands to shoulder height, palms outward, in a gesture of surrender. "Hey, I haven't slept with any of the members, so I can't put my hand on the Bible and swear, but that's my understanding."

"I'm impressed. An integrated organization of dyke golfers that's existed for half a century."

"Lesbians, Wanda. Only lesbians are allowed to call lesbians dykes."

"Oh, really? How is it you know so much about dyke—I mean, lesbian—etiquette?" I tease. "Is there something you're not telling me?"

"Nope, not that I wouldn't. I might. Just haven't had the opportunity."

"Whatever. Let's go meet them anyway. Whatever they're into sexually, they must be some badass women and you may be wrong about the lesbian thing. Even if you're not, who knows? Maybe some of 'em like a penis every now and again."

"Maybe. But if they do, they've got plenty of ways to hook it up without getting a man involved. Vibrators, strap-ons, dildos, I'm sure they've figured it out." Jeanette falls into step beside me and we walk toward the group of women. They look to range in age from their thirties to eighties, their varying body types and sizes tanned, strong, and firm. The muscles on their calves and thighs are sleek beneath their shorts, and their arms are sculpted and hard. They stand in a circle, talking softly, and low bursts of laughter drift our way. As we cross the last yards between them and us, they turn, look toward us expectantly.

"Sorry," a short, chubby woman with a shoulder-length page boy, impeccable makeup, and a neck laden with gold chains calls out in greeting. "Are we slowing down your game?"

"Not at all."

"Hope we're not interrupting an important conversation," Jeanette says.

"Glad you did. We were just talking politics," an Asian woman with gorgeous short-cropped silver hair and fabulous turquoise jewelry responds.

"And don't worry, you couldn't slow down my game, I have none," I add, chuckling. The women give us a friendly version of the "so what can we do for you?" look.

"I'm Jeanette Tiger, and this is my friend LaShaWanda P. Marshall. Sorry to bother you. We don't mean to interrupt, but I wanted to say how honored we are that the Back Nine has chosen to play the Vineyard," Jeanette says quickly. Their faces soften.

"Thanks, we're happy to be here. Beautiful island," responds a tall, dark brown woman with thick locks wound in a bun protruding from the top of her visor.

"Farm Neck's a great course, too. We'd heard a lot about it from friends. Thought they were exaggerating until we arrived," a woman adds.

"How are you enjoying your time here? I mean, off the golf course?" I ask.

"Eating well."

"Getting a lot of sleep."

"Reading that stack of books I don't have time for during the year."

"Taking naps."

"In short, not bored yet, but probably soon," I say, to a few chortles and nods of agreement.

"Any suggestions?" This from a short, pigeon-breasted blonde wearing an armful of gold bangles and a hungry expression.

"I'm glad you asked." I reach into my pocket. "My girlfriend Lydia and I recently opened a day spa on a yacht not far from the island. We offer massage, reflexology, gourmet cuisine, manicures and pedicures, and other, more personalized services."

"Such as?" the tall woman asks. I give a quick group wink.

"Come see us and find out. Let me give you some passes on the water shuttle; it leaves every two hours from the dock in Oak Bluffs," I say, putting a card in each woman's hand. "Come visit, check us out. If you're not interested in any of the services we offer, we'll whisk you right back to shore."

"Sukey, the manicurist, is a genius," Jeanette chimes in, flashing her nails. Sukey's adorned them with the shape and topography of Martha's Vineyard island, floating in a sea of blue. I have to admit, my cousin's great at what she does. Too bad she's so damn slow.

"We have two wonderful masseuses," I add, "and much, much more."

"I could definitely use a massage," a woman says, pocketing her card.

"And my nails are ruined," the blonde adds.

"Your reputation will be joining them if you don't pick up your game." The chubby sister who'd first spoken to us laughs. She turns to me and Jeanette and briskly extends her hand. "Great to meet you both. I'm sure some of us will visit your spa, LaShaWanda. Now, if you'll excuse us, we've got fifteen holes to play before cocktail hour."

Jeanette and I say hasty good-byes and continue toward the clubhouse, a sprawling one-story shingled building with white trim, beautifully landscaped with deep purple hydrangeas and wildflowers. The building houses a golf shop, locker rooms, restaurant, and bar. From where I'm coming from, it looks to me like an oasis in a desert of heat, insects, grass, and outdoor sports. I can already feel and taste the cold iced tea, upgraded to Long Island style, sliding down my parched throat. I glance at my watch and see it's just past noon, time for lunch.

The restaurant at Farm Neck is packed at lunchtime. Open to members and nonmembers, it has become the lunch spot of choice for a wide swath of island residents. Those who've finished a round of golf, those soon to begin, folks looking to see and be seen in a setting a sight more upscale than more casual island restaurants, and people simply in search of a meal. Waiting for a table, Jeanette and I sit at the bar, order drinks, and survey the dining room. Three men and a woman who I recognize from the *Vineyard Gazette* as selectmen, the elected officials in town, are huddled at a table simultaneously studying a spreadsheet, talking, and trying to eat lunch. The small tables on the long porch whose windows overlook the golf course are occupied by couples, most wearing golf shoes and a few arguing over scorecards, although at one table a couple dreamily hold hands on top of the table while attempting to fork up salad. At the big round table in the corner, a group of people laugh boisterously, clearly celebrating something. Across from them I notice Ma Nicola, Mavis, Audreen, and Evangeline Worthington chatting and laughing. The maître d' passes the bar as he leads a group of five to a large table for eight, next to a small table where a man in a dark nylon tracksuit sits alone, his back to the room, a baseball cap pulled down low on his forehead, intently reading the *Vineyard Gazette*. I recognize three of the newly arrived gang of five from a few weeks earlier in Post Office Square: B. T. Lincoln, Lulu Langlais, James Winbush. One of the faces is familiar from C-SPAN, BET, and the backs of book covers: William "Stretch" Smith, academic, rhyming orator, and the author of twenty-two slim, provocatively titled books, most recently *Momma's a Bitch & Ho: Reconstructing Black Femininity in the Age of Hip-Hop*. Also in the group is the Reverend Dr. Herman P. Rutledge V, the youthful pastor who took over San Francisco's Last Shall Be First Baptist Church from Acey's father.

"That's Stretch Smith," I whisper to Jeanette. "I didn't realize he was so short."

Jeanette snorts. "You know how black folks' nicknames are, the opposite of reality and another way to play the dozens. If he were tall we'd call him Shorty."

"B.T., Lulu, Winbush, Stretch, and Rutledge—looks like a meeting of the local chapter of black public intellectuals is in full effect." The five people around the table order drinks and study menus, their voices adding to the restaurant's din. Every few minutes B. T. Lincoln's voice rises above the cacophony when he bellows, "Niggah!" apparently his universal sobriquet. He includes the young white male waiter who is obviously nonplussed when addressed as such while taking B.T.'s drink order. Hell, for all I know, he takes it as a compliment.

"Damn, I haven't heard *niggah* this much since I left the city." Jeanette laughs.

"I hear you. Even on beautiful Martha's Vineyard, surrounded by other successful African Americans, some of us still don't believe we're authentic."

"I guess it's not authentically black to only be smart, educated, powerful, and rich, huh? You gotta be gangsta, too. Who knew?"

"I can almost smell the testosterone. It's a wonder Lulu can stand it."

"I guess someone's got to represent the sisterhood. Besides . . ." Before I can finish my sentence the room quiets and all heads turn toward the doorway. I follow them straight to the handsome face of Judge C.

Virgil Susquehanna, and am relieved that he's not looking my way, since from the heat on my face, I'm pretty sure I'm blushing.

He stands in the doorway wearing linen slacks, a white golf shirt, and taupe golf shoes, looking impossibly imposing and regal even without his judicial robes. A delicate, pale brown hand rests lightly on his right wrist, attached to a tiny, wiry, erect woman who looks be anywhere between sixty-five and ninety. There is something delicate and birdlike in her diminutive stature, but a look at her sharp angular face and huge brown eyes that seem to throw sparks makes it clear she's no sparrow but a bird of prey. Her abundant salt-and-pepper hair is woven into a thick braid and wound, crownlike, about the top of her head. The lobes of her ears sag under the weight of glittering diamond studs the size of dimes, and a pair of rhinestone-encrusted spectacles hang from a silver chain around her neck. She is dressed in a long black linen skirt, matching jacket, and white, high-collared blouse, her appearance an intriguing mixture of past and present, hip and unhip, then and now. She and the judge stand at the top of the two steps that lead down to the dining room, posed and poised, surveying as they are surveyed. I hunch over my drink, scoping them out in the mirror behind the bar, relieved I've kept my gold visor and shades on and hoping C. Virgil doesn't notice or recognize me. In my fantasies I've played out my first meeting with him outside the courthouse in San Francisco, and my being hot, sweaty, and in ill-fitting golf clothes isn't a part of my scenario.

"Judge. Dr. Crawford. Over here," B.T. calls out, standing up and gesturing from his table.

"Well, at least he didn't call Dr. Angelique Shorter Crawford and C. Virgil 'niggah.' Guess he knows better. " Jeanette giggles.

"Is that his wife?"

"Dr. Crawford? Not now, although rumor has it they had a brief but torrid fling years ago, when she was sixty and Virgil was an up-and-coming lawyer in his early thirties. She's almost ninety, but with that figure and flawless skin, you'd never know it. As for the judge, he's been a widower for at least a decade with, I hear, a respect and affection for women of all ages, in and outside the bedroom. Witness his abiding friendship with Dr. Crawford."

"Tell me about her."

"Dr. Angelique Shorter Crawford was head of the African American history department at Harvard, where she did groundbreaking research on slavery, the Civil War, and white supremacist groups. She's been emeritus for years but maintains an office and goes in several days a week. I met her through Terry; he's known her since they marched with Dr. King in the sixties, and probably C. Virgil from back then, too, during his stint as a civil rights attorney. She was at the house last week when I got back from the Floating Spa, having a drink with Terry. I caught the tail end of their conversation; it seems she's near finished with a book she's been working on forever about white supremacist groups after the Civil War."

"Ah. Me and Lydia heard B.T., Lulu, and some other people talking about that a few weeks ago at Post Office Square."

"Every season B.T. holds an event, usually a panel on an important contemporary issue. He charges fifty bucks and packs the house, not so much because of the subject matter—frankly, I'm convinced half the people don't know what it is and the other half don't give a damn—but it's something to do and another place on the island to see, be seen, and connect."

"What do Dr. Crawford and the judge have to do with that?"

"Don't know, but the waiter's beckoning us to the window table close to theirs, and I'm not averse to eavesdropping," Jeanette says, sliding off her stool and pulling me along with her.

I'm relieved that our table is behind theirs, nestled in a corner, and that Judge C. Virgil Susquehanna's back is to me. "Dr. Crawford, let me say how profoundly honored and grateful I am that someone of your stature, with your many, many years of important scholarship and busy schedule, with all the years you have devoted to your work and I am sure numerous other invitations, would take the time out from your seminal work to join us."

"It's lunchtime, B.T. I have to eat somewhere." Crawford's voice is light and teasing.

"Yes, yes, of course, Doctor. Again, I am just honored it is here with me and my friends who, like me, attempt to humbly follow in your academic footsteps at Harvard."

"You sound suspiciously like you're delivering a eulogy, B.T. Virgil, pinch me so I'll know I'm still alive."

"Stretch Smith. A true honor to finally meet you, Dr. Crawford." Smith reaches across the table, hand extended. Crawford's hand remains in her lap.

"Yes, yes, no need for formality, Professor Smith. There's butter on your cuff. Lulu, how's your mother's health?"

"Better, Aunt Angelique, thank you. You, as always, look wonderful."

"Thank you, dear. Appearances can be deceiving, but that's all to the better sometimes, don't you think, Virgil?"

"Whatever you say, I agree completely, Angelique." Virgil laughs his booming laugh. Maybe it's the cool breeze coming in through the window, but my nipples stand at attention.

"Dr. Crawford, have you considered my invitation to present your new research at my annual event at Union Chapel?"

"I have, B.T."

"And . . ."

"Lulu, are the crab cakes here still mostly crab, not bread crumbs?"

"I haven't had them in years. I have high cholesterol."

"A yes or no would suffice. Medical history is not necessary."

"I had them the other day, Doc, and they were slammin'," Stretch Smith offers eagerly.

"Please don't call me Doc. I speak neither slang nor ebonics."

"My bad, Dr. Crawford. I've been doing so much research on the homeys at night, I forget how to talk, what is wrong, what is right, 'cause a niggah in the hood can't do nothin' but fight; if he can't, he'll be dead 'cause his shit just ain't tight."

Dr. Crawford stares at him wide-eyed and snaps her menu closed. "I'll have the Cobb salad."

"I'll have the same and a martini," C. Virgil adds.

"What're you having, Stretch, humble pie?" Lulu inquires sweetly.

"You know, I think I'll eat some crow, that'll show I'm in the know and can go with the flow."

"Niggah, enough of that rhyming bullshit, ain't no cameras here," B.T. yells at Stretch.

"Or books for sale," Lulu mutters. Stretch sits back and slathers a roll and the side of his hand with butter as his eyes dart about the room.

"About that invitation, Dr. Crawford . . . Or may I call you Aunt Angelique?"

"Absolutely not." Crawford shudders, a look of distaste on her face. "I'm quite sure we are not related." B.T. looks hurt. C. Virgil roars with laughter.

"I meant more as a term of respect and affection."

"Ah, in the same way you young people use *nigger*?"

Stretch perks up. "With all due respect, Doctor, it's *niggah*, a term of respect and affection. The dropping of the *er* and substitution of *ah* signaling the linguistic liberation and transformation of the vocabulary of the master into the vernacular of the masses, giving them the agency to use the language of oppression in a sweet hymn of ghetto liberation." Stretch Smith grins at Angelique Crawford, panting like the last puppy in the pet-shop window.

"*E-r* or *a-h*, young man, I do not use the word. Or appreciate hearing it, either. By the way, when did *agency* become a synonym for *license*? Perhaps you should turn your attention to your chowder. If you allow it to cool, the clams become chewy."

"She told you, niggah, she told you," B.T. yells, laughing. Stretch obediently picks up his soup spoon. "Will you present your research at this year's event, Dr. Crawford?" B.T. asks.

"I suspect my research into the Keebler Conspiracy may not have the mass appeal you are so enamored of, B.T."

"The Keebler Conspiracy? Wasn't that the group that plotted to assassinate Abraham Lincoln?" James Winbush asks. I had almost forgotten he was there; maybe that's the way he wanted it.

"Ah, James Winbush, a serious scholar." Crawford breathes what sounds like a sigh of relief. "Yes, the Keebler Conspiracy was a group of Confederate representatives of each of the slave states who developed a plan to assassinate President Abraham Lincoln and force a negotiated settlement of the Civil War. Their objective was to partition the United States and perpetuate slavery. It has long been rumored that Vice President Andrew Johnson was a key player in the Keebler Conspiracy and that during his tenure was simultaneously acting president of what would have, had the conspiracy succeeded, been called the Confederate States of America, although there was no definitive proof." She pauses as the waiter delivers drinks to the table.

"Why no proof?" Winbush asks.

"The plot was revealed by a slave woman who was used as sexual property by the conspirators, proximity which made her privy to the details of their plot. When they received word that they were found out, she was dismembered alive and the conspirators scattered. Of the eleven men eventually captured, none talked and all were hanged. The bodies of another dozen of those believed to be involved in the plot were found dead of self-inflicted wounds in several Confederate states. No others were apprehended."

"Fascinating. What have you discovered in your research?" Winbush asks.

"It has taken nearly twenty years, but through a careful search of birth and death records, a variety of deeds, and other sources, I have identified by name most of the heretofore unknown conspirators and many of their descendants who are alive today."

B.T. looks disappointed. "Interesting, but not groundbreaking, and I'm not sure it'd fill the house."

"Not all of us do research in order to, as you put it, fill the house." Crawford shrugs.

"Come on, Angelique, don't be uppity or get offended, tell them more," C. Virgil urges quietly.

"Did I say I have found the name of the slave woman who revealed the plot and those of her surviving descendants as well?"

"Really?" Lulu Langlais perks up.

"Yes, really. Did I mention that many of the descendants of the conspirators have remained involved in white supremacist activities and organizations for the more than one hundred and forty years since the Keebler Conspiracy and that more than a few hold prominent positions today?"

"Dr. Crawford, are you suggesting that vestiges of the Keebler Conspiracy survive today?" Winbush asks incredulously.

"Professor Winbush, you are an attorney. As such, perhaps you offer suggestions. I am a historian, I do not. Mine is an unequivocal statement of fact."

"I stand corrected," Winbush says easily. "As well as unequivocally fascinated by your new research. It's exciting," he adds, his voice full of admiration.

"And perhaps dangerous. I've been urging Angelique to allow me to provide some round-the-clock protection, at least until she publicly announces her findings, but she won't hear of it," C. Virgil says. "Why is it that bright women are usually also stubborn?"

"Virgil, would you pass me the pepper mill?" Crawford ignores his comment.

"I agree, Judge, this material sounds explosive. Of course, if you would agree to present your findings at our event, I'll arrange for security," B.T. says.

"Wonderful, B.T., I'm sure people on the island would be fascinated by Auntie Angelique's research," Lulu says. "Besides, it's about time we had a sister as the keynote speaker. Last year it was 'The Black Male Academic: Is He an Endangered Species?' The previous year it was 'The Pedagogy of Spoken Word: From the Pool Hall to the Lecture Hall.' I can't remember what the topic was the year before that, but I'm sure it was all about the brothers."

"As you know, Dr. Crawford, the event is a fund-raiser. Those of us who summer on the Vineyard are committed to giving something back to this island that has given us so much. Perhaps I can get C-SPAN or PBS to come down and film the event. Dr. Crawford, would you be willing to reveal the names of the slave woman and her descendants as well as those of the conspirators and their descendants at the July Fifth event? Perhaps to a national television audience?"

"Why not? The material is copyrighted and it is my intention to submit my book on the Keebler Conspiracy to my publisher before Labor Day."

"Well then, it's settled." James Winbush smiles, reaches over, and pats her hand. She gives him a coquettish smile.

"Remember, B.T., you said you'd provide security and I intend to hold you to it," C. Virgil says. "I've read Angelique's material, and to characterize it as explosive is an understatement."

"No problem, no problem, settled!" B.T. responds. "I know some brothers from the Fruit of Islam who'd be happy to come over here and provide security, gratis, if it means a weekend away from having to listen to tapes of Louis Farrakhan lectures. That niggah's lost his mind, if he ever had one, really believes Elijah Muhammad descended from outer space . . ." His voices fades and his eyes momentarily lose focus as he begins to bore even himself.

"Niggah! Bring us the dessert menus," B.T. yells so loud that more than a few heads in the restaurant turn. The man sitting at the table behind him reading the newspaper has apparently had enough. He throws a bill on the table, jumps up, pulls his hat low, and hustles out of the restaurant, ignoring the waiter who calls after him, "Sir, do you need change?"

"The cranberry crème brulée is the shit," Stretch offers. Lulu looks repulsed.

"I've never been partial to sweets," Dr. Crawford says, delicately wiping her mouth and rising from the table. "If you would, Virgil, I'm ready to go home. One must conserve one's strength when almost fourscore and ten."

CHAPTER 17

Lydia

W AIT A SECOND." I BEND DOWN AND
peel off my sweat socks, afraid that I will
slide across the polished wood floors if I don't,
then turn back to the edge of the bed, steady
myself by placing my palms, about a yard apart,
on the rumpled sheets. Naked now, I plant each
foot on the cool floor, spread a bit wider than my
hands. Like trying to steady a piece of furniture
on an uneven floor, I adjust my position by rock-
ing gently from side to side until I feel firmly
grounded.

"Ready," I say. I look up at the man poised
above me, his smooth, hairless chest, brown
muscular legs, calves, and his hard penis, the
foreskin already drawn back. I close my eyes,

the better to sense you with, my dear, and the musky, sweaty, masculine smell of sex envelops me, the only sound our heavy breathing and the voice of Dianne Reeves singing "I've Got My Eyes on You."

He places one hand on either hip, his fingers sliding up to caress my waist, slightly adjusts my position. Moving downward, his hands caress my waist, stomach, and move down to that place where the cheeks of my ass meet my thighs. He gently pulls my legs apart, and eyes closed, I can feel the coolness as my bush parts and air touches the wetness of my vagina. His fingers brush lightly against my clit, already swollen and distended, and I moan, reflexively push my pelvis up to allow him easier access, wait to feel the head of his penis against the moist opening of my vagina. Holding my breath, I wait for the first thrust.

He obliges, slides fingers inside my love box, pushing it in and out. I push up and back on my hands, my fingers clutching the tangle of sheets. With one hand, the man reaches up and caresses my nipples before his hand slides down and he begins feathering my clit with his thumb. I hold my body as still as possible, not wanting to disturb the delicate balance our bodies have achieved. My breasts, stomach, clit, and head get heavier and the temperature of my body increases. I open my eyes, look down, and watch him slip a sheath on with one hand.

He stands, contact between us momentarily suspended, places a hand on either side of my waist, leans forward, and I feel the head of his penis against my now-sopping pussy. I spread my legs wider in welcome, feel his penis slip inside me.

I reach down between my legs and with my fingers caress the base of his penis and the underside of his balls as he pulls back, my swollen clit as he thrusts forward. I can hear his breath quicken and mine does, too. He picks up the pace and I thrust toward him, feel the tightening of a building orgasm dance through my body. He reaches forward and takes a nipple in each hand, rolling them between his fingers. It feels so good that I am holding my breath, have to remind myself to breathe.

"Pull almost out, then back in slow!" I command, and he obeys. I come hard and slow, grunting, mumbling, and speaking in sexual tongues, his long thrusts seeming to pull orgasm after orgasm from my wet, quivering body until finally my legs are shaking so hard from coming they give out from under me and I slide down, my butt on the cool floor, one cheek on the side of the bed, a dozen fabulous orgasms offered up as tribute.

"Would you like more?" he asks politely as I lie in a liquid puddle on the floor. My body feels as if it has no bones or shape, nothing but the vestiges of my satiated need.

"No, but thanks for the offer," I manage to mumble, pulling myself up on the side of the bed. "Go on to bed, tomorrow's a busy day," I add, gesturing toward the door.

"Thank you, goddess," he whispers as the door closes quietly behind him.

I wiggle my way up to the pillows, lie down. Slowly, the room, and my body, stop pulsating, my senses come back to me, my bones solidify again. Second to orgasm, this is my favorite time in sex, the transition back to myself and the real world from that space where there is only physical desire, need, and finding satisfaction.

I lie in bed enjoying the afterglow, my legs bent, knees up, and my thighs shaking gently, releasing the last shreds of orgasmic bliss. A chime rings faintly, signaling that it is ten o'clock and the last water shuttle will be leaving soon. There are no clocks in the rooms of the Floating Spa. We want our clients to have a feeling of timeless pampering while they are here. The chimes signal the time to the sex workers, who know exactly what package each guest has purchased and when to wrap it up.

I pick up my cell from the bedside table, hit Acey's number in Reno. I miss my best friend. I miss laughing and talking together, miss those Acey Allen arched eyebrows that wordlessly speak volumes. Most of all I miss the familiarity that comes from knowing someone for almost a lifetime, the way we can talk to each other in our own personal shorthand because we know most, if not all, of each other's history. Loath as I am to say it, I miss Acey's caution, the way she has of getting me to slow down, breathe, and consider a question or problem from a different perspective. That's not to say she doesn't sometimes make me crazy—she does—but she also helps me see life from different angles, a necessity since, much as I'd sometimes like to be, I'm not queen and supreme leader of the world.

"Lydia. I was just thinking about you," Acey answers.

"Well, I guess I'll have to live a long time, like it or not."

"Hey, it's the only game in town." Acey chuckles. "What's going on?"

"You mean other than having just had marathon, multiorgasmic, damn near earthshaking sex?"

"Tell me something I don't know, or at least suspect. How's everything out there?"

"Mostly good. Word of mouth is strong, the bookings are steadily increasing, and Wanda's been doing some outreach."

"Which means?"

"Going to the island, meeting folks, letting them know, discreetly, about the spa and the services we offer. You're not going to believe this, but she actually had a golf date last week, a sport she describes as hot, annoying, and profoundly pointless. The good news is that she met a bunch of women from a golf club, and more than a few have visited the spa."

"No problems? Lucky you."

"Knock wood, but nothing urgent. Sukey's still not generating the income, and you know Wanda, she's on her ass about it."

"What's the plan?"

"Wanda says if she doesn't speed it up, she's out after this season."

"Too bad. I know Wanda wanted to help out her cousin."

"Yeah, well, how's everything going out there?" Acey releases a long, loud breath.

"Besides being extorted by the Providence Mafia and worrying about our government banning sex, great." Acey's laugh is bitter.

"Ace, chill, there's no point in anticipatory anxiety."

"Sounds good, but I think the shit's about to hit the fan," Acey snaps.

"But it hasn't yet. You and Odell will be here in a few days and I'm sure that the five of us can figure something out."

"Five?"

"You, Odell, Wanda, me, and Chef Marvini."

"Give him my love. Tell him his assistant's food is delicious, but it sure doesn't have that Marvini touch."

"Who you telling? Between living on the yacht and eating Marvini's food, I've picked up a few pounds. Speaking of Odell, how's my favorite male business partner doing?"

"He's your only male partner."

"I know that. I asked how he's doing."

"Busy, thinking about expanding, and in his downtime figuring out what to do about Eddie Sollozzo."

"Are you two fucking, er, I mean, making love and melding together in orgasmic bliss yet?"

"No, you idiot. I told you we're business partners, not a couple. Period."

"Yeah, well, things change."

"This hasn't."

"Acey, I want you to know that if it does, that's cool with me. If you and Odell find comfort in each other's arms, I ain't mad at you."

"Thanks for permission, not that I need it." Acey sniffs. "So much is happening, there's no time to deal with much else."

"Maybe there's nothing to deal with."

"Which means?"

"That maybe you should just relax and go with the flow, instead of looking at the vibe between the two of you as a problem that has to be dealt with. It's obvious Odell cares about you. Maybe you should let yourself care about him. I say grab that joy while you can."

"Of course by *joy* you mean sex, right, Lyds?"

"Hey, that's my joy; you've got to define your own. All I'm saying is that you'll never get what you say you want—a great husband, kids, happily ever after, whatever—thinking about the good old days and not taking any risks. I mean, clearly Earl was the one. Isn't it possible Odell's the *next* one?" Acey laughs and I join her companionably. The faint tinkling of the chime tells me that it's ten thirty, all aboard for the last ferry to the island, and time for me to make my final rounds.

"Love you and miss you, Ace, can't wait to see you in a few days. Give Odell my love and tell him not to work too hard or worry too much."

"Back at you, Lyds. I'll tell Odell and try to take your advice myself."

"What's the alternative? Anyway, as you often say, everything works out for the best." I think I hear her ask, "Who's best?" before I flip the phone off.

I jump off the bed, grab a cover-up from my closet, and slip it over my head. In the bathroom, I throw some water on my face and pat my short natural into shape. I walk rapidly through the ship, knocking quickly and then opening the doors to the staterooms to make sure there are no stowaways. Then I check the massage and reflexology rooms and knock on the door of the nail salon. I'm about to turn the handle and enter when the door swings open.

"I heard the chime; sorry, Lydia, I'm a bit late finishing, sorry," Sukey says, her voice apologetic. Behind her, Jeanette Tiger gathers her belongings from beside the chaise.

"Hey, Lydia, sorry to hold you up. Thanks so much, Sukey. Same time next week?" she says, walking toward the door and slipping what looks like a hundred-dollar bill into Sukey's hand. Since all spa services are paid for in advance, I'm impressed. I've never tipped more than ten dollars at the nail salon and that was mostly because I didn't have a five.

"Absolutely, Jeanette, see you then."

"Let me walk you to the launch," I offer, leading her in the direction of the steps. "You don't want to be stranded here overnight," I tease. She smiles.

"Actually, I can imagine that might be quite pleasant." Then we're on the deck beside the small lift down to the boat and the last four clients, already waiting with Cap'n Chubby in the water shuttle for the trip back to the island.

"Good night. Hope you had a wonderful time. Come again," I call down. The voices of the four women drift up, their responses affirmative.

"Wonderful experience. See you next week," Jeanette calls out as the boat pulls away, waving with both hands. It's probably an illusion caused by the reflection of the moon on the water and the dim lights of the boat, but her nails look whipped.

CHAPTER 18

Odell

I STAND OVER THE LEATHER SUITCASE lying open on my bed and take inventory. Shorts, shirts, slacks, jeans, a sport coat, toiletries. I throw in a baseball cap, socks, sneakers, and a pair of sandals, and remind myself that I'm going to Martha's Vineyard, USA, not Mongolia. I close the bag, start to zip it, and then go into the bathroom. From the small drawer next to the sink I grab a handful of condoms, stuff them into one of the small side compartments, and close the bag. Then I open it again and take the condoms out. Hard as it is for a brother to admit it, I'm not interested in recreational sex, even though I've heard that the ratio of women to men on the Vineyard makes Washington, D.C., look like an equitable division of resources. I'm interested in making love to Acey and being made love to by her. I'm interested in the commitment where you get tested, throw the condoms away, and try to make babies. Odell Overton is ready to settle down.

That said, I'm not sure about Acey's feelings toward me. I don't think she is, either, but most of the time we're so busy it's hard to tell. Running the spa doesn't leave much time for a personal life or serious conversation, plus whenever the talk turns that way, Acey slips away. I've been thinking on it and decided to put my cards on the table while we're on the Vineyard, tell her how I feel, and hope she feels the same. I'm restless and ready to take the next step.

I sit down on the edge of my bed, turn on my laptop, google "newspapers on Martha's Vineyard," click the link to the *Vineyard Gazette*, and check the weather forecast. Temperatures in the low eighties during the day, sixty-five to seventy at night, no rain expected. I glance at my watch, still nearly an hour before we leave for the airport. I scroll down, reading the headlines until one catches my eye.

Famed Historian to Reveal Details of Plot at Union Chapel

Dr. Angelique Shorter Crawford, former head of African American studies at Harvard University, the author of eighteen books, recipient of the Pulitzer Prize in history, and a lifelong summer resident of Oak Bluffs, will be the keynote speaker at B. T. Lincoln's annual event on Sunday, July 5. Since her retirement from Harvard, Dr. Crawford has focused her research on the Keebler Conspiracy, a little-known and often-dismissed Confederate plot to assassinate Abraham Lincoln, partition the states, and perpetuate slavery. Dr. Crawford's remarks at the event will be her first concerning this groundbreaking research and will, she says, "change the face of American history."

"How exciting," commented Carrie Tankard of the African American Heritage Trail of Martha's Vineyard. "Dr. Crawford is a brilliant historian, an island treasure, and her home has long been a stop on the Heritage Trail. We look forward eagerly to celebrating this new work."

"Dr. Crawford's latest discovery will blow minds," said B. T. Lincoln, event organizer. "It's so explosive we've arranged for tight security at the event, attendees must all enter through one door, and no cameras or recording devices will be allowed inside. We urge the folk to forget C.P. time and come early if they want to witness this historic event."

Soon to celebrate her ninetieth birthday and diminutive in stature, Dr. Crawford remains a sassy woman with a razor-sharp wit. Her presentation will be followed by a panel discussion with Harvard luminaries and island summer visitors Lulu Langlais, William "Stretch" Smith, James Winbush, Reverend Herman P. Rutledge, and, of course, B. T. Lincoln. Admission is $50 and doors open at 6 P.M. Light refreshments will be served.

Just as I finish reading there's a light tap at the door before it opens enough for Acey to stick her head in. "Hey, Odell. You packed and ready?"

"Yep, just checking out the island weather." I close my laptop, slip it into my briefcase. "You?"

"Absolutely. I am really looking forward to getting away from here for a few days, even though it's not really a vacation."

"Me, too."

"You think Christian will be able to manage the spa while we're gone?"

"Absolutely, he's smart, has been with us from the beginning, and wants to prove himself so he can move from sex work to management," I reassure Acey. "He'll be great."

"I can use a change of scenery. And perspective."

"I'm with you there. Besides, I'm looking forward to meeting Eddie Sollozzo."

"Ugh. Why?"

"I want to see if he's actually for real."

"And if he is?"

"Then we can deal with him once and for all, one way or another, and go on with our lives."

"I like your confidence, O."

"Why not? There really is nothing to fear but fear itself."

"You think?"

"I know."

"I wish I had your confidence. Or Lydia's or Wanda's, for that matter."

"I've got some to spare," I say, grabbing my suitcase in one hand and wrapping the other arm around her shoulder as I steer her toward the door. For once, she doesn't flinch or pull away, but leans into the crook of my arm.

CHAPTER 19

Wanda

S O THEN THE BROAD SAYS, 'I WANT THE nail package.' So I'm like, 'Okay, fine, you want a manicure and pedicure?' And she says, 'Yes, and the complete package, just as I had the last two sessions.' We don't offer a nail package, but the customer's always right, so I booked her with Sukey for later this afternoon. Now I'm wondering what's going on?" Lydia and I are sitting on the deck of the *Lady Lay,* going over the books and trying to catch some sun at the same time.

"They're clients, Wanda, not broads. Clients."

"Whatever," I say, spritzing my sunburned face with a can of Evian water spray. "I'm just stressed. My cousin's up to something, and if I know her, it's no good."

"Why do you say that?"

"Look, Lydia, it's right here in black and white," I say, waving a sheaf of papers. "Her bookings are pretty good, but her receipts are half what we projected and her sessions take twice as long as expected, sometimes longer. Something's up."

"Such as?"

"Hell if I know. I'm worried she's started drinking again."

"Do you think she's stealing?"

"Do you?"

"I haven't given it much thought, but the other night I had to roust Jeanette from the salon before she missed the last boat, and as she was leaving I saw her slip Sukey some folded bills. The one I saw was a hundred," Lydia says. "I figured it was a tip."

"When was the last time you tipped a manicurist a hundred bucks? Don't bother to answer that," I say, glancing down at Lydia's short, unadorned nails. "You probably can't remember the last time you had your nails done."

"Wanda, I don't believe Sukey'd steal from us."

"Not us, me."

"Why?"

"Damned if I know. Might be some bullshit that happened when we were seven. Maybe I cut off her Barbie's hair, liked the same boy, took the biggest piece of chicken. Family's twisted in that way."

"So I've heard. Guess I'm lucky to be an only child."

"I don't want to think she'd steal from me, either, especially after I moved her ass out here, bought all the equipment, gave her a chance."

"Wanda, you don't know she's stealing."

"I don't have any proof, but look at the evidence. Her salon is bringing in half what we projected. Half the sessions run way overtime. And you saw her taking money."

"Wanda, nothing you've said proves Sukey's a thief; it's all speculation. You got no evidence."

"Not yet. But I'm going to find out what's going on. Today."

"How?" I leaf through the day's schedule lying in my lap until I get to Sukey's page.

"She's got a client coming right after lunch. While she's chowing down I'm going to slip into the salon, hide out, and watch what goes down. And if I see her pocket one thin dime, I'm gonna—"

"Do nothing until the client leaves, right, Wanda?"

"I was about to say jump out and commence with an old-school Bronx beat-down, but you're right, don't want to scare off the customers. I'll wait until afterward to kick her narrow ass."

"I know you fancy yourself a secret agent, but have you thought about just asking Sukey what's up?"

"I've tried, but *nada*. I don't want to accuse her of anything without some evidence, you know? She's pretty fragile since she left New Orleans, but she's getting better."

"Yeah, I noticed her hands don't tremble nearly as much."

"Right, and while she may be secretly juicing, I haven't seen her take a drink in the six weeks she's been here, and I sure don't want to push her over the edge. That said, I *am* going to find out what's going on. Stay tuned."

Forty minutes later I've grabbed a quick lunch, changed into my spook outfit—black shorts, a matching T-shirt, and sneakers—and slipped unobserved into Sukey's Sea Salon. It's a small space and not easy finding someplace to hide. In the end I wedge myself behind the fabric that drapes the wall behind the clients' chaise. A tight fit, but I can see the whole room and everyone in it.

I'm already fidgety and perspiring lightly when the door finally opens a few minutes after one and Sukey ushers in a woman with blond hair who I recognize as a member of the Back 9 golf club. As she settles herself in the chaise, Sukey slips a CD into the player and Alice Coltrane's haunting, mellow harp on "Journey in Satchidananda" fills the room. Sukey begins the standard manicure ritual: soaks each hand, trims nails, cleans, buffs, pushes back and trims cuticles, files nails into a rounded shape.

"Would you like a nail-art design today?"

"Something simple and golf-ish."

"What about two clubs crossed, one maroon and one powder blue. Aren't those your colors?"

"Perfect, but nothing too fancy, Sukey. What I really need is a pedicure."

Before she begins work on her nails, Sukey lifts the woman's legs, separates the chaise, and fills the foot tub with hot water and fragrant salts, carefully lowers her feet into the steaming water.

"That feels wonderful," the blonde purrs dreamily. "I know it's only going to get better."

Sukey rapidly paints each nail in maroon and powder blue, her face bent low and her expression intent, concentrating as she works with brushes so small they have only a few strands of hair to them. Even though she's done my nails dozens of times, watching her do someone else's is a revelation. She may be my relative, sometimes trifling, and possibly a thief, but she's also an artist. I can be a cold hard-ass if need be, but watching Sukey's delicate work, her concentration and the tiny images come to life, I can't help hoping there's an explanation for the low revenues and long sessions other than larceny.

"Let your hands relax on the table and dry while I begin your feet." I watch her slide down so she is on her knees between her client's legs; then she washes and pumices, cuts and files, firmly massages the pressure points of the feet, kneads and manipulates the blonde's toes until she moans with pleasure. Sukey finally pushes the basin aside, kneels, and dries the woman's feet with a soft towel.

"Same design here?"

"No."

"Clear polish maybe?"

"Don't bother. Most of the time I'm wearing golf shoes, and the rest of the time, who gives a damn?"

"Leg massage?"

"That would be delightful." The blonde wiggles in the chaise, adjusts her body into a more comfortable position. I glance at the luminous face of my watch. From where I'm standing behind a hot curtain, it seems I've been here for hours, but it's only been forty minutes, and nothing left to do but a leg massage. I should be out of here soon.

Sukey rubs lotion on the palms of both hands, begins stroking the client's muscular calves. She spreads her long fingers and runs them inch by inch up the leg to the knee; I can see the depressions her fingers make in the flesh. She runs an index finger up each shinbone simultaneously. When she is just underneath the knee, she slips her fingers behind them to the soft spot there, caressing with four fingers. A slight smile plays on the blonde's lips as Sukey's fingers move slowly down, kneading the backs of her muscular calves. When her fingers reach the ankles, she starts up the legs again, repeating her ministrations at the same languid pace. In the chair, the blonde's head has fallen back and her mouth is slightly open. As Sukey repeats the motion, each time her hands venture a little higher above the spread knees until they are between the woman's legs. Four fingers of each hand knead the outside of her thighs while her thumbs move in circles against her inner thighs, each spherical motion moving upward until her fingers cradle the cheeks of the blonde's ass and her thumbs tease and flutter at the opening of her box. In the chair the woman shifts her hips, wiggling so her skirt rides up to her waist, revealing both a lacy, transparent thong and her vagina, hidden under a bush of hair. I note that her natural color is brown.

With one thumb, Sukey pulls the crotch of the panties aside, still drawing circles with her thumbs as she moves up toward the hidden clit. Her mouth falls open, and as I watch, so does mine, as Sukey slips a finger inside. I am not sure if the quickening of breath I hear is the client's, Sukey's, or mine, perhaps it is all of us. Sukey's other hand snakes up to caress first one breast, then the other, cupping the underside in her fingers and smoothing her thumb in a languid back-and-forth, caressing flesh and areolae. I watch as the blonde's nipples grow longer and strain under the sheer fabric of her blouse, the flesh around them flushes with heat and desire. With her other hand, Sukey works her cunt, fucking her with first one finger, then two, until three of her fingers thrust in and out. In the orangey light I can see her fingers gleaming with creamy wetness as they slide out, watch as the woman's hips raise to meet Sukey's fingers as they ease into her. She moans and arches back to push her swollen nipple into Sukey's hand and grinds down to swallow her pumping fingers. Sukey reaches up and unbuttons the blonde's blouse, reveals a lacy black half bra. She leans forward, now tracing the outline of the nipple with her tongue, her fingers still moving insistently in and out. Beginning just where the breast begins to slope downward, she draws circles with her tongue, their circumference growing smaller as she approaches the nipple, her tongue lingering on the almost maroon darkness surrounding it, coaxing and teasing, lazily moving in for the thrill. Finally, she takes the tip of the nipple between her teeth, begins the softest of chattering, nibbling like a horse at a bag of oats. The blonde groans, shifts, pushes her chest into Sukey's waiting mouth, gasps.

"Too much?" Sukey whispers.

"Not enough." Three fingers still buried inside her, Sukey uses her thumb to stroke the hood until the clit thickens and emerges. The woman arches up to meet Sukey's hand.

"Enough?" Sukey purrs, her voice teasing.

"More. Like last time." Her clit is swollen, pink, protruding. Sukey unhurriedly slides down the length of the blonde's lush body, her hands stopping to play under the arms, along her stomach, run up and down her sides, along her hips, massage her buttocks. She stops above her clit, gradually lowering her mouth toward it, swiping her tongue against the swollen tip again and again, teasing as it swells. At last, her mouth closes softly around it and I can see her lips purse and tighten as she latches on and the muscles just above her jaw expand and contract in a sucking motion. Someone moans, and again I'm not sure if it's the client, Sukey, or me. Still gently tonguing the woman's clit, Sukey slides two fingers inside and begins easing them in and out as she eats her. With her other hand she reaches up, begins to roll one of the blonde's nipples between thumb and forefinger, changing the pressure as she alternately squeezes her breasts. I watch, my own nipples hard, my pussy wet. The woman moans and shudders as Sukey coaxes little waves of orgasm from her body, a brilliant conductor eliciting music from all the parts of the orchestra and building to the crescendo. Sukey's fingers begin to slide deeper inside with long, steady strokes. She buries her face in her mound, her mouth working like one of the Three Bears at that bowl of porridge, determined to eat it all up. Hands and mouth move in unison, steadily faster and harder. The client opens her eyes, looks along the length of her body, her eyes resting on Sukey's head. It is a look of wonder. Then she opens her mouth and the sound that comes out is a combination of moan and scream as she presses her mouth hard against her, legs tightening around Sukey's head, and comes, crying out and bucking, legs quivering, arms flailing, and an exhausted, sloppy grin on her face.

After a few minutes, she rouses herself, pulls her clothes back together, and does a quick washup. At the door she splays her fingers, turning each hand from side to side as she examines her nails. She reaches into her purse, hands Sukey a wad of folded bills. "Perfect. Thank you. Until next week," she says, giving Sukey a long kiss. Then she's out the door.

Sukey walks to the small sink. She cleans her hands, brushes her teeth, washes and moisturizes her face before she sinks into the chaise and counts the bills. In the dim light it looks like a few hundred dollars. She opens a drawer in her worktable, tosses the money in, extracts a cigarette, lighter, and smokeless ashtray. She lights up, takes a long drag, and leans back, eyes closed, her smug expression one of sexual triumph.

"I didn't know you smoked!" I stumble out from behind the curtain, sweaty, horny, and pointing.

"Wanda! What the fuck?" Sukey's eyes fly open. She sits up and stubs out her butt. "What're you doing hiding in here?"

"I should be asking you that."

Sukey looks at me angrily. "Did you check the sign on the door? It says 'Sukey's Sea Salon,' not 'Wanda's Weird Hideaway.' What the fuck, you've been hiding behind the curtain all this time? You must have lost your damn mind. Look at you." That's when I realize I'm clutching a few yards of orange mirrored fabric, my hair is plastered to my head, sweat's dripping from my chin, and after an hour and a half of almost being suffocated by heavy drapes and taking shallow breathes, I'm gulping for air like a beached fish.

"Okay, maybe I went a little overboard," I concede, embarrassed. "But I had to find out why your sessions were so long and the revenue so short."

"Why didn't you just ask, instead of pretending you're Agent

Double-O Soul? You know, you could have given me, or my client, a heart attack, and the truth is, you look as if you might have one yourself. You better sit down." Sukey gestures toward her work chair and lights another cigarette. "Oh, of course; you didn't trust me."

"So, what's your racket, Suks? Obviously it ain't just nails."

Sukey shrugs. "Just doing what comes naturally."

"What does that mean?"

"I'm gay."

"Gay? Since when?" She shrugs again, takes a long drag of her cigarette.

"Listen, Sukey, don't bullshit me. Gay? When did that happen? Or have you been in the closet—sorry, on the down low—ever since you starting fucking boys at fourteen?"

"You know what, Wanda? Probably."

"Are you serious?"

"And a lesbian."

"Damn."

"Damn what, Wanda-babe? Statistically speaking, there's at least one queer in every family. Don't tell me you're a homophobe?"

"Fuck no; I'm a shocked-aphobe."

"Get over it. It's not exactly as if you're Miss Straight. You told me yourself you'd been with women, and from the looks of those big nipples pressing against your shirt, you must've liked what you saw." She smirks, looking into my eyes. What can I say? Nipples don't lie and it's eighty-five degrees outside. "Don't be embarrassed, cuz, ain't nothing wrong with that. When a woman makes love to you, if she's good, it's like making love to yourself. She knows all the best, most secret places and points because she's got them, too. Needs no direction, just a little nonverbal encouragement."

"I'm just surprised."

"Get over it, Wanda-babe, it's like that."

"Are they paying you for your services?"

Sukey snorts. "I wish. Unfortunately, the Floating Spa doesn't offer same-sex services."

"Do you think they would?"

"What?"

"Pay you." Sukey tosses her head, apparently a Marshall family trait, opens her fist, and begins counting a wad of bills.

"Shit, yeah. Anya, the chick from the Back Nine who just left, gave me a two-hundred-dollar tip. Add that to seventy-five for the nails and that's nearly three hundred bucks for nibbling her nugget in a chaise," she brags. "Imagine how much money we could charge if I had a bedroom and could take care of some serious business."

"Two hundred dollars for an hour and a half of work. Not bad."

"It's great. Did I mention this was her third visit in ten days?"

I calculate three women a day times six days a week: $3,600. Minimum. Hell, if Sukey brought in $2,000 a week, I'd be happy.

"Plus, we could charge more if we were up front about the specialized services I offer, have a set price instead of settling for tips."

"Confident, aren't you?"

"Why not? I've been doing this a long time."

"Do you do everyone?"

Sukey laughs until tears roll down her cheeks. "No, Wanda, only the ones who indicate they want it."

"How's that?"

"Some clients want a mani-pedi and to be on their way, no leg massage. Others want their legs massaged, but only below the knee. As a rule, if they let me rub them down above the knees, odds are they're amenable to the full Sukey experience."

"Just the golf lesbians?"

She laughs again. "Nope, though I've made love to a few of them, as well as the so-called straight clients. Lydia almost busted me and Jeanette Tiger the other night. What's that line in your rap? 'At the Floating Spa we believe that sexuality is not static, but part of a continuum.' Don't forget that continuum, Wanda-babe," she chortles, glances at her watch. "Matter of fact, one of the Doyennes is due shortly."

"Damn. I've got to shower, change, and go to the airport to pick up Acey and Odell. We need to talk more, Suks. Apparently we've ignored a significant constituency and an important source of revenue, huh?"

"No doubt, Wanda-babe, no doubt."

CHAPTER 20

Odell

"YOU OKAY?" I LEAN DOWN TOWARD Acey, my arm still linked through hers as we walk along the narrow pathway toward the gazebo in Ocean Park. It sits cradled in a natural depression, the green and white paint sparkling in the late-afternoon sunlight, the heart of the park. The air is balmy, smells lightly of salt. What a peaceful, beautiful place, and romantic. I smile to myself at the incongruity of meeting Eddie Sollozzo on such a gorgeous day and in such an idyllic place. Rain, cold, wind, and the crashing of waves seem more appropriate, not an azure sky, brilliant sunlight, and the faint sensuous echo of water caressing sand as waves break tenderly against the shoreline.

A few yards ahead, Lydia and Wanda stroll along together. An occasional burst of raucous laughter wafts back. Beside me, Acey is tight-lipped, the expression on her face both troubled and determined.

"Acey?"

"As okay as possible," she responds to the question in my voice.

"I hear you, but try and relax. It's important that we put up a strong, united front. We don't want Sollozzo to see any weakness." She nods and holds my arm a bit tighter.

I squeeze Acey's forearm, run the upcoming discussion through my brain. I've already asked Lydia and Wanda to let me do the talking, and it's a measure of how tense and worried they are that they acquiesce. Under normal circumstances, my request would have been greeted by accusations that I'm macho, sexist, controlling. As much as I try not to be any of those things, I have to admit I kind of miss that response. The absence of the two of them selling woof tickets and challenging me grimly underscores the stakes.

"I think that's him, to the right," I say softly. At the base of the gazebo a plump woman in a bright yellow shorts set emblazoned with an enormous sequined anchor in oranges, purples, and greens poses, one hand on her hip. A top-heavy man with a sunburned face, bulging stomach, and scrawny ghostly white legs protruding from Bermuda shorts hovers nearby. He holds a digital camera awkwardly, alternately pressing it against his eye and thrusting it out at arm's length. The woman's mouth is moving and the man looks hot.

"Lydia, Wanda, remember, let me take the lead on this."

"Cool, Odell. We'll be your backup."

"What Wanda means is if Eddie won't agree to our deal, we'll jump his evil ass and beat him down." Lydia laughs.

"Let's hope it doesn't come to that," Acey interjects. "Remember your mother's report: he's likely packing."

"Packing?" I repeat, my voice teasing. Acey looks up and gives me a sharp glance, but there's no time for her to respond, we're there. I let go of her arm, step forward. If it's possible, I can feel a testosterone rush in my bloodstream and every aggressive alpha-male cell in my body go into high alert. I feel more than see Acey, Lydia, and Wanda close ranks behind me, my gang of three. I lift my hand, start to tap the man on the back, then think better of it. Startling a mobster probably isn't the best way to go. Instead, I clear my throat.

"Mr. Sollozzo?" He turns around, looks me up and down, glances at the diamond-encrusted Rolex on his hairy wrist.

"Overton. Right on time. Call me Eddie. That's the wife, Madge."

"A pleasure, Mrs. Sollozzo," I murmur. Madge Sollozzo doesn't look at me or break her pose, simply nods disinterestedly in my direction.

"So, Madgie, excuse yourself and lemme take care of some business for a few minutes." Eddie's voice is a combination of commanding and beseeching.

"Before you start doing business on our big-deal one-day vacation, take the fucking picture, Eddie. And get out of the nineteenth century; it's a digital camera, you don't have to smear it on your eyeball. Just hold it in front of you, and when you see me, press the button."

"You married, Overton?" Sollozzo asks, backing away from his wife and pressing the camera against his face.

"Nope."

"Smart. Stay single. Love 'em, leave 'em, and no alimony."

"Eddie, cut the fucking phisopholy and take the picture."

"Madge, relax. I'm trying to get all of you in the frame. It ain't easy."

"Well, hurry it up, same for whatever business you have to take care of. I want to take some pictures by the water, over there." She points toward the beach, the direction from which we came.

"Sure, sweetie. Now smile for Daddy." Eddie clicks a few photographs, still pumping the camera back and forth as if he doesn't quite believe in digital technology. "Okay, Madge, time for your personal paparazzi to take care of some business," he says, handing the camera to his wife. "Why don't you and the girls"—he jerks his head back toward Lydia, Acey, and Wanda—"walk over there and look at the water," he says, pointing his finger in the direction of the ocean.

"Unless one of us has that fast-aging disease in reverse and is sixteen or under, there are no girls here," Wanda snaps. So much for that vow of silence.

"Actually, Mr. Sollozzo, Acey Allen and I, Lydia Beaucoup, are the founders of the spa; LaShaWanda Marshall and Odell Overton are our partners. If there's business to be discussed, we're all going to participate." Sollozzo shrugs, nods slightly at each woman, and then turns to his wife, who's leaning against the gazebo, looking hard and pissed, her soft pose for the camera vanished.

"Don't say anything, Eddie, nothing," she barks, holding her hand, fingers spread, in front of her. "You got ten minutes, that's all. I'm going to walk over there and admire the water, and if you're not there when time's up, I'm gonna walk my ass onto the ferry to the other side and drive myself back to Providence." Eddie opens his mouth to speak but Madge stops him with the hand.

"Don't ask me how you're going to get back, Eddie. Call one of the boys to come get you, hitchhike, take the damn bus, it don't matter to me. This was supposed to be a little vacation for us, you promised. I should have known when you suggested coming here you were up to something, you're always up to something." She leans down, picks up her sequined straw purse from beside her feet, ties a thin red chiffon scarf around her hair, and pivots on her toes. "The clock's ticking. Ten minutes. No bullshit." She turns and walks across the grass toward the water, the heels of her mules taking small clumps of earth with them as she goes. She never acknowledges any of us. For what? We're nothing besides more of Eddie's dreaded business associates.

Her husband watches her stomp away, shakes his head, shrugs. "Foul mouth, great ass." Sollozzo turns to me. "So, you ready to join my church?"

"We need to talk, Mr. Sollozzo."

"I thought we already talked. It's time to make a deal."

"Right now your church is a little rich for our blood, Mr. Sollozzo."

"Call me Eddie, Mr. Sollozzo's my father's name. 'Rich for your blood'? What's that mean, you don't have the money?"

"Because of a few challenges in Reno, we're a bit short."

"What challenges? Women still want to get fucked, don't they?"

"Perhaps you aren't aware of the president's No Child, No Behind initiative."

"Cut the shit, Overton, I'm not stupid. Our people are working on that fuck-wad's plan as we speak, we're gonna make sure it'll never happen. Now, how much is a bit short?" Sollozzo asks sarcastically.

"We'd like to pay five percent for the next six months. By then, our finances should be straight and we can revisit our arrangement," I say smoothly.

"Fucking half? Revisit the arrangement? What kind of shit is that?"

I take a deep breath and release it slowly before I respond, hopefully expelling my disgust and anger with it. I can feel waves of tension, anger, and in the case of Lydia and Wanda, potential violence emanating from the three women.

"What the fuck, Overton? I don't need any shit, this is business. Talk to me," Eddie Sollozzo says, raising his raspy voice and stepping closer. Even though he's a senior citizen and from the look and sound of him not in the best of health, I can see and feel my fist smashing into his upturned face in my mind's eye. I step back, both to move my fists out of range and so that me and my partners stand together in one strong line.

"Eddie, there's no need to use obscene language or raise your voice. We should be capable of negotiating peacefully and respectfully."

"Negotiate? Peacefully? This ain't the United Nations. Who the hell do you think you are, Kofi Annan?"

"Nope. Small businesspeople trying to work out a difficult situation."

"Difficult? You don't know from difficult. But you will unless I get the necessary donation."

"As my grandma used to say, you can't get blood from a turnip. Ever heard that before, Eddie?" Wanda asks, and does that black-woman neck thing. The cowrie shells threaded through her twists clink together musically.

"It means, to quote Billy Preston, who no doubt you've never heard of either, 'Nothing from nothing leaves nothing.' I'm sure you've heard of nothing, right?" Lydia chimes in.

"What we're saying is we don't have it," Acey concludes. "In our case, you can make a deal for something or get nothing."

"Who're they, the fucking Andrews Sisters—excuse me, Kofi, make that the Supremes—your backup trio, Overton? Here's what I know, Overton: broads are bad for business. You should have sent them over there with Madge to look at the pretty water."

"Who're you calling broads?"

"Sounds like he said 'bitch' to me."

"Who you calling bitch?"

"Not bitch, I said 'broad.'"

"That's not what I heard," Wanda says indignantly, turning to Acey and Lydia. "What about y'all, did you hear 'broad' or 'bitch'?"

Before Lydia can say a thing, Acey steps forward. "I heard an insult, I know that for sure. Your ten minutes are more than half over, Mr. Sollozzo. Don't you think it's time to stop arguing and work this out?" she asks sweetly, a faint smile on her lips. I'm not surprised that the expression on Eddie Sollozzo's face is incredulous. It's late afternoon on the Fourth of July and he's standing in the middle of a hot park on Martha's Vineyard with four spooks who have the temerity to try to negotiate. Not to mention Madge waiting by the water, ready to abandon him and simultaneously concocting the tortures in store for him once they return to Providence. No doubt his head is spinning, because he moves it like a boxer trying to shake off a hard right.

"What it's time for is me to catch Madge before she stomps off and leaves me on this crummy little rock. I promised her a stroll along the boardwalk and a lobster roll before we leave and I'll never hear the end of it. As for you, Overton and Company, nice try, but I don't negotiate. The contribution's nine and a half, period. I'm willing to give you a month's grace, finito. Your first payment, in cash, is due August fourth. I'll send Tony to Reno to pick it up. Ya know, even though you fired him and he still gets his salary, he says he misses work." Sollozzo shrugs indifferently. "Go fucking figure. August fourth. Nine and a half. No bullshit or you'll be out of business. Painfully and permanently." He turns and heads toward the water and Madge, his bony knees bowed and his white loafers sinking into the lush grass.

"I wouldn't say that went well," Acey says to his receding back.

"Who you telling? Can you believe that SOB called us broads?"

"I thought you said 'bitches'?"

"What's the difference? An insult is an insult."

"Yes, well now we've been extorted and insulted," Acey says. "And bad news always comes in threes. I shudder to think what's next. Could things actually get worse?"

"Maybe, but hopefully not this afternoon. I think we've all had enough. We're going to go to the clambake and enjoy ourselves. Have a few drinks, eat some lobster, bond with the crème de la crème—"

"And as Scarlett O'Hara put it, think about this crap tomorrow," Lydia finishes my sentence, not exactly as I would have said it, but the gist is the same.

"We did buy some time, just not as much as we wanted," Acey says hopefully.

"Yep, it coulda been worse," Wanda says. "Let's relax, try and have a good time tonight, and deal with this crap in the morning. To hell with Eddie Sollozzo. I'm happy to be on land with my best friends and have an evening off."

"Amen. Don't forget that besides Ma Nicola's insistence, one reason we're going to the clambake is to do some low-key advertising for the spa. From what I've heard, everyone who is, thinks they are, or aspires to be anyone will be there," Lydia says, slipping her arm through Acey's.

"I'm with you, let's postpone discussion of Eddie Sollozzo until tomorrow." Before I can finish saying "All in favor?" I'm drowned out by a chorus of "aye's." Relieved, I loop my arm through Acey's other arm and try to turn her body in the direction of the Inkwell, but she's immovable. "Lydia, I know you're not into prayer, but before we go, let's say the Serenity Prayer together, for luck."

I glance across Acey's body at Lydia the adamant agnostic, trying to will her, through telepathy or the glare in my eyes, to go along and if she doesn't want to pray, just bow her head and pretend. We're all hot, tense, hungry, and thirsty, and I'm not interested in Lydia's familiar diatribe about religion as a tool in the oppression of women or Acey's sermon on the church as a transformational institution in black communities. The truth is, at this point I don't really care one way or the other; like Rodney King, I just want everyone to get along.

You know, maybe I do have telepathic powers, because Lydia nods agreeably. We move together, our arms linked. The only sound the cawing of a lone crow swooping overhead, and, when the wind blows just right, the music of Wanda's cowrie shells.

"God, grant me the serenity to accept the things I cannot change . . ." Acey begins softly, her voice resolute. "The courage to change the things I can; and the wisdom to know the difference." We say this last line loudly and in unison, and it is no longer a simple prayer but a chant, a cheer, our very own declaration of independence.

CHAPTER 21

Wanda

YOU KNOW THAT SAYING, IT AIN'T OVER till the fat lady sings? Well, I haven't heard a peep out of her, but from the gloomy silence between the four of us as we walk through the park toward the Oak Bluffs Doyennes' clambake at the Inkwell, you'd think she'd sung so long and hard her vocal cords were permanently busted. Me? Like Bob Marley sings, *'He who fights and runs away lives to fight another day,'* that's how I felt. We hadn't beaten Eddie Sollozzo or wrangled six months from him to figure out how, but I'm damn sure not ready to concede defeat.

"I don't know what the Doyennes are serving at this event, but whatever they're pouring, I'll have a double," I say.

"Make mine triple." Lydia sighs. "I'm so tense I feel as if my shoulders are about to fuse to my chin. Or tits."

Odell laughs. "I wouldn't know about that last bit, but I'm with you on the tension."

"Amen to all that," Acey adds.

As we get closer to the beach, other people fall into step and we all promenade to the cookout. It's a parade of the who's who of successful African Americans. The women are in brightly colored dresses of silk, linen, or some diaphanous material that undulates and shimmers in the ocean breeze. Slacks, shorts, and capri pants abound, topped by slinky blouses or skimpy halters. Many of the women wear wide-brimmed summer hats or upscale baseball caps. Some of the them are clad in bathing suits with matching cover-ups or sarongs, but from their meticulously applied makeup, coiffed hair, and definitely not costume jewelry, I suspect they're more interested in showing off buffed bodies than their prowess, if any, at water sports. The men are more casually dressed in shorts or slacks, polo or camp shirts, and summer-weight casual sport coats.

"Damn. Look at the folks," I say as we near the wide wooden steps that lead down to the beach. Several hundred people are on the beach, the sand nearly hidden under a blanket of humanity, a moving tapestry.

Children play at the edge of the water, elderly folks too old to mingle sit in groups in the many beach chairs scattered about or at one of the round tables set up for the event, eating and talking stuff. Everyone in between congregates in groups large and small, some with heads bent together conspiratorially, others chatting casually, and nearly all clutching tall, frosty glasses. Groups of people stand along the shoreline talking. They wisely hold their glasses high enough to avoid the possibility of salt spray from an errant breaking wave polluting the alcohol. Far out, at the end of one of the two rock jetties that frame this length of beach known as the Inkwell, a man with a fishing rod methodically casts out his line and slowly reels it in. Just beyond the end of the jetty, a man swims parallel to the shore with long easy strokes, all that can be seen of him his long dark arms and hands as they lift in an easy freestyle.

The music of relaxation, laughter, and camaraderie muffles the turning of waves as they break on the shore, and the voices of Dinah Washington and Brook Benton singing their sexy, teasing duet "Baby, You've Got What It Takes" weave in and out and around the assembled crowd, seeming to knit them together in the commonality of good feeling and relaxation that superb music creates. Like the water, the music ebbs and flows, occasionally drowned out when the laughter or conversation reaches a crescendo. A line of people snakes up to the long serving tables placed against the wall of the boardwalk, sagging from the weight of enormous pots filled with lobsters, clams, corn, and new potatoes; punch bowls heaped with potato, tossed, and fruit salad; a platter piled with lobster rolls. In a sandy corner an enormous grill sends up a steady stream of smoke from baby-back ribs, barbecued chicken, grilled bluefish, and the ubiquitous hamburgers and hot dogs.

The four of us stand at the top of the steps, surveying the lively scene on the beach. "What're you smiling about, Wanda?" Acey asks, lightly pinching my arm. I hadn't even realized I was grinning, but it figures.

"You know, I just love my peeps, truly. Sometimes just seeing a bunch of black folks together having a good time makes you grin," I say, putting on my shades as Acey nods. I walk down the steps, slipping out of my sandals and tucking them in one of the open bins provided for that purpose. The cool, soft sand feels wonderful under my feet and between my toes. After living on the boat for weeks and our otherworldly meeting with Eddie Sollozzo, it's a relief to sink my feet into terra firma, even if it is shifty sand.

"I know what you mean, girl. As my mother used to say, it's a comfort."

"All that, but I won't be totally comfortable until I get a drink in me," Lydia says. "The bar's over there. Y'all coming?"

"I'm going to take a walk along the beach first, shake out all vestiges of Eddie Sollozzo," Odell says.

"Mind if I come with you?" Acey asks.

"Not at all." Odell takes Acey's arm and pulls her away from the crowd. "Catch you two in a few."

"Ya think they're boning?"

"I doubt it, Wanda. Acey and Odell are too serious for that. They don't bone, they make love."

"They doing that?"

"I doubt that, too. If they were, they'd probably sit us down like we're their children and explain the situation."

"What a waste, huh, Lyds?"

"You, me, and Odell know that. Now, if Acey would only get with it. Or, more precisely, him."

"I'm with you." I laugh. "Whatever, here's the bar."

"Lydia, Wanda, let me tell you again what a marvelous time I had on my visit to the Floating Spa," Ellen Canning, one of the Doyennes, who today is also a bartender, greets us. "I'm hoping to sneak back once my company goes back to the mainland." She winks. "May I offer you a Get Well?"

"A Get Well?"

"That's a drink Ma Nicola concocted for this evening. Two fingers spiced rum, three fingers mango juice, ginger ale to the top, a dash of grenadine, and a sprig of mint from her garden."

"Sounds good to me." I take the frosty pink drink from Ellen and gulp a generous mouthful. "You know, I think I feel better already."

Sipping our drinks, Lydia and I wander through the crowd, stopping to talk with the people we know, most of them Doyennes, Mansioneers, or unaffiliated women who've visited the spa. It's clear that our reputation, or more accurately the Floating Spa's, has preceded us, and there's little need to work the crowd. If anything, the women in the crowd are working us.

"Wanda! Yoo-hoo, over here. I want you to meet the members of my club from Philly," a deep, gravelly voice calls from the direction of a table crowded with women and nearly veiled by the smoke from a dozen cigarettes. I walk toward the cloud, and when I get close a hand grabs my arm. "It's me, Audreen. Sit down and have a drink with us, unless you're one of those antismoking Nazis." What can I say? I used to smoke myself, quit ten years ago, and still sometimes happily dream of that first rush from a drag of tar and nicotine. Besides, Audreen and her club members look to be in their seventies and eighties, old enough to do as they please and not have to take shit for it. I've already decided that if I live to be seventy-five, I'm going to start smoking again. If I make it to eighty, I will have lived a long life and it likely won't be smoking that kills me. Besides, I'm all for clean and healthy living, but let's not take it too far: no one gets out of here alive.

"How are you ladies doing?" I say. The women around the table smile, give polite, positive responses.

"Yeah, yeah, they're fine, but they're going to be fabulous once they visit your spa," Audreen interjects, winking broadly. "I told them all about it."

"Yes, yes, Audreen has talked it to death since we arrived a few days ago."

"On and on about your lovely yacht."

"And unique services."

"Which she swears will be a life-changing experience."

"One she insists we shouldn't miss."

Audreen chuckles and pulls on her cigarette so hard her cheeks collapse. What begins as a laugh abruptly becomes a cough as well. "What I told them was that I'd forgotten what sex was, if I ever knew, until my first session with Jamal, and now I can't get enough. I've been a widow for twenty years and never was much for diddling myself, and the men our age . . ."

"Are usually too old and sick to do much—"

"Or want to do it with a younger woman—"

"Who can blame them? I'm not interested in any old man, either."

"Already had someone to cook for and take care of."

"Been there, done that."

"For forty years of marriage."

"The truth is, when you get to be old, you know what you like and what you don't."

"Who knows how much time's left?"

"Which is why the twelve of us would like to book the whole spa for a day next week," Audreen declares, slapping her American Express Platinum card on the table littered with glasses, ashes, and lobster shells. Her club members giggle agreeably and raise their near-empty glasses in a group toast.

"No need to pay in advance, and I'll see you all next week."

"Tell Jamal and the rest of your employees to get ready, the old gals are coming to get 'em!" Audreen yells at my departing back as I dance away to the sound of Mary J. Blige's "Just Fine."

"What was that about?" Lydia asks, nodding toward the smoke cloud.

"It's all good. You know there's no one more serious than a born-again anything, and Audreen the cynic is definitely a convert."

Lydia and I float through the crowd, trying to be cool as we spot a well-known civil rights attorney here, a major D.C. restaurateur there, a brother who's a six-hundred-dollar-an-hour partner at a major law firm in Chicago over there, a sister from Los Angeles whose novels we both love and who's a regular visitor to A Sister's Spa in Reno. There are even a couple of familiar actors and music-business folk, trying to blend in and, perhaps much to their chagrin, succeeding. What I've noticed here is that while people may discreetly stargaze, it's considered crass to overtly acknowledge or harass. Besides which, most of the people here think they're stars, too. We swing past a second bar tended by the Conover sisters, three cyclones who've created their own assembly line to take orders, mix drinks, absorb the latest gossip, and all the while keep the line moving.

"Wanda! Lydia! The spa is wonderful," Faith declares.

"Absolutely!" Hope chimes in. "And that Sukey. She's fabulous!" The three sisters stop their feverish activity for the few seconds it takes to hold up their plump hands and display thirty fingernails, each painted with one of my cousin's tiny designs, although I'm too buzzed and exhausted to see exactly what.

"As soon as the holiday weekend is over, we'll be back!" Charity declares, handing us fresh drinks.

"Bye. Enjoy the party," they call in unison, our cue to get gone and not hold up the line.

"I wonder which of Sukey's many services Hope Conover found so fabulous," I whisper to Lydia, giggling.

"Niggah, tomorrow is going to be the bomb!" A voice rises above the rest, quickly swallowed by ensuing laughter. I follow the commotion to a group of folks standing in a loose circle, at the center of which stands B. T. Lincoln, and around him Stretch Smith, Lulu Langlais, Herman Rutledge, and five or six other people who look both professorial and vaguely familiar. Unless they're customers, I'm not all that good at names, but maybe I've seem them on *Book Notes*, trying to get a word in edgewise on *Tavis Smiley* or *Charlie Rose* or someplace else serious.

"I've talked C-SPAN and three local news channels into covering Dr. Angelique Shorter Crawford's presentation, told them there'd be some breaking news and they'd better get their asses down here."

"We're almost sold out. People have been calling me trying to get tickets, folks who never come to our event," Lulu Langlais adds.

"Do you still want me to say a prayer before we begin tomorrow?" Herman Rutledge asks.

"Yes, yes, put that black-church mojo on 'em and protect us from any and all surviving Confederates." B.T. cackles.

"Yep, and the prayer you say better be tough, else my new book's gonna be titled *Murder in the Bluffs*," Stretch Smith says.

"Niggah, you have lost you mind with those rhymes. Now you tryin' to drive the rest of us mad, too."

"Tell me something new," Lulu barks. "Why do you think James's gone fishing on the jetty?"

"I'm going to find something to eat. I'll catch up with you, Wanda." Lydia scurries off and disappears into the packed crowd. I take a break from schmoozing, walk down to the water, and stand looking out at the ocean. It's moving toward that time of evening when the world is bathed in that orangey-golden light that comes just before twilight, one of my favorite times of day. Past the end of the jetty the water is flat, although the motion of the currents running underneath it trace random patterns on its surface. A sprinkling of gulls float regally atop the darkening water, heads and yellow beaks pointed toward shore, no doubt on the alert for a falling morsel of food. The lone swimmer I noticed earlier swims lazily in to shore, his strokes easy, measured, seemingly effortless. A dozen yards from land, he stands up and begins walking out of the water. As he moves he wipes salt water from his eyes with the thumb and forefinger of one hand. Squinting, he looks up and gives me an impersonal but dazzling "I don't know you, this isn't a come-on, but we're all in this place together, so presumably you're okay" smile.

Even in the fading light, slightly buzzed, and after a long day, I know that smile. Judge C. Virgil Susquehanna, my savior, the man who gave me my fortune back, parting the waters in a pair of loose black swimming shorts. Standing in water just below his knees, he runs a hand across his eyes one more time, squints, and then a smile of recognition spreads over his face.

"Ahhh, Ms. LaShaWanda P. Marshall," he purrs. "The woman who challenged Goliath and won. What a surprise." He extends his wet hand and we shake. I know I'm not imagining the electricity that runs up my arms, wonder if he feels it, too.

"Judge Susquehanna, it's great to see you. I want to thank you for your decision—" I begin.

"Don't thank me; thank the American system of justice, which, while deeply flawed, is all we've got and does, at its best, offer fair recourse. What brings you to the Vineyard?"

"Business and pleasure. I've always wanted to see this island that everyone's talking about. After I won my case, I decided to spend the summer out here and open a business. Here I am."

"What sort of business?" C. Virgil asks, picking up a towel from the beach and drying his torso. I manage to refrain from offering to do it for him.

"A floating day spa for women. It's on a boat off Oak Bluffs and—" Before I can finish my sentence, a voice I wish I'd never heard and never hear again bellows, "C. Virgil Susquehanna! Well, I'll be screwed. Fancy meeting you here!"

"No more fucking business, can't we just eat our lobster rolls in peace?" a woman's voice whines. I look up and Eddie Sollozzo is barreling toward us, his hand outstretched. Madge follows slowly behind him, an overstuffed lobster roll clutched in either hand, her heels sinking into the sand with each step.

"Do I know you?" C. Virgil's voice is aloof.

"Damn straight you know me. Ya might not recognize me, it's been forty years and I've put on at least forty pounds, but you, goddamn if you don't look just like you did in the sixties. You work out, huh?"

"Ah, but the name escapes me."

"Eddie, Eddie Sollozzo, from Providence. Remember, we met in 1965, in Mississippi. You were working for that colored group right around the time my baby sister was killed, remember her—"

"Vivian. Vivian Liotta. Unforgettable."

"Fuckin' A she was, you can say that again. Not a day goes by I don't miss her, you know?"

"She came to Mississippi to walk with Dr. King, first time she'd marched. She stopped on a road at night to help some folks pretending they had car trouble and they lynched her. An unforgettable travesty."

"Exactly. Vivian was my baby sister." Eddie stands in front of us, hand extended, panting from the exertion of walking ten yards.

C. Virgil takes his hand, shakes it. "I was working for Racial Solidarity Now! back then. We helped identify your sister's murderers, three good old boys, all members of Crackers Against Niggers and Nigger Lovers, better know as CANAN-L, if I remember correctly."

"Yep, CANAN-L." Eddie nods vigorously. "Fuckin' bastards."

"As I recall, they never made it to trial—"

"You got that right."

"Their truck spontaneously combusted in broad daylight in front of the courthouse. Burned them to a crisp."

A smirking Eddie nods enthusiastically. "Yep, those were some crispy crackers, or so I heard. Me, I was in Rhode Island at the time."

"I bet you were," Virgil Susquehanna murmurs.

"Good riddance to bad rubbish, huh, Judge?"

"Would that it were so, Eddie. CANAN-L's still in business; in fact, it's at the top of the government's domestic terrorist list."

"Ya don't say."

"Oh, but I do. In fact, my friend Angelique Shorter Crawford has discovered information that traces the roots of CANAN-L back to the Civil War."

Eddie shrugs indifferently. Obviously history is not his forte. "Anyway, like I told you back when you found the bastards, I owe you a big one, Virgil."

The judge shrugs elegantly. "No need. Justice has been served."

"I'm even a lifetime member of Racial Solidarity Now! thanks to you."

"I'm sure they appreciate your support."

"Yeah, whatever. I been following your career on and off all these years, you done very well for yourself. Guess you haven't needed any help from Eddie Sollozzo. Offer still stands, just in case. Anytime."

"Eddie, isn't that one of the girls from the gazebo?" A heavily breathing Madge has finally reached us, leaving a trail of fallen lobster chunks and battling gulls in her wake. Virgil Susquehanna looks from her to Eddie to me, raises his lovely eyebrows.

"You know each other?"

"Unfortunately. Eddie's like a bad penny that keeps coming back."

"Just doing a little business, Judge."

"Unless you've changed radically, Eddie, I suspect that doesn't bode well for Ms. Marshall."

"Extortion. He's wants a percentage of the profits from the spa my friends and I own in Reno or he'll put us out of business."

C. Virgil's chuckle is condescending. "Business must be bad if you're going after the spa set."

"It ain't simply a spa, Judge, get real."

"And what more would it be?" C. Virgil looks from Eddie to me.

"Well, sir, along with all the traditional spa services, we offer our exclusively female clientele the unique services of men trained to provide women with the ultimate in pleasure—"

"Blah, blah, blah, cut to the chase; they're selling dick. Male ho's," Eddie interrupts. "Nobody runs ho's in Nevada or the tristate region unless the Sollozzos get a piece."

"Pun intended, I'm sure," the judge says. "Is this true, Ms. Marshall?"

"Yes, sir, it is. And not illegal," I add hastily. "But we'll be out of business if we have to pay this creep ten percent."

"Nine and a half," Eddie interjects. "There's no need for name-calling," he adds huffily.

C. Virgil Susquehanna stands in the dusk looking thoughtful. "Eddie, the time is now."

"For what, Judge?"

"To call in your debt."

"You name it."

"I would ask you to cease and desist in your efforts to extort money from Ms. Marshall, her partners, and their business endeavors, now and in perpetuity. That will settle, in full, any debt you feel you have to me."

"What? Why? You bonking this broad or something?"

"Woman, Mr. Sollozzo, woman. And I don't 'bonk' women, I make love to them," C. Virgil says, giving me a sly smile. "Are we in agreement?"

"I ain't Aladdin, there're no three wishes, just one. Why waste it on her? You might need something important down the road."

"It is my wish, to use as I please, isn't that right?"

"I'm not so sure about that, Judge. I wasn't expecting you to ask for something that interferes with my business, you know?"

"Ahhh. I misunderstood." C. Virgil's voice drips sarcasm. "When you said you owed me one, you failed to explain that even though I am the one to be paid, it's your choice how the debt is repaid."

"Not exactly, Judge. I'm just asking you to consider your options. Maybe we can work out something that works for both of us, you know?"

"This works for me," C. Virgil says firmly. "Do we have a deal?"

C. Virgil's and Eddie's eyes meet and they hold their gazes for what feels like forever, or maybe that's just because I'm so stunned by the judge's request and busy hoping Eddie will acquiesce that I forget to breathe.

It's Madge Sollozzo who finally interrupts the staring contest at Inkwell Beach and breaks the silence. "Enough business, Eddie. I wanna 'nother roll and a drink before we catch the ferry," she demands through a mouthful of lobster, bread, and chips.

Before Eddie or C. Virgil can respond, a shocked shriek escapes from my mouth as two cold, wet, and sandy paws gallop over my instep, dragging a loose leash behind them and followed in short order by a winded voice calling, "Mr. Boule! Bad, bad boy! Come back here! And don't you dare go in that water!"

CHAPTER 22

Chef Marvini

ME, CHEF MARVINI, I'M A WEED HEAD. I've been a stoner since I smoked my first joint at thirteen. One thing I've observed is that most straight people don't really see me. That's okay, I'm content in my under-the-radar groove. I'm not oblivious to what's going on around me. More like what's going on is oblivious to me. I'm like a stoned fly on the wall that most people don't notice, and if they do, as long as I'm not buzzing and annoying them, they let me be. That's fine. Gives me more time to check everyone else out, or not, depending on the circumstances.

I'd been drifting from restaurant job to gigs as a private chef for more than a few years before

I came to work at the spa. I didn't want to be in a crowded, hot kitchen with a bunch of egomaniacs dashing around shouting and acting as if cooking a piece of mahimahi was tantamount to finding a cure for sickle-cell anemia or pancreatic cancer. I've traveled around the world as a private chef to the wealthy and can tell you this: it doesn't matter if you're living on a pristine beach in Maui or a villa in Tuscany; it's a serious downer to be awoken at three in the morning because someone wants a butterscotch sundae or sautéed duck breast.

Along with cooking, I also watch everyone's backs and keep my ears, the sharpest of my senses, open. I listen to the sex workers talking about their prowess, Jamal, Sekou, and Isaac saying morning prayers and reminiscing about home late at night. I hear DeJuan, DeQuan, and DeMon trying to decide whether to stay at the spa or go to grad school. I listen to Lydia and Wanda worrying about cash flow and the extortionist Eddie Sollozzo and the president's No Child, No Behind initiative and why Sukey isn't bringing in more cash. I listen to Cap'n Chubby when he comes down to the galley searching for something to eat and tells tales of braving fifteen-foot swells to deliver our insatiable clients. To the housekeepers complaining about staterooms left as if a tornado hit them and trying to keep up with the fast turnover. The only one I don't listen to is Tollhouse, because he is mostly silent. This bothers me.

You have to try hard to slip past me, I'm the invisible one, yet that's exactly what Tollhouse does. More than a few times when I open the kitchen just before dawn, I've caught him climbing the steps to the deck, shoes in hand, like he doesn't want anyone to hear him. And how about him swimming around the boat at daybreak when he told me he couldn't swim? I seldom hear Tollhouse. I know he's in the room, but while other people are laughing, talking, singing, chanting, when it comes to him, *nada*. Not a peep. He's there but not there, the weed head's way of being, but he isn't one of us. There's nothing laid-back and mellow about him, just secretive. Our tribe isn't a secretive one, we're not trying to hide, we're just not trying.

I stay in bed most of the Fourth of July, smoking a spliff and alternately drifting and reading a book by the brilliant scholar and historian of slavery John Hope Franklin. We were closed for the day; it was the sex workers' first day off in over a month; Acey, Lydia, Odell, and Wanda had gone to the island; and the Floating Spa was deserted. Just after dark I got hungry and started to fantasize about a big salad with grilled shrimp and eating it on deck watching the fireworks down in Edgartown. I like to be close to my kitchen, so I've appropriated the storage room behind the galley for myself, it provides all the comfort and privacy I need. I stretch, pull on a Steel Pulse T-shirt over my shorts, and go into the galley to fix myself some dinner. That's when I see Tollhouse, the silent wonder, crouched underneath the sink in jeans and a white sleeveless undershirt, his hand wedged in the space behind the sink and the propane tanks for the stove. I watch him for a few moments, then take a long drag of my joint and grab my ten-inch cleaver from the magnetic strip along the wall.

"What're you up to?" Startled, he bangs his head against the edge of the deep stainless-steel sink, but the space is so tight he's leaning on one hand for balance while the other one remains out of sight. He manages to turn his head toward me, his eyes blank.

"Hey. Chef, help me up." He grins and his face is suddenly sweetness and light. "I seem to have gotten myself all twisted up." No lie. One leg rests on the floor, bent at the knee, while the other knee sticks up in the air, supported by a foot pushed into his side and flat on the floor. From the waist up, he's mostly jammed behind the deep bowls of the double sink, just able to turn his face to one side. His right shoulder juts up in the air.

"What're you up to?"

"I dropped something. Help me up."

"I didn't hear anything."

"What've you got, X-ray hearing? Gimme a hand, man. I'm stuck."
I relight my joint, take a long toke, keep my eye on Tollhouse, and shake my head thoughtfully.

"I think you're an ill wind, man."

"What the shit does that mean?"

"You're blowing no good."

"All you're blowing is that weed smoke, it's fucked up your vision. Help me up," he orders, squirming to no avail. He can't work himself free without help and mine isn't forthcoming. I watch him impassively.

"What're you messing with down there?"

"Nothing. I told you I dropped something."

"What?"

"A key."

"A key? None of the rooms on the boat need a key."

"Not a door key, a windup key. But never mind, just help me up."
I don't move.

"What's that on your shoulder?" I point to a two-inch square tattoo, three rows of three parallel holes run across it.

"Nothing, an old tattoo."

"What's it mean?"

"Nothing, just a design."

"Looks familiar."

"Yeah, well, you're tripping off that weed, ain't nothing but a design. It don't mean nothin'." Tollhouse's voice now has a pronounced southern drawl.

"You could say the same about the swastika until the Nazis got hold of it."

"It ain't a swastika."

"No, it's not. That would be too obvious," I say, reaching into a drawer and removing the twine I use for trussing fish, fowl, and meat. I squat down to eye level. "I'm going to tie your feet and legs up tight so you can't run off, then help you get out." I pull his feet together and start at his ankles, wrapping the string around and around as if I'm preparing a mummy.

"What the fuck are you doing, you nigra piece of shit?"

I turn, exhale. "Did you call me nigger?"

"Fucking right, nigra, that's what I called you, ain't that what your homeys call you?"

I kick him in the gut, ask politely, "Homeys?"

"Other nigras. Not to mention wigger traitors and the white bitches who love black dick."

"Huh? What happened to the silent sex worker?" I laugh. Then I kick him in the side of his head and laugh some more. Tears of pain flood his eyes.

"Laugh now, but the day of divine retribution is upon us. Chaos will reign, thousands shall die, and the white race shall return to its rightful place."

"Which is?"

"On top, you stupid baboon. On top."

"Who's going to make that happen, you?"

"As soon as I get this engine started, the Floating Spa will head toward the mainland and Harvard, center of elitism, diversity, and latte sippers," he says derisively. "Once in the Charles River, kaboom! No more Harvard. The ensuing carnage and destruction will be a signal to my Aryan brothers around the nation to rise up and take America back."

"It's gonna be a long trip back to those good old Neanderthal days, huh?"

"To the days when the white man was in his rightful place!"

"Tollhouse, huh, like the crackers," I say thoughtfully, slowly exhaling a narrow line of smoke. "What's that, kinda like a racist gang name?"

"The revolution begins today! The day of transformation is at hand!"

"Yeah, well, you're not going to get to those days in this vessel. I knew you were up to some shit the moment I saw you. I disabled the engine."

"Motherfucker, you're going down! The Keebler Conspiracy lives! The Confederacy will rise again!" Tollhouse bellows, writhing on the floor like a mad dog, complete with yellowish foam forming at the corners of his mouth. I think I hear his collarbone crack as he wrenches himself from behind the sink and struggles to stand from his cramped position.

"Them days are over. The dying white culture is here. You don't believe me, look in the mirror. Or at Fox News," I say, and can't help laughing at my own joke.

"Make jokes if you want, you black ape, but you're going down," he shrieks.

Enough is enough, he's blowing my high. I kick him in his ribs so hard his head and torso slam back against the wall, knocking him out and dislodging the shelves above him. He slides to the floor followed by boxes of dry goods that tumble open, covering an unconscious Tollhouse with flour, grits, and saltines. I stare at that white man covered in white food for a long minute and finally a light goes on. I go into my room, grab the John Hope Franklin book I'd been reading, and leaf through the pages, glancing at the photographs and drawings. There it is, on page 175 of the chapter on white supremacist hate groups, a replica of Tollhouse's tattoo. I quickly reread the page below it.

This tattoo of a cracker was chosen for its visual subtlety, and in an effort by white racists to reclaim the derogatory reference to a poor white as a "cracker" in the same way that some black Americans believe they can reclaim "nigger." The tattoo is worn by those in the military arm of Crackers Against Niggers and Nigger Lovers, commonly known by its acronym, CANAN-L. Likely the most virulent domestic terrorist group, CANAN-L is a loosely organized group of white racist, sexist homophobes.

Although CANAN-L came to public attention after the lynching of Vivian Liotta during the civil rights movement of the 1960s, it is suspected that its roots go back to the Civil War and perhaps earlier. Like many white supremacist groups, CANAN-L came to prominence advocating the continuation of slavery and allied with the Confederacy. Though the organization, along with many others, disappeared after the exposure of the Keebler Conspiracy during the Civil War, it is thought that these organizations reconstituted themselves and may well continue, sub rosa, to this day.

CANAN-L and groups like it are responsible for numerous acts of violence around the country targeting blacks, Latinos, Asians, Catholics, Jews, and Muslims, women, and gay, lesbian, bisexual, and transgendered individuals. They are believed to be responsible for hundreds of violent attacks on abortion clinics and civil rights and antiwar marches, resulting in the death or maiming of several hundred citizens. It is also suspected that members of these groups have infiltrated the highest levels of business, industry, and government and that more than a few elected officials are affiliated with such white supremacist organizations.

Most recently, the group's energies have been focused on domestic bombings in an effort to create terror and initiate a white power revolution. Their focus has been on institutions of higher learning, businesses, and monuments it views as standing in the way of the reinstatement of slavery and aiding and abetting the demise of the white man. Their targets have included historically black colleges and universities, the Statue of Liberty, the University of California at Berkeley, Harvard, and the headquarters of Taco Bell, Sean John, and Viacom, owners of BET.

I walk into the kitchen to finish securing the unconscious Tollhouse, but he's gone. A trail of twine, white flour, and cracker crumbs leads to the spiral staircase. I sprint upstairs and find him standing in the bow pulpit of the yacht, leaning against the railing and fiddling with a black metal device the diameter of a large pizza. He's got what looks like an old-fashioned metal skate key inserted in the round thing and is turning it laboriously.

"Tollhouse, man, it's over," I say, walking toward him. "It's time for prison, some serious meds, and years of intensive counseling courtesy of the—as you call them—homeys in lockup."

"It is just beginning!" he yells. He's too far away for me to see what he's doing, but a flashing red light comes on on the object in his hand. "Plan B is about to commence," he screams, tying either end of what looks like a giant rubber band—and looks vaguely familiar from observing Lydia's torturous exercise regimens—around the boat's railing. Clearly this is not one of those wait-and-see moments. I toss the rest of my joint overboard and move rapidly toward him. He turns, cradles the round thing in the band of rubber, and moves backward, leaning his whole body into it until the band is stretched taut. Then he angles his body until the makeshift slingshot is aimed toward shore and lets go. The disk sails through the air until, like a golf ball launched by Tiger Woods, I can barely see it and it hits the water, and, still flashing, begins rapidly skimming the surface toward shore. Tollhouse stands in the bow pulpit with his hands aloft and head rolled back, a frightening keening sound coming from his mouth. I tackle him and he falls sideways, the upper half of his body bent over the yacht's railing. I grab him both to choke him and keep him from going overboard and my eyes meet those of Cap'n Chubby, halfway up the rope ladder to the deck, Tollhouse the white meat sandwiched between us. Bob Marley's voice wafts up from *Phish Tales*. The Cap'n looks from me to Tollhouse, susses out the scene, and then, seeing who the cap fits and like the good brother he is, hits Tollhouse upside his head with an oar.

"What's up, chef?" Chubby's stands on the ladder, leaning against the side of *Lady Lay*, holding Tollhouse's torso with one arm and bracing himself against the railing with the other.

"Not quite sure. Cracker been messing with the engine. Stopped that, then he threw something in the water, maybe a bomb," I say, shifting Tollhouse's limp legs in my arms. "Think we'd better head toward shore." We lower the unconscious Confederate into *Phish Tales* and I jump in after him.

"Better tie him up. Don't want any problems when he wakes up. I got just the spot for him. Lift his legs," Chubby says. We half carry, half drag Tollhouse to the bow of *Phish Tales*. Chubby sets him on his knees and props his stomach against the bow pulpit. "Hold him upright." He removes the mooring rope from the deck cleat and threads the thick rope around and around the prostrate Tollhouse until he is wound in rope from knee to chest, a doomed white supremacist figurehead lashed to the front of *Phish Tales*.

"Where to?" Chubby turns the key and the boat's engine roars to life.

"Follow the bouncing red light, Cap'n, and step on it," I say. We head toward shore as Bob's voice fills the evening air.

CHAPTER 23

Lydia

WITH HIS SALT-AND-PEPPER FUR, HE sure looks like an elderly long-haired rat, but Mr. Boule's sprinting toward the jetty so swiftly he could be a greyhound at Derby Lane Racetrack in Florida chasing after that mechanical rabbit. Aaron Semple Stone makes a poor second when it comes to speed, but he's kicking up enough sand weaving through the crowd on the beach and ineffectually hollering at Mr. Boule to draw people's attention. Even if conversations don't actually stop or decrease in volume, most eyes follow him as he scampers toward the water in hot pursuit of the nasty little critter. Me, I've eaten, slurped down several Get Wells, and in my tipsy state can think of nothing more entertaining than to enjoy the inconvenience and stress Mr. Boule is inflicting upon Aaron Semple Stone. I follow lazily after dog and master, but before I get to the water, I stumble upon Wanda, C. Virgil Susquehanna, and Eddie and Madge Sollozzo, an odd quartet if there ever was one.

"What's up, Wanda?"

"Girl," Wanda says, throwing up her hands, "where do I begin?"

"What're Eddie and Madge doing here?" I think I'm whispering, but you know how liquor throws off your perceptions.

"It's a free country, ain't it, missy?" Eddie says.

"Besides, I wanted a lobster roll and the shack on the other side of the beach only sells dogs and burgers," Madge adds.

"It turns out Judge Susquehanna was the man we saw swimming out past the jetty and it just happened I was standing here when he came in to shore," Wanda says happily.

"Fortuitous for all of us," C. Virgil says in his deep baritone. Is it me or does this man have one of those voices that could make reading the grocery list seductive?

"Mr. Boule! Halt!" Aaron Semple Stone hollers in what's supposed to be a commanding tone, and while he succeeds in getting a number of heads to turn in his direction, Mr. Boule is having none of it. He leaps from the sand onto the rocky outcropping, bounds past the sign that warns PLEASE DO NOT CLIMB ON THE JETTY. What choice does his dedicated and now deeply perturbed master have but to follow? Aaron Semple Stone tries to hurdle himself from the beach onto the dark, glistening rock of the jetty. Without claws or paws to cling with, his foot slips on rock swathed in slimy, odiferous seaweed and jagged barnacles and for a moment it looks as if he is doing a split, straddling the jetty with one foot on either side.

"Hey, watch it!" a familiar voice shouts, and Odell's head appears from the far side of the rocks followed by Acey's flushed and excited face. "The cookout's to the right of the jetty. We're trying to talk over here," Odell yells. Aaron Semple Stone ignores him, manages to stand up again, pick his way around slick seaweed, pools of water in depressions in the rock, and the ubiquitous barnacles, and resume the chase. His unfaithful featherweight canine friend bounces from rock to rock. In the advancing twilight, Odell and Acey stand up and gently brush sand off themelves, each with an arm around the other's waist.

"Damn, Wanda. You see that?" I say, gesturing toward Acey and Odell.

"Yeah, but what the fuck is it?"

"Hey, what's with you? Even I know love when I see it."

"Love? I'm talking about that thing in the water," Wanda says, pointing out to sea.

"Mr. Boule, heel, heel!" Aaron hollers. Need I say that Mr. Boule keeps on getting up?

In response to the commotion, people at the clambake have moved down toward the shoreline to watch the drama unfold, drinks in hand, and the DJ has lowered the volume. Mr. Boule, yapping steadily, is almost at the end of the jetty, which stretches about a hundred yards into Nantucket Sound. Standing on the last rock, James Winbush has stopped casting out his line and turned around to see what all the yelling is about. Aaron Semple Stone, slipping, sliding, dripping salt spray and smeared with seaweed slime, continues to gingerly make his way, shouting for Mr. Boule to stop! halt! heel! even as his voice grows fainter with the growing distance.

"What's the matter with the puppy?" Madge asks no one in particular.

"Fuck the mutt. Whatta ya say, Judge? Can't you come up with a favor that doesn't take money outta my pocket?"

C. Virgil exhales vehemently. "Eddie, I said you owed me nothing, you insisted you owed me something, when I ask you to leave Ms. Marshall and her business partners alone, you tell me you don't want to owe me that. Your line of reasoning is both nonsensical and un-American."

"Which means what, you're not going to change your mind?"

"Exactly. I expect you to be a man of your word."

"What're they talking about?" I whisper to Wanda. She links her arm through mine and pulls me a few feet away so we stand looking out at the ocean.

"It turns out that Judge Susquehanna and Eddie Sollozzo go way back to the civil rights—" she starts to say, then interrupts herself. "Look!" She turns me in the direction of her extended arm. "Is it the heat, the drinks, my imagination, or is that light coming toward us?" I follow her arm to see a blinking red light. At first I think it is an anchored buoy marking the channel, but it is too low to the water, and squinting, I realize that the light is growing stronger, so it must be moving toward shore.

"Sure looks like it."

"Strange," Wanda says, walking into the water up to her knees and peering out. By now Mr. Boule has reached the end of the jetty, where he stands growling and barking hysterically at the blinking light a few hundred yards out. Aaron continues to scrape and scrabble his way toward his canine companion. I can hear him faintly calling, "Mr. Boule, stay. Stay." For his part, James Winbush squats beside the nasty little critter and looks out to sea.

It's a strange tableau, but not an exciting one. The DJ turns the volume back up and Marvin Gaye's creamy voice crooning "Let's Get

It On" fills the fading twilight. Folks begin to talk again and move lazily away from the shoreline toward the bar or the food or something more appealing. Disappointed, since it looks as if Aaron will make it to Mr. Boule without the humiliation of tumbling into the ocean, I'm about to go for a fresh drink myself when B. T. Lincoln, standing with his posse at the water's edge, shouts, "Hey, isn't that a motorboat heading to shore?"

I peer out through the dimming light and damned if I don't see the lights of a fast-moving launch zooming toward the beach, the twinkling light now almost parallel to the end of the jetty. The ship's bell is ringing frantically. I recognize it as Cap'n Chubby's and at the same time hear Chef Marvini's voice shouting, although in the wind and at this distance I can't make out what he's saying. Apparently James Winbush can hear him loud and clear because he jumps up from beside Mr. Boule and begins running toward the beach, yelling unintelligibly and waving both arms in the air. Between the liquor, music, and babble of voices, it takes a while to understand what he's saying.

"Run! Run! Off the beach! It's a bomb!" Although a few people on the beach back away from the water's edge, no one runs anywhere. Most people don't even move. Either they don't hear him or, if they do, figure it's a prank like when people yell, "Shark!" on a hot day when the beach is crowded. After all, Martha's Vineyard is where the movie *Jaws* was filmed.

"Isn't that Marvini and Cap'n Chubby?" asks Odell. I hadn't even realized he and Acey were standing with us.

"What's that thing in the water, Eddie?" Madge Sollozzo asks.

"Hell if I know. Looks like a floating Frisbee with a light on top."

"A bomb? That damn Winbush, always the prankster." Stretch Williams guffaws.

"I think it's time for us to move away," C. Virgil Susquehanna says firmly. "I was in the marines and that floating Frisbee looks suspiciously like an amphibious explosive."

"Oh shit," Wanda says.

"Let's go," Odell agrees.

"Eddie, I'm going to kill you if I die," Madge shrieks.

"I love you, Odell," Acey blurts out in what I guess is her "I think I'm going to die" moment.

"Later for that, let's go!" I say, but before we can, Aaron shouts, "No, Mr. Boule! Don't!" I look out to the end of the rocky outcropping just in time to witness Mr. Boule lunge off the jetty and fly a dozen feet in the dusky air before he splashes into the water and begins paddling toward the light. Like shadow dancers or silhouettes come to life, I see Aaron kick off his shoes and James grab him and shout, "Don't do it, man! It's a damn dog!" Then Aaron pushes him away and dives into the water after Mr. Boule. In the murky light between twilight and night, I can't see Aaron, Mr. Boule, or anything in the water but the blinking red light at the tip of the jetty and James Winbush as he sprints along the rocks toward shore. I can't see him in the gloom but I hear Chef Marvini's voice, now clear as that damn bell calling out after him, "Run! Run! It's a bomb!"

Then everyone's scrambling away from the water and toward the stairs to the boardwalk and I'm running in the sand, stumbling and trying to find my mother and Ma Nicola, whose running days are over, when I trip over a mound of seaweed and fall on my face. Before I can get up, there's an explosion so loud that it obliterates sound; the world goes silent for what seems like forever but is only seconds. Then, abruptly, salt water displaced by the explosion pours onto the beach from the sky, drenching everyone and putting out the fire under the grill, the lobster pots, Audreen's ever-present cigarette. Along with water I am drenched by hunks of something moist, slippery, and fragrant falling from the sky like hail. I squeeze my eyes shut tight, wrap my arms around my knees, tuck my head down, and yes, Lydia Beaucoup fervently prays for the air attack to cease. When it does I peer out through squinting eyes at a beach littered with the ragged heads, tails, fins, claws, and other body parts of thousands of detonated fish and crustaceans. Several hundred stunned but alive people, soaking wet and covered, as I am, in a gumbo of fish guts and crab legs, surround me on the beach. Just when I think it's all over, something lands in the seaweed at my feet with a moist, squishing sound. Eyes half closed, I look down hesitantly, anticipating a leg, arm, or other body part. Lying beside my ankle is a sodden, lifeless but intact Mr. Boule. Even though I still haven't forgiven the mongrel for attacking my leg on the ferry, I certainly didn't wish him dead. I touch his damp fur in a final benediction and look around the beach. Amazingly, I don't see any dead bodies. I catch sight of my mother and Ma Nicola, Wanda and C. Virgil, Madge and Eddie. Chef Marvini and Cap'n Chubby are alive and well, out past the jetty waiting for the churning water to calm down before they come in to shore. I must still be drunk and possibly suffering from a concussion because, oddly enough, it looks as if there's a figurehead awkwardly lashed to the bow of Chubby's boat, although this one is no wood carving but alive, writhing, and looks suspiciously like our sex worker Tollhouse. As for Acey and Odell, they're obviously very well, since they're standing in the midst of chaos as if they're in one of those man-goes-off-to-war scenes, their bodies entwined, tongue-kissing like we did when we were virginal adolescents.

Maybe the music never stopped and I just couldn't hear it over the silence after the blast, but out of the blue and unexpectedly, Marvin Gaye's voice fills the twilight: *"There's nothing wrong with me loving you, baby no no / And giving yourself to me can never be wrong if the love is true / . . ."* Must be the music that's turning him on because I'll be damned if scrawny Mr. Boule doesn't lift his front paws, fasten onto my calf, and start humping.

CHAPTER 24

Wanda

IT'S FUNNY HOW THE KNOTTED-UP, TWISTED strands of life sometimes untangle themselves and come right in the end. Who would have thought that the Floating Spa would end up leading to the capture of Tollhouse, a member of CANAN-L and a real-life homegrown terrorist? He was plotting to steal the Floating Spa, sail it across to the mainland and up the Charles River, and blow up Harvard University. Once he heard about Dr. Angelique Shorter Crawford's research into contemporary white supremacist organizations involved in the Keebler Conspiracy, including CANAN-L, Tollhouse moved on to Plan B. He intended to detonate a bomb at the Inkwell and kill Dr. Crawford before she could announce her findings that white terrorist organizations were alive and actively working to foment a second Civil War, one that would result in the partitioning of the United States and the resurrection of slavery. It was feared that such a revelation would force the government to turn some of its focus inward, toward domestic terrorism, scrutiny that would seriously hamper white racist organizations. Tollhouse hoped to obliterate Dr. Crawford, a significant percentage of Harvard's black faculty, and three hundred members of the black bourgeoisie gathered on the beach for the Doyennes' annual clambake.

"He was going to blow up Harvard?"

"Not a place I consider a hotbed of leftist thought," the judge says.

"Nor the Inkwell. It might be a hotbed of something, but it's not socialism. More like socialite-ism."

"Tollhouse or Keebler, that's one stupid cracker."

"And useless. I'd just as soon weight him down, throw him overboard, and be done with him," I say.

"He's worthless dead, Wanda," C. Virgil reminds me. "Alive he may have value as something to barter."

"In exchange for what? Who'd be stupid enough to want him?"

C. Virgil smiles his charmingly predatory smile. "I know a president who'd give just about anything—including his absurd effort to control Americans' sex lives—in exchange for a real live apprehended terrorist. He needs something to show for eight years of terrorizing the nation and the world. While I'm certain the home-grown variety of terrorist isn't at the top of his list—he'd doubtless prefer one with a beard and a Muslim name—I've no doubt he can work with this one."

"Ah. A terrorist in hand is worth whoever's in the bush, even if it is unmarried, nonprocreating, recreational fornicators. Good-bye, No Child, No Behind. C. Virgil, I like your style," I murmur. I don't think he hears me since he's flipped open his cell phone and is punching in the president's private number.

As for Eddie Sollozzo, in the end he agreed, unhappily, to settle his debt to C. Virgil and stop extorting any and all of our businesses in perpetuity. In exchange, he requested a half hour alone with Tollhouse before he was handed over to the FBI. All we asked was that he leave Tollhouse alive and without any fatal injuries.

Aaron Semple Stone was never seen again. James Winbush credited him with throwing his body over the floating explosive device and sacrificing himself to save hundreds of lives. We've ordered a bench from the Friends of Oak Bluffs to honor him and plan to place it on the boardwalk just above the jetty. IN MEMORY OF AARON SEMPLE STONE, WHO GAVE HIS LIFE FOR HIS PEEPS, the plaque will read. I'm not quite sure how he'd feel about that epitaph, but I like it.

Dr. Angelique Shorter Crawford wasn't even at the Doyennes' beach party: she fell asleep watching *Oprah* and never made it to the event. She did, however, deliver her lecture exposing the contemporary Keebler conspirators to a packed audience and major media the next evening. Soon afterward she was spirited away to Washington, D.C., in a military plane, accompanied by a rather attractive bodyguard from the Fruit of Islam. It's said that she'll be testifying before both houses of Congress for the foreseeable future, but the details are top secret.

William "Stretch" Smith never again spoke in rhyme. Some say the explosion blasted the verse out of him, but if you ask me, it knocked some sense into him and his academic buddies. He grew up and realized he has more to offer as a serious scholar than a pretend-to-be hip hop homey. B. T. Lincoln and his Harvard cohorts became more politically active after the blast, venturing down from the ivory towers to do equal-justice and antiracism work.

Maybe the best to come out of all the drama is Acey and Odell finally hooking up after years of pretending their feelings for each other were strictly business. I guess it took Mob extortion, No Child, No Behind, a demented sex worker, and being pummeled with, if not fire and brimstone, seawater and fish guts, for them to figure it out. In the fall, they're going to take a month off, go to Tahiti, and in Acey's words, "figure out where we're going." Damn, what's to figure?

Who would have thought that my little cousin Sukey would turn out to be a hardworking, sober employee and inadvertently tap into a revenue source we didn't anticipate? If it hadn't been for Sukey's seductive leg massages and her passion for women, we wouldn't have known our patrons were interested in pushing the sexual envelope into the girl-on-girl realm, not to mention the thriving dyke—sorry, lesbian—market. Need I say we're on it?

Strange as it is, Lydia's become attached to Mr. Boule since he landed at her feet after the explosion. She plans to spend her days off at Ma Nicola's with her new best friend, nursing him back to health and giving him some obedience training—Lord knows he needs it. I was getting worried that maybe she'd suffered a brain injury and lost her mind and libido until she told me Jamal would be staying with her and assisting in the training. Now, that's my girl.

Chef Marvini? He's going to stay on the Floating Spa and read the manuscript of Dr. Crawford's book that C. Virgil slipped him after he heard how he'd figured out Tollhouse's tattoo.

Me? Judge C. Virgil Susquehanna's invited me to stay with him in his house in Aquinnah for a few days of rest and relaxation. The esteemed judge has promised to teach me how to swim and I've vowed to show him, to the best of my formidable ability, my deep appreciation for all his assistance. He may be old enough to be my father but thank goodness he isn't. After years of enjoying the pleasures of the young studs who work at the spas, experience is my aphrodisiac.

I've given all the workers a week off with the warning that they are absolutely not to give away any sex on vacation, at least not on the Vineyard. That goes for my pie-gobbling cousin, too, although she argues that free love is free advertising. Hopefully, I've implored and threatened her enough that she'll keep her mouth and legs closed and her hands to herself for a few days. But then, when was the last time she listened to me?

Ahhhhhh, Sukey, Sukey, now.

About the Author

Jill Nelson's work has appeared in numerous publications, including the *New York Times*, *Essence*, the *Washington Post*, the *Nation*, the *Chicago Tribune*, and the *Village Voice*. Her books include *Volunteer Slavery*, which won an American Book Award; *Straight, No Chaser*; *Finding Martha's Vineyard: African Americans at Home on an Island*; and *Sexual Healing*, the prequel to *Let's Get It On*. An avid swimmer, gardener, and explorer, Nelson lives in Harlem with her husband. She blogs at www.NiaOnline.com. Please visit her Web site, www.jillnelson.com.